LOVE DIES

For Charles,
Best of luck on the
next step – have fun!
[illegible]

REVIEWERS PRAISE TIMOTHY SHEARD'S LENNY MOSS SERIES!

This Won't Hurt A Bit

Things get off to a macabre start in Timothy Sheard's offbeat procedural…when a student at a Philadelphia teaching hospital identifies the cadaver she is dissecting in anatomy class as a medical resident she once slept with. Although hospital administrators are relieved when a troublesome laundry worker is charged with the murder, outraged staff members go to their union representative, a scrappy custodian named Lenny Moss, and ask him to find the real killer. Since there's no merit to the case against the laundry worker to begin with, Lenny is just wasting his time. But Sheard, a veteran nurse, makes sure that readers do not waste theirs. His intimate view of Lenny's world is a gentle eyeopener into the way a large institution looks from a workingman's perspective.

New York Times

Some Cuts Never Heal

This well-plotted page-turner is guaranteed to scare the bejesus out of anyone anticipating a hospital stay anytime in the near future.

Publishers Weekly

Sheard provides realistic details of hospital routine and budget-cutting politics…polished prose and elements of warmth and humor. Strongly recommended for most mystery collections. **Library Journal**

If your pulse quickens for ER on Thursday nights, you'll want a dose of Timothy Sheard's medicine … The well-meaning, hard-working hospital folks will warm your heart, while the cold realities of modern medical care will raise your blood pressure and keep you turning the pages.

Rocky Mountain News

It's hard putting the book down. I raced through it but hated to see it end…The hospital scenes ring true. For mystery lovers, this one's a must!

Challenge

A Race Against Death

Looking for a murder mystery whose hero is a worker instead of a cop? Try this One! While most shop stewards do not get involved in murder mysteries, they solve tough problems at work every day. Now they can look up to a fictional role model—Super Steward Lenny Moss.

Public Employee Press Review

Timothy Sheard provides a delightful hospital investigative tale that grips readers from the moment that Dr. Singh and his team apply CPR, but fail.

Mysteries Galore

Slim To None

A fast paced mystery with more than enough twists and turns to keep you turning the page!

Grace Edwards

Here's a page flipper, a murder mystery set in a hospital where the invisible, everyday workers are the key...Their practical knowledge, solidarity and smarts solve this confusing case that leads us down all sorts of blind paths with lives on the line...a great read, a complicated mystery, good friends, comradeship in hard times, and union workers shown in full humanity. Get it now!

Earl Silbar, AFSCME 3506, City Colleges of Chicago,

In *Slim to None*, Tim Sheard's' fourth and most exciting and unnerving Lenny Moss mystery to date, you won't be the only reader to say 'Yes… Lenny should have an action figure in his likeness!'

Sue Doro, Pride and a Paycheck

This novel is a work of fiction. Names, characters, places and incidents are either the product of the author's imagination, or, if real, used fictitiously.

To contact the publisher, visit www.timsheard.com

Cover art by D. Bass and Tim Sheard. To contact the artists, email: Sheard2001@gmail.com

Published by Hard Ball Press,
ISBN: 0981451853.

Library of Congress Cataloging-in-Publication Data

Love Die, A Crime Novel/Timothy Sheard.
1. New York City (NY) – Fiction. 2. Medical – Fiction. 3. World Trade Center. 4. Ground Zero. 5. First Responders. 6. Public Health Policy.

For Forest & Abba

Beloved teachers; treasured friends.

And all my friends, they had such big dreams
Of all the things they'd do with their lives;
Some turned out to be bankers,
Some turned out to be gangsters,
Can't none of them sleep at night.

Chris Sheard, *THE TIMES*

LOVE DIES

A Crime Novel

By Timothy Sheard

ONE

A woman attains her greatest beauty in death.

He entertained this simple truth as the light came on in the bedroom window. Six A.M. Right on time. A slim figure moved behind the sheer curtain. Moments later the frosted bathroom window brightened.

And aren't punctual people the easiest to kill? Another simple truth.

Pulling down the car visor, he checked his face. Saw the cocoa-colored makeup had smudged along his cheek, revealing white skin beneath. He applied a dab of foundation to the spot and blended it with the rest, then checked the black wig with the dreads.

Perfect.

He sipped a cold cup of coffee as he watched her figure move across the bathroom window. She was pinning up her hair; spritzing her throat with a bit of perfume.

When the bathroom light winked out, he patted his jacket pocket, checking for the vial of liquid soap. She would finish dressing, walk to the living room for her jacket and hat, then make a final check: office keys, cell phone, lipstick and powder. No breakfast for this babe, she was all about work and keeping those aristocratic cheekbones prominent. Show off the legs and a little cleavage; give the clients the promise of a little heaven.

He stepped out of the car, mailing envelope in hand. His brown UPS shirt was embroidered with the name "Henry." His pants were crisply ironed, his shoes glossy black. "I'm a credit to the company," he told himself, dodging traffic as he crossed East 23rd Street.

He approached the building entrance, looking for a resident on the way out. The spinster with the little fluff-ball dog was usually an early riser. So were the Wall Street guy in pinstripes and the nurse in scrubs. This was the only part of the plan left to chance. If he failed to gain access before she left her apartment, he would have to wait for another day. No problem; patience was the mother's milk of success.

The briefcase guy in the pinstriped suit strode through the lobby toward the entrance. Holding the door open, briefcase said, "Here you go. Unless it's for me."

In a vaguely Caribbean accent he asked, "You mistah Schermerhorn?" A name *not* listed in the lobby.

"No, Fallon. Oh, well, have a nice day."

"You, too, Mon."

He stepped into the lobby, saw that the night porter was nowhere in sight and the doorman hadn't come in yet. The pinstriper would be a witness, but so what? Nobody was going to investigate. And even if someone *did* nose around, they'd look for a black UPS guy from the Islands.

He opened the door to the stairs and climbed, taking the steps two at a time. Midway between the third and fourth floor landings he removed a spool of twenty pound monofilament fishing line and tied the line between the posts supporting the railings.

He exited on the fourth floor landing, pulled a cardboard sign from the mailing envelope and taped it to the elevator door. The sign read, "OUT OF ORDER."

Loitering at the end of the hall, he heard the lock on her door turn. As he moved slowly from apartment to apartment scrutinizing the numbers, he listened to her heels click on the marble floor. The clicking stopped in front of the elevator.

"Oh *shit*," the woman said in a shrill voice. "They damn well better have it fixed by tonight or the board will hear from me!"

He was now doubly happy that she was the target.

At the sound of the stairwell door opening, he hurried back to the elevator and snatched the sign, then hurried after her. The heavy stairwell door, fireproof *and* soundproof, closed just as her scream pierced the silence of the stairs.

He found her crumpled on the third floor landing. One shoe had flown off and skittered onto the stairs. Cutting the fishing line and pocketing it, he stepped down to where she was lying, lifted her head in his large rough hands, and with a fierce motion slammed the head onto the concrete floor, generating a fearsome *crack!*

He put his ear to her open mouth and listened. No breath whispered to him.

He felt at her neck for a pulse. There was none.

Letting his fingers glide lightly over her still breast, he felt a powerful urge to rip open her clothes and take her there in the dark stairwell. He had never before felt so aroused. But he knew some early riser might come trotting down the stairs at any minute. Besides, only a fool left his DNA on a corpse.

He smeared liquid laundry soap on the sole of the errant shoe and dribbled more on several steps, then took up the package and moved silently down the stairs to the street. He drove south to 14th Street, turned east and picked up the southbound FDR Drive. As the pink tongue of the morning licked the gray Manhattan skyline, he went over the kill in his mind, savoring every moment. She was so sexy. So utterly beautiful. And so dead.

TWO

Alex Germaine stared at the thick manila envelope on his kitchen counter, the bitter taste of bile rising in his throat. He didn't have to open it to know exactly what was inside. Addressed to him in his own handwriting, the package announced the rejection of his latest manuscript as if the word was stamped across the front in big red letters for the whole world to see.

Taking a mouthful of scotch from his glass, he swirled the golden elixir around in his mouth before swallowing, then he slit open the package with a razor-sharp letter opener and pulled out the form letter. *We have reviewed the enclosed manuscript with great care . . .Our editors are not sufficiently enthusiastic about your work to warrant publishing the material . . . Be assured that this decision does not constitute a criticism of your work. Publishing is a subjective experience. . .*

"Blind bastards!" He crumpled the letter and hurled it at the wastebasket. It bounced off the rim and landed on the floor. He let it lie.

Germaine knew what the rejection was really about. His books had never been bestsellers. The first title had sold four thousand hard covers. Each subsequent book sold less, until the publisher began losing money on a mountain of unsold books. It was all a numbers game. If your book didn't quickly sell out its print run, the publisher branded you a loser and refused to even look at your next work.

He finished off the glass of scotch, noting that the gallon bottle was low. He'd have to fill up on the weekend. Opening the fridge, he saw dried up corned beef from the corner deli and a jar of pickles. The celery stalks in the tray were turning black. He forced the meat and the celery down the garbage disposal, listening to the grinding blades tear up the food, and enjoying the sense of power that came from obliterating a living thing, though it was only a vegetable and some tired beef.

Alex imagined forcing the hand of the editor who had rejected his manuscript into the disposal. Heard him screaming in terror and pain as the blades chewed through his fingers. Saw the blood spurting up from the sink. He would continue forcing the arm down until he reached the shoulder and the editor passed out from loss of blood.

Replaying the revenge fantasy in his mind, he dropped his glass in the sink and left the apartment for his dinner with the mystery writers, wishing he could kill somebody.

THREE

Stanley Bezlin broke his stride as the WALK sign turned red and began to blink. He took in a deep breath; as deep as his lungs would allow.

"Do you want to use your inhaler, dear?" his wife Fran asked. She saw that her husband had no desire to hustle across the street, as he would have done before that dreadful day in September. "I really thought we should have taken a cab to the dinner."

"The doctor said I should exercise as much as my lungs can tolerate," said Stanley. When the WALK sign lit up once more, he took his wife's hand, saying, "C'mon on, I'm not ready for a body bag yet," and strode across Seventh Avenue. A spring shower had tapered off, leaving pools of water in the street that reflected the white headlamps of the passing cars and the colored lights of Rosie O'Grady's restaurant.

Entering the noisy, crowded restaurant, the couple descended a stairwell and passed a sign reading, MYSTERY WRITERS INTERNATIONAL. DINNER & LECTURE. They entered a hushed room where people stood in small groups chatting, drinks in one hand, hors d'oeuvres in the other. The men wore jackets and ties; the women, dresses and pearls.

Stanley greeted several friends as he escorted his wife to the bar. He had a crooked nose from too many fights with belligerent suspects, a few missing teeth, and a partial plate he usually left at home. "False teeth are a pain in the ass. They can take me as I am," he had told Fran when they were getting dressed.

"You're looking good, Stanley!" said a bearded fellow in a corduroy sport coat and bow tie. "Can't keep a good man down!" said another. "That man of yours gets younger every day, Fran," said an elderly woman in a swooping hat with a fake canary pinned to the brim.

"The doctor has him walking twenty minutes a day," said Fran. "And no more than one drink a night."

"A shot of Jameson and a pint of Guinness *is* one drink," said Stanley, giving the bartender a wink. He ordered a beer for himself, a glass of white wine for his wife, and slipped the bartender a tip. They approached a table where Alex Germaine was lecturing several people seated at the table.

"I don't care how many copies the damn thing sold," said Alex. "The Dragon Tattoo trilogy was a verbose, third rate thriller." Germaine was a man of fifty, with receding dark hair that owed its color to a bottle. His large hand engulfed a glass of red wine.

A young man new to the group said, "They were runaway best sellers, they must have had *something* going for them to garner such a huge audience."

Alex took a long pull on his wine. "The publishers are all in bed with the reviewers. Best sellers come from the marketing, not the writing."

"Yeah, but the publisher didn't really market the books, the author was dead," said Stanley, taking a seat beside his wife. "It was all word of mouth that sold them." He shook hands with the new member at the table. "Stanley Bezlin's the name, pleased to meet ya. This gorgeous gal is my wife, Frannie. How she ended up with a broken down ex-cop with a bad ticker and crappy lungs beats the hell out of me, but I'm not complaining."

"Do you have a book out?" Fran asked the new man.

"No, I'm still struggling with the story line." Turning back to Alex, the young man asked, "What is your latest novel about?"

"I'm between publishers," Germaine grumbled. He looked around for the waiter to refill his glass, a sour look on his face.

"A lot of veteran authors have been dropped by their publishers," Stanley explained. "These editors are ruled by the bean counters. It's all a numbers game to them."

"They want every book to be a fucking bestseller!" said Alex. "If your books don't sell out in six weeks, the store sends them back for a refund and your publisher drops you like a shitty diaper." Alex's lips were glistening with wine and mucous.

"It's all so unfair," said Fran, seated beside Alex. "Stanley's first novel got wonderful reviews, but the publisher wouldn't spend a *dime* to promote it."

"Well spoken, my dear," said Alex, leaning in toward her. "You have beauty *and* brains. A deadly combination." He dropped his glazed eyes to Fran's cleavage, amply revealed by a low cut dress.

Embarrassed, she turned toward her husband, trying not to think of Germaine's dirty eyes looking her over. He was a vulgar, hack writer. She hoped the guest speaker would begin his talk soon, it would shut

Germaine up. She hoped.

While Fran remained facing away from him, Alex let his eyes run over her curvaceous body. She was a mouthful. What did a beauty like her see in a sick cop like Bezlin? So he was a 'First Responder'. Big deal, the city was full of them. There was talk some of them were getting sick from working the pile. Good. Let them get sick. Let them all die. The sooner Bezlin was in the ground, the sooner he could drive his tongue deep into Frannie's lovely, sensuous mouth.

FOUR

As the desserts were being served, Alex signaled to the waiter, who appeared not to see him. Irritated, he raised his wine glass over his head. The waiter finally acknowledged his signal and approached with a bottle of red.

"Fill'r up this time," said Alex, slurring his words.

"Sir, perhaps you've enjoyed enough of our spirits — "

"Don't gimme that crap, I can drink any man here under the table!" He held his glass up with a hand so shaky, the waiter had to grasp Alex's wrist and steady it to pour.

As the speaker was introduced, all eyes turned to the podium to hear his remarks. A forensic anthropologist, the man offered a brief explanation of his work, then launched into a grisly case involving a woman who murdered her husband and kept his body in her deep freeze until a blackout killed the electricity. She tried to keep the body preserved with bags of ice, but the local bodega ran out of ice within hours of the power failure. Her neighborhood didn't see its power restored for a week, by which time the stench had attracted the attention of the neighbors. And the police.

While the anthropologist got to the part where the police were about to stumble on the body, Alex stole a glance at Fran, who was staring at the speaker. Savoring the gentle rise and fall of her chest, he cast a glance at Stanley, whose eyes were focused on the speaker as well.

With everyone staring in rapt attention at the lecturer, Alex leaned into Fran and slipped his arm around her waist. He cast his eyes down to enjoy the fullness of her breasts. "My dear, you must stop wasting your feminine wiles on that broken down hack."

Fran pulled her body away from Germaine, bumping into her husband and knocking over a glass of wine.

"You sleazy bastard!" she cried, her face red with fury. "You keep your filthy hands to yourself!"

Alex held both hands up as if held at gunpoint. "Hey, don't blame me, honey. You wear a dress so low your tits are showing, you're asking for a little stroking."

Stanley jumped up from his chair. "You got a lotta nerve, Germaine.

If I was still on the force I'd cuff you right here and throw you in a cell!"

"Well you're not a cop anymore," said Alex.

"I'm still gonna kick your ass." As Stanley stepped toward Germaine, Fran grabbed his arm, trying to restrain him. "Please, dear, remember your heart."

Alex turned away from Stanley, a bemused look on his face. Stanley hesitated, looking back at his wife. Alex suddenly spun around and drove his fist into Stanley's face. Stanley stepped back, tripped on the chair behind him and fell backward. His head made a loud *crack* as it hit the marble floor.

He lay on the floor as motionless as a corpse.

"*Stanley!*" cried Fran, her heart pounding in fear that he had died.

Another writer bent down over the stricken figure and placed his ear over the stricken man's mouth. He heard the soft *sssh, sssh* of air entering Stanley's lungs. "He seems to be breathing all right." He grasped Stanley's wrist and felt his pulse for a moment. "His heart beat is steady. I think he's okay."

A few seconds later Stanley opened his eyes, looked up, and saw several people standing over him. He shook his head trying to clear his mind.

"*What the hell . . .* What am I doing on the floor?"

"You better lie still," said the new member. "I'm no doctor, but I think you could have a concussion."

Stanley pushed himself up to a sitting position. "Where's that bastard Germaine?"

Several heads turned to scan the room. Alex Germaine was nowhere to be seen.

"Looks like he split," said another member.

"The next time I run into that prick I'm gonna murder him." He struggled to his feet, his wife holding him by the arm. "I can't believe I let that drunk sucker punch me. I'm off my game."

Fran said, "Dear, let me take you to the hospital and have them check you out."

"I don't need a hospital, I'm fine."

"You didn't hear the sound your head made when it hit the floor. It was terrible!"

"You always said I was a hard head. Come on, let's get the program going." He signaled to the local chapter president, who escorted the speaker back to the podium while the other members returned to their seats.

As the anthropologist apologized for telling what had obviously been a bad joke, Stanley felt the anger simmer inside him. He felt a powerful urge to hunt Germaine down and beat the crap out of him. It wouldn't be hard to do, he could get the address from a buddy on the force, wait outside the building, then…

But Fran was right, he had to be careful, he shouldn't exert himself. If he didn't have enough wind to dash across an intersection, he couldn't go running after Alex Germaine. Stanley decided to start carrying his service pistol whenever he went out on the off chance he ran into the bastard. Pulling the trigger would require no exertion.

No exertion at all.

FIVE

After the dinner and lecture, Fran insisted that she and Stanley take a cab back to their apartment.

"Je'ez Louise, a cab to Flatbush costs a million bucks! I'm on disability. Remember?"

"I don't care, I don't want you bouncing around on the subway, you could hit your head again." With much grumbling, he let her flag down a cab.

As soon as they were home, Fran made sure her husband got undressed and into bed. While he watched the eleven o'clock news, she sneaked out of the apartment, went down the hall, and knocked softly on a neighbor's door.

After a moment, there was a rustle inside and the door opened. She was relieved to see that Nicholas Andreas was not yet dressed for bed.

"Nicholas, I'm so sorry to bother you this late at night."

"That's all right, I was reading." His face darkened. "What's the matter? Is Stanley short of breath?"

"No, it's not that. For a change." She described the incident at the dinner, Stanley hitting his head and briefly passing out, and her husband's refusal to go to the hospital. "If you could just give him a quick look see?"

"Of *course*. Let me get my keys."

Nicholas walked with Fran to the other apartment, where he found Stanley in bed cursing the broadcaster, who was describing another loss by the Yankees.

"Hey, Stanley. Fran here tells me you were going one-on-one with a big bruiser tonight. Didn't I tell you to avoid bar fights?"

"Jesus H. Christ, did my wife drag you out of your apartment at this ungodly hour? Have you no shame, woman?" Stanley continued as Nicholas sat on the edge of the bed and studied him. "I've taken worse punches in my day. Two guys once broke three of my ribs with baseball bats and I *still* stayed on my feet."

"You were lucky they didn't puncture a lung." Nick held out a finger and told Stanley to follow it with his eyes. "Any dizziness?"

"No."

"Blurred vision?"

"Nope."

He told Stanley to count backward from a hundred by three's.

"That's hard, lemme do it by two's" said Stanley, beginning to count. Fran stood at the foot of the bed, arms across her chest, worry lining her face.

"What do you think, Nick. Is he okay?"

"His *head* is doing fine." To Stanley he said, "Have you coughed up any blood today?"

"Nah, just the usual yellow and green crap. I brought up a mess of it cursing the Yankees on the tube. That A Rod…"

Nicholas noted the bluish tint to Stan's lips and the pallor of his skin. *Chronic oxygen deficit.* He estimated his friend had maybe 40% of his normal lung capacity. Lose any more and he would be bound to a bed or a wheelchair, on oxygen.

Nicholas felt a familiar ache deep in his heart. Looking at his friend, he wanted to break something. Curse someone. He wanted to rewind history and go back to the days following the two planes crashing into the World Trade Center, only he would do it differently. He would be better. Smarter. More courageous.

But it was only a pathetic dream. It was two-thousand three, and there was no going back.

"Maybe it's time to order that oxygen tank," Nicholas said gently. "Do you still have the prescription I gave you?"

"I don't need any fricking oxygen. I'm fine."

Getting up from the bed, Nicholas told Fran that if Stanley showed any signs of dizziness or double vision or if he became confused, she should call 911 and get him to Downstate. "They have a first rate stroke unit. And be sure and wake me, it doesn't matter what the time is."

As he turned to go, Dr. Andreas didn't bother repeating for the hundredth time that he wanted to get Stanley on the waiting list for a heart-lung transplant. Stanley always brushed off the idea. Maybe he was afraid of going under the knife, it *was* a horrific procedure. And the anti-rejection drugs made your body vulnerable to all kinds of infections.

"Don't send me any bill for your house call!" Stanley called after the doctor, trying to summon a real yell. The effort brought on a spasm of coughing. He spat a thick wad of green phlegm into a tissue, then lay back, exhausted.

After giving her neighbor a hug and thanking him profusely, Fran went to the kitchen to make Stanley a cup of hot tea with a splash of Jameson's, and for herself, a pot of strong coffee. She intended to sleep very little this night; she wanted her man alive and complaining when the sun came up.

SIX

In the window seat of a local coffee shop, Alex Germaine bit into his breakfast sandwich, a bacon, egg and cheese on a roll. He watched the pedestrians streaming by on their way to work, school, or some illegal enterprise. He washed the food down with black coffee. Milk was for sissies; they might as well drink *decaf*.

High above Seventh Avenue the sun bathed the streets and sidewalk in a shower of Spring warmth. Pedestrians rolled up their sleeves and bared their heads. Even bald ones. A construction worker across the street took off his shirt and tied it around his waist, showing off a muscular physique that drew the eye of a short-skirted young women walking by.

Alex loved the anonymity of the city. From the noisy streets and crowded sidewalks to the long rows of subway cars loading and unloading around the clock, his presence went unnoticed, like a trained assassin hiding in plain sight. He could watch people at will, free to snatch fragments of conversation and pass on, writing down the words when the speaker was safely out of sight. New York City was the perfect milieu for a writer. Especially a crime writer.

He glanced at the front page of The Post, saw a pouting Laura Metcalf-Reinhold on the cover with the headline, LET THE CREEP SLEEP IN THE STREET! The youngest daughter of the Metcalf real estate mogul, Laura declared that she would never give her cheating husband a thin dime in their divorce.

Opening the paper, he read a classic story of a good looking stud with big ambitions and little talent who met a wealthy woman at the gym, where he worked as a personal trainer. After they married he borrowed money from Laura to launch his own gym and spa. The business was in trouble, and she was about to withdraw her line of credit, leaving him bankrupt. Laura really knew how to turn the screws on the guy, no doubt about it.

The divorce proceedings promised to be explosive. Steven Reinhold claimed that the internet videos of him cheating on Laura were simulated sex. He'd been trying to land a part in a movie and had hired a model to act out love scenes with him. Trying to be a porn star, no doubt.

The videos must have appeared around the time that Laura realized a marriage can't survive on sex and partying alone, no matter how well-endowed the partner. Laura swore she would never settle out of court, she was going to win the case and leave him out on the street. "Let him go back to using his hands to make a living," she declared.

What an iron cast bitch, thought Alex. The hubby should put her out of her misery. Bump her off and he was set for life. The problem was, the cops would make him suspect *numero uno.* Reinhold had motive. In spades. He was poor, she was rich. End of story.

He'd need a solid alibi. Alex knew from reading hundreds of crime stories that manufacturing an unbreakable alibi was a tricky piece of business.

Another issue: opportunity. No doubt he knew her routines. Her favorite haunts; when she would be alone. When she would be *alone and vulnerable.* That could work in his favor, except the cops would know that, too.

Means. The method had to be fast and reliable, and not leave any signs that the husband was the perpetrator. Slow poison, a bullet to the head, a hit and run; any kind of foul play might be traced back to the hubby. It wouldn't be easy to do the deed and not be connected by physical evidence, as well as the timing.

Alex swallowed more coffee as he thought about the dueling divorcees. The husband could always hire somebody to kill his wife. But concealing the fee was a huge problem, the cops had forensic accountants who were as cunning as IRS investigators. They would look at phone records, emails, bank receipts, stock redemptions…The whole nine yards.

A final problem: if the husband hired a killer, someone might see them together plotting the murder, the hubby's face was on the front page of all the papers. Hell, snippets of his "love scene" that Laura released on YouTube had gone viral. Steven had the phony good looks that a Plain Jane remembers, and New York was full of lonely women. Let a spinster librarian take the stand and testify she witnessed the hubby chatting it up with the muscle-bound hired gun on trial and the show was all over.

As he chewed his breakfast sandwich, he contemplated the difficulties the husband faced. One of Alex's favorite aphorisms from his books came to mind: *Murder seeks those who need to die.* Steven Reinhold's wife was asking to be knocked off. Did the husband have the balls to get it done?

SEVEN

Fran pressed the button on the espresso machine and watched the deep brown coffee stream from the spout, the heady aroma cheering her morning. "Want me to froth the milk before I go to work?" she said.

"Yeah, thanks," said Stanley from behind his newspaper. She placed the cup in front of Stanley and kissed the top of his head. He reached for the cup without taking his eyes off the paper.

"That Alex Germaine made me so mad last night," she said, pouring a cup of tea into her travel mug from a diminutive teapot painted with tiny flowers. "What a letch. I'd like to scratch his eyes out." She added a spoon of honey and a little milk and screwed down the top.

"He always was a sleaze ball. And a lousy writer. Sucker punching me…" He sipped his coffee. "You make the best damn coffee in all five boroughs."

"I always knew you married me for my cooking."

He lowered the paper, gave her a lascivious look. "It wasn't your cooking caught my eye."

She smiled and sipped her tea. The phone rang. Seeing he was ignoring it, she shook her head and answered it.

"Hello? Yes, this is Fran. Hi, Nicholas! How nice to hear from you. What? No, Stanley isn't busy, he's just having his coffee. Hold on."

She pulled down the top of Stan's newspaper and held the phone out to him.

"It's Nicholas Andreas."

"Ah." Stanley put down his paper. "Hi ya, doc. What's the word?"

"I called to see how you're feeling. Did you have any dizziness this morning? Headache? Ringing in your ears?"

"No, I'm fine. I got a lump the size of an Easter egg on the back of my head, but I'm okay, thanks."

"I wanted to be sure you didn't lapse into a coma during the night. Fran could sue the hell out of me, and the Department of Health doesn't offer malpractice insurance."

"I was shot and left for dead one time, don't worry about me."

"I'm a public health doctor, worry comes with the job."

"It's the same with cops. What'cha doing today?"

"I'm going out in the field testing high school students' lung function."

"No kidding. Hey, could we get together for a drink later? I want to hear more about what you dig up. It might tie in with my condition."

"Uh, we're not supposed to talk about our findings, there are confidentiality issues. I could lose my job if I let any information out. You understand."

"Sure, sure, it's the same with us. We can't discuss a case that's under active investigation. Besides, anything connected with the World Trade Center fallout is touchy stuff. There are people making all kinds of claims, the dust made them sick."

When Nicholas didn't pursue the topic, Stanley said, "Hey, how's about we get together and talk about our wives? After all, they talk about us all the time."

"I don't think I can make it for a drink, Stanley, work's crazy. But I will stop by tonight to see how you're feeling."

"Great. I'll have some beers on ice. See ya later." As he hung up the phone, Stanley turned to his wife with a grin on his face. "How 'bout that? I've got my own personal physician."

"You need a jailer, not a doctor," said Fran. "Why don't I make up an ice pack for your head before I go to work?"

"Leave my head alone, there's nothin' wrong with it!"

Fran slung her tote bag across her shoulder, picked up her mug of tea and kissed her husband on the top of his head. Walking to the front door she said, "Don't you go drinking with Nicholas tonight. I want that heart of yours to keep on ticking."

"One shot and a beer!" he told her. "Promise!"

"I'm getting a breathalyzer for you, mister," she said and waved to him from the door. Once out in the hall, her smile washed away. When was that hard head ever going to realize he couldn't go on living in the old way? That he had to be careful and not push himself?

Punching the button for the elevator, her mind recalled the days when Stanley was in the hospital and the doctors were telling her there was little they could do for him, there was no effective treatment for the strange new disease eating away his lungs.

She stepped into the elevator feeling a terrible sorrow. And fear.

EIGHT

Finishing his breakfast, Alex left the little coffee shop and walked the streets with no destination in mind. That was often the key to unlocking his muse: to wander through the city, unnoticed; anonymous; letting his mind meander along with his legs. Eventually his muse whispered in his ear, revealing the story.

He considered how Steven Reinhold could free himself from his bitch of a wife Laura Metcalf. A professional killer was his only solution, but how could he connect with one? He couldn't post a *Killer Wanted* ad on Craig's list. Hell, they were even taking down the ads for the massage artists. Whatever happened to freedom of the press? And if Steven *did* try to contact somebody via the internet, he'd end up with an undercover cop, just like the perverts caught looking for some young plaything.

Divorce was a damn, dirty business. The husband shouldn't have to take his chances before some lame judge the rich wife bought off. The poor slob didn't have a chance.

Crossing a street in a stream of pedestrian, Alex suddenly stopped in the middle of the intersection, an idea starting to form in his mind. *What about a professional killer who plies the divorce courts seeking clients?* He studies the warring parties and determines who has guts enough to hire him, then offers to murder the other in a way that looks like an accident.

A cabby leaned on his horn and stuck his head out of the window throwing curses. Alex held out a hand like a traffic cop and continued across the street, savoring the ideas as they streamed through his mind. The Medical Examiner would rule accidental death; that would eliminate any serious police investigation. The killer could even offer to wait for the first payment until after the case is closed.

It was brilliant! Pure genius! A breakthrough novel, with movie rights screaming to be bought at auction. Was DeNiro too old for the part?

He realized that with one stroke he had created a unique criminal for his story line. The killer not only had a modus operandi that had never been used in a crime novel, but he could make trenchant and pithy observations about marriage and the human condition as he plans his kills. The story had action *and* philosophy.

This was going to be a best seller! An MWI award winner! A major motion picture!

He decided to use the Reinhold-Metcalf divorce case as the template for his first murder scene, they were already caricatures of feuding divorcees. Alex had no doubt the hapless husband was a shallow, unscrupulous wannabe actor who married Laura for her money. The poor sap would be glad to be rid of his ball-busting wife as long as no evidence pointed to him.

The method was Alex's first order of business; the death had to fool the Medical Examiner. With many options at his disposal, Alex was confident he could work out a scheme that would convince the husband that his killer was a pro with a string of successful contracts. Accidents were common enough, and the papers said Laura was a heavy drinker. Kill her when her blood alcohol level was sky high and there'd be no questions asked, case closed.

Collecting the fee without arousing suspicion was a lot trickier. The killer would have to receive the payments without providing any kind of paper trail. Not even phone records or email. First contact would have to be person-to-person. After that, the killer would have to make any phone calls from a pay phone or unlisted cell, in case a suspicious detective applied for a subpoena just to be thorough.

The problems in the story line fired up his imagination. Alex could feel his creative juices bubbling inside him. He needed to observe the couple in court in order to develop his characters. He would even steal some snatches of dialogue if he could get close enough. Then there were the lawyers, the judge, the court personnel...He didn't want to rely on scenes from *Law & Order* for his research, he wanted to get it right. Telling the truth on the page was the important part of writing. *Truth* was the only part that mattered.

As he walked along the crowded street, the joyful noise in his heart subdued the old gloom that had gripped him after the latest rejection. The incident at the MWI dinner the night before now seemed like a joke. Who did that Stanley Bezlin think he was, threatening to have him arrested? Alex's hasty retreat had been a strategic necessity; no sense putting himself at risk. What if he *did* give her a little squeeze? It wasn't even her tits or ass.

Maybe he wouldn't be back at the MWI any time soon, but so what?

What did they ever do for him? Did they help him place his latest manuscript? Hell, no! All the agents and editors who came to the conferences and dinners were caught up in young, virile writers, like Jason Starr and Steve Hamilton. Like their stories were any better than his. He dyed his hair to make himself look younger, but it didn't help, they still turned him down cold.

But hadn't it felt great when his fist connected with Bezlin's chin? He showed those milksops at the dinner what a *real* tough guy was all about.

And then when the clumsy oaf fell backward and hit his head and it looked like he was *dead:* now that was thrilling! Alex hadn't felt so excited since he deflowered a virgin his senior year in high school. To think he could have killed the man with his bare hands. What a revelation. What a kick. And in front of everybody! He showed *them* who had the balls in that crowd of pansies.

Seeing in the newspaper that Laura and her husband were scheduled to be in court today, Alex hurried back to his apartment to change his clothes. He was going to become a hard-nosed old lawyer.

NINE

Dr. Nicholas Andreas rode the subway to his first testing assignment of the day, a high school in Manhattan. Settling into a seat, he opened the newspaper and read the obituaries. During his residency he'd begun reading them as a mental exercise, trying to determine the cause of death when the obit left out the fatal diagnosis. He took what little history was available — age, ethnicity, occupation, and so on — and worked toward a diagnosis. In the two years since 9/11, Nicholas found himself drawn more intensely to the dead.

He read about an elderly cat lover, Agnes Allen, who left her estate to a pride of felines. Nicholas wondered if the old woman died from an infection she acquired from the cats. Had the Medical Examiner taken the proper cultures, some of them required special media to grow? If the dead woman's family physician was willing to sign the death certificate, there would be no autopsy, and no tests for infections that crossed species from cats to humans.

He put away the newspaper as the train neared his stop at Chambers Street in lower Manhattan. Stuyvesant High School. On the steps to the building a tall, hefty Hispanic man with an earring in his left ear, black leather jacket and aluminum case was leaning on a railing watching the girls enter. Nicholas recognized the young man's Department of Health ID tag.

"Hi, I'm Doctor Andreas. You must be the respiratory technician."

"That's me, Steffan Iregui." Steffan held out a meaty hand. "Call me Stef."

"Call me Nicholas."

"Cool."

Nicholas led the way into the building. They showed their DOH identification to the guard and made their way to the Health Office. The school nurse was a worn out white woman with thinning red hair that was gray at the roots, tired eyes, and age spots on her hands. Nicholas introduced Steffan and himself.

"Yeah, the A-P told me you guys were coming. Have a seat." They sat on rickety plastic chairs that listed to the side. "I gotta tell you, I'm up to my armpits in work. I don't have time to help you perform these tests."

"That's okay, my assistant and I can do the studies. We just need a space to work in."

"*Ha!* Space? We're so packed in here, sardines would be laughing! But I cleared out the exam room for you. As long as nobody comes in bleeding to death, I guess you can use it."

Steffan set up the pulmonary function machine, an electronic meter with a corrugated tube and disposable mouthpiece. The machine measured lung capacity, force of expiration, and lung elasticity.

Telling Nicholas he had to calibrate the machine, Steffan turned it on and ran it through the diagnostics. Nicholas saw him attach a plastic mouthpiece to a flexible tube.

"There isn't any risk of exposure to the previous user's mouth flora, is there?" asked Nicholas.

"No way," said Steffan. "Each mouthpiece is disposable and has a one-way valve. We've never had a case of infection linked to the tester."

As Nicholas took out a clipboard with a sign-in sheet, a group of students began to line up outside the room. "You got your first victims!" called the school nurse. She steered a skinny girl with a butterfly tattoo on the back of her neck into the exam room.

"Be sure and check their photo ID," the nurse told Nicholas. "These kids have all kinds of tricks."

"I have a daughter in high school, I know all about it," said Nicholas. He gave the girl the sign-in sheet and told her to be sure and put down her height, weight and address.

"Which one, my parents are divorced?" she asked.

"Put down the one you spend the most time with," he said. As she scribbled on the page, Nicholas asked to see her school ID.

With a dramatic sigh, the girl unfastened a button on her shirt and pulled out her ID from where it hung in a pouch between her breasts. She leaned in close to Nicholas, bringing her chest within inches of his own.

"You won't have to strip for this test," said Nicholas.

Steffan grinned and handed the girl the mouthpiece. "See, you first take a deep breath and then you exhale as hard as she can into the machine. You keep blowing out until — "

"I *know* how to give a blow job, thank you. What do you think they teach us in this school?" She put the mouthpiece between her teeth and rolled her eyes.

Steffan winked at Nicholas as he pressed a button on the machine and said, *"Breathe in! Deep! Deeper!"*

The digital meter rapidly increased until stopping at a value. *"Now blow out hard as you can!"* The girl blew until her face was red and she was hunched over from the effort. She went through the test a second time. Satisfied with the second pass, Steffan tore out a printout from the machine, clipped it to a paper and told her she was finished.

"What's it say?" said the girl.

Steffan looked at Nicholas, who said, "We're studying the whole school, not individuals. Your values will be a component of the study."

"That's fucking great," said the girl, turning to the others in line. *"We're dying 'cause they brought us back to school four weeks after nine-eleven, and they're not even gonna tell us how sick we are."*

Nicholas wanted to tell the girl that the Department of Health would release a summary of the aggregate data once it had been analyzed, but he knew that explaining that to her was as pointless as reasoning with his teenage daughter Christine, who was always angry with him.

The worst part was, he knew their accusations were true.

"Next student, please," said the school nurse, hustling the first student out of the room.

Nicholas handed the sign-in sheet to the next student, an overweight boy with acne and a pale mustache, trying to look grown up. As the boy took the fresh mouthpiece in hand, Nicholas felt the gloom descend on him. He worried that his wife and daughter would show signs of lung damage. He worried because they lived in Brooklyn Heights, less than two miles from Ground Zero. The wind had blown the toxic plume south for weeks, carrying a horrible odor. Everyone in the Heights had been exposed, but Nicholas had reassured his family they didn't need to take any special precautions. That the EPA's tests showed there would be no long term health threat from the malodorous air.

The memory brought to mind how his friend Stanley volunteered to join the patrol around the smoking site where the Twin Towers once stood. Four officers from each precinct in Brooklyn were sent to help. Stanley felt like one of the lucky ones when he was chosen to guard the site.

The second night on his apartment terrace, watching the smoke drift over the northern end of Brooklyn, and knowing that his friend was in the middle of it, Nicholas considered taking a respirator-type mask and isolation suit from the DOH and giving it to Stanley. But he didn't do it. *Why?* Why didn't he knock on that door just down the hall and insist that his friend take the precautions that any prudent occupational health officer would insist upon?

Nicholas didn't know. Or perhaps he didn't want to know. Didn't want to look into the face of his irrefutable failure.

TEN

Returning to his apartment to prepare for his 'court appearance', Alex changed into an old pinstripe suit he once picked up at Goodwill and had dry-cleaned and pressed. He set off the suit with a lavender handkerchief in the breast pocket, making him look the quintessential lawyer. An old attaché case had a bruised look that spoke of years battling hard-nosed opponents and carrying the day. Even his shoes, polished broughams, proclaimed *serious attorney!*

He rode the subway to the courthouse, showed his driver's license to a bored guard, let his attaché case be scanned, and signed in. The guard didn't seem to find it odd that Alex was not flashing his lawyer's bar card. That was a good omen. If security was lax he could come and go as he wished. He would observe the Metcalf-Reinholds fighting it out in court, steal lines of dialogue from overheard conversations, and get a read on their deepest passions and flaws.

Finding the courtroom, he selected a seat close to the front where he estimated one of the spouses would be seated, and waited. The courtroom was almost empty. A middle aged couple dressed in shabby clothes was standing before the judge. A pair of reporters sat off to one side trading whispered stories, waiting for the fireworks to erupt when Laura and Steven's turn came up. A sleepy clerk with a clipboard leaned in to a female security guard and said something that she ignored, while the judge glanced at his watch, ignoring the big clock mounted on the wall.

The husband and wife before the court were angry as a pair of dogs fighting over a bone. Their sniping went into Alex's notebook. Complaints, charges of abuse, appeals for the welfare of the children. It was a string of tired clichés. Stanley wrote in his notebook: *The sniping spouses were hostile but poor; the murder business has no room for charity cases. Cash and carry rules the day.* His killer would ignore them and wait for a spouse with deep pockets.

The next case was free of fireworks. The divorcing couple looked tired and despondent. They couldn't wait for the marriage to be ended. When the judge asked the soon to be ex-wife if there was any hope for reconciliation, she shrugged her shoulders and said, "Look at him: what's to love?" Alex scribbled the line in his notebook along with a description of the sad sack sitting with his head down as if half asleep.

Alex realized he was seeing the rotting entrails of a moribund institution. Maybe the Mormons weren't so crazy after all. Two people locked in a marriage for eternity with no legal options for variety? For fresh flesh? It was an absurd idea. Why in hell did the gays and lesbians want *this*? Were they *crazy?*

Finally Laura Metcalf made her entrance. The dark haired beauty walked through the room with a confident gait, her tall, slim body ramrod straight. The look on her face proclaimed, *Get out of my way, peasants!* Even her long, manicured fingers looked made for clawing.

Laura's lawyer, a handsome, tanned fellow in a beautiful pin striped suit, struggled to keep up with her as she strutted down the aisle. Once seated in the first row, the lawyer leaned over and spoke in her ear. She listened without reply, her face a mask. Cold. In control. She would take no prisoners.

A moment later Steven Reinhold strode in. The sculpted figure in an elegant suit was light on his feet. Reinhold was handsome and muscled. The man was made to star in a porn film. Maybe the judge would believe the story that his liaison was simulated sex. Steven smirked when he saw Laura, as if the entire procedure was a joke to him. His lawyer was a rotund, pink-faced fellow with a diamond ring on his pinky. Alex took the lawyer for a smug bastard who slavered his bread with butter and caviar and ordered his wine by the year.

The court crier announced the case: *"Laura Metcalf-Reinhold v. Steven Reinhold!"*

The judge asked Laura's lawyer if he was ready to proceed. The lawyer produced a raft of papers and put forward several motions, arguing that Steven had failed to produce accurate and complete financial statements. Steven's lawyer rose to object.

Alex ignored the legalisms and the jousting lawyers, studying the couple instead. It was clear that Laura was heartless enough to want her husband dead. She was arrogant, vain, and a ferocious snob who seemed fully capable of killing her husband in cold blood. She would jump at the chance to hire a professional.

But with her video of hubby in bed with an actress, Laura clearly had the stronger hand. Why would she take a chance on a hired gun when she held the winning cards? On top of that, the judge appeared sympathetic to many of her lawyer's motions. Steven's lawyer protested, argued, and pleaded, but lost most of his objections. Alex decided that, having the upper hand, his Laura character would be a poor prospect for a killer for hire.

On the other side, Steven was clearly a degenerate, narcissistic stud with everything to lose. He would have no compunction about paying to have his wife killed, but did he have the cajones to go through with it?

The judge set a trial date for two months hence. As he stood to leave, Steven winked at Laura. If he was facing a losing battle, the cocky bastard wasn't letting it show. Hoping to study his subject further, Alex followed him out onto the street. When Steven walked into the first pub in sight, Alex followed him in. The double promise of a scotch and a colorful character to observe was irresistible.

ELEVEN

Stepping into the dimly lit pub down the street from the courthouse, Alex wondered how he might strike up a conversation with Steven Reinhold. He was hoping to dig up some juicy dirt on the wife that he could use in the manuscript. Alex knew all too well that disgruntled husbands loved to talk trash about their wives.

He watched Steven lean in close to a leggy hostess, stuff a ten dollar bill in her hand and whisper in her ear. She threw the handsome lothario an appreciative smile and led him to a table in the back. In a heartbeat a waitress took his order and went to fill it.

Alex settled at the bar, ordered a scotch and considered how to broach the interview. Some people were prickly about talking to writers, especially when they were in a court case, their words could be used against them. Alex had no problem feeling sympathy for the poor bastard, his own wife had fucked him over in their divorce years ago. *Took the rights to his first four novels, the bitch.*

Not that they brought in any revenue stream any more, but you never know, Hollywood could come knocking any time. You get a movie deal, they bring back the book in trade paperback to coincide with the movie release and it's found money. *Screenplay based on the novel by Alex Germaine.* Is that ever a sweet sight or what?

Bringing his glass to his lips, Alex recalled the latest rejection from another brain dead book editor. The jerk was into 'Zombie' stories. *Zombies?* Wasn't the world full of enough crazed fanatics killing people at random, did they need to imagine walking *dead* people?

Alex's spirits sank as he swallowed the whiskey. Here he was, mining this couple for a *great story,* one that was fresh and had plenty of juicy murders, and what was the chance he'd even get an editor to look at it?

Zero. Nada. Nil.

The future was bleak. Even the scotch failed to lift his gloom. The landlord would throw him out in the street soon if he didn't come up with some income pronto. His life was shit. The excitement over his new story line withered before the reality of the literary marketplace.

He set his drink down on the table. As he stared into the empty glass bemoaning his fate, the glimmer of an idea nudged his consciousness. As the idea grew and took shape, his spirits began to lift. He felt his failure transforming into a shining opportunity, like an alchemist turning a slab of lead into solid, shimmering gold.

In the same way that the solution to a tricky story line sometimes struck him without warning, the answer to all his problems reared back and hit him between the eyes. It was an epiphany with a solid left and a roundhouse right.

I, Alex Germaine, am perfectly suited to embody my own fictional killer. I have the skills, the motivation, and the guts to carry out the very murders I've been plotting for my novel. He was destined to become the heroic figure he'd spent his whole life creating. He would become a professional killer.

Alex especially enjoyed the fact that he wouldn't have to run his story line by some twenty-something junior editor fresh from Vassar for her approval. He had only to convince the client that he had a foolproof plan with a hundred per cent guarantee, and his financial future was assured.

Ordering a refill from the bartender, he marveled at the beauty and simplicity of the solution. There would be no royalties, which meant *no taxes.* No scathing revues from wannabe writers masquerading as 'critics.' No returned books from book stores, turning his advance payment into a debt to the publisher.

And the best part of all was, *he got to kill people!*

Alex picked up his drink from the bar and sauntered toward Steven Reinhold. Holding the attaché case in one hand, he reached out the other, saying, "Excuse me. Rene Anabasian, sorry to disturb. I saw you went before Judge DeSantis today."

"Uh, yes, that's right. How did you…"

"I'm representing a fellow in a case right after yours. Unfortunately, he's been arrested for violating a restraining order, so I had to explain to the judge why he was a no show."

"Tough break for your client."

"Indeed. He will find no sympathy from the judge after his latest transgression."

Alex looked at the empty chair opposite Steven. When Steven invited him to sit, Alex put down his scotch and settled into the chair. He looked into the golden liquid. "Such a beautiful color, don't you think? A woman with eyes that color will bewitch you, and then she will break your heart."

Steven shrugged. "They're all bitches."

Alex took a sip and savored the elixir. "I sympathize with your situation. Your wife is holding a winning hand."

"I'm happy with my lawyer, Mister Ana . . ."

"Anabasian. As well you should be. I'm not here to poach on another man's territory. Your situation reminds me of my own divorce years ago. The scars have yet to heal." He tilted his glass, swirling the liquor in the glass.

"The world's fucked up when even lawyers get screwed in a divorce."

"Indeed it is," said Alex. "I often wished my wife had suffered a fatal accident. A car wreck, say. Or a drowning." He set the glass down and glanced at Reinhold. "Do you ever feel like that?"

"Of *course,* every husband does. But I don't have that kind of luck, my wife will live to be a hundred." He took a long pull on his drink.

Alex looked into Steven's eyes. "I believe I have some information that will give you a measure of comfort." He signaled to the waitress to bring Steven another drink. Leaning closer to Steven, he said, "Permit me tell you how you can bring this troublesome divorce to a totally satisfying conclusion."

TWELVE

Once Steven's drink arrived, Alex began his pitch. "From time immemorial men have wished that they could rid themselves of a mate without any messy complications. Like any other need, this desire was eventually met by a service provider. Several of these service agencies have been established over the years, each with its own unique methodologies and terms of payment."

"You mean, like divorce lawyers?"

"No, my friend, not lawyers. Our company has been in the eradication business for over seventy years. *And,* not only can we brag of a one-hundred percent success rate, the best in the industry, we also have the most affordable payment plan."

Steven looked at Alex as if he were speaking a strange tongue. "Exactly what sort of 'elimination' are you talking about here?"

"The only completely permanent kind," said Alex, enjoying his role of storyteller. "The kind that's been on your mind for some time, I daresay."

"You don't mean…"

"Oh, yes, Mister Reinhold. I am speaking of terminating a life. A quick, efficient death."

"Now wait a minute." Reinhold looked around the bar to be sure nobody could hear them. "This elimination thing is some kind of joke. Right?"

Alex calmly sipped his scotch. "I assure you, we are a serious business."

Steven looked hard at Alex. "Laura put you up to this, didn't she? You're wearing a wire."

"If you wish, we can retire to the bathroom and you can search me from head to foot. I'll even give you my briefcase to examine."

Steven stared at Alex, wanting to believe him but wary of being caught in a trap.

"Nah, this is nuts, I'd never get away with it. I'm the first guy the cops would come to. They'd be sweating me in the precinct all night."

"Not when we are involved. You will at most encounter merely the briefest of interviews. It will be nothing more than a formality."

"Yeah? What makes you so sure?"

"Several reasons. First of all, our eliminations perfectly resemble an accident. The Medical Examiner will so rule, ergo, the police will have no reason to suspect you."

"They're not dummies, they'll still be suspicious."

"Of course they will, but with no forensic evidence to support the theory that a crime has been committed, the police will be handcuffed." Alex savored his little play on words while he watched Steven begin to imagine the possibilities suddenly open to him.

"Secondly, we will activate the procedure at a time and place that give you an ironclad alibi. You will in point of fact be thousands of miles away."

"That's smart," said Steven, beginning to warm to the idea. "Speaking theoretically."

"Thirdly, your payments will be on a monthly schedule, and *you will pay nothing until you have the Medical Examiner's final ruling of accidental death.*" Alex waited while the part about paying no money up front sank in. "After the report, you will pay in a form that will not arouse the slightest suspicion. You will continue the payments until the bill is paid in full."

As Steven weighed the proposal, Alex delivered the coup de grace. "The judge is going to rule against you. You'll end up with zip. We know your spa business is in financial trouble."

"The bitch is calling in the debt. I have to repay her share of the company, and I don't have it. I don't know what I'm going to do."

"This is the only way to secure your financial future."

Steven nodded his head slowly at this last statement. His wife had him in a financial vise and she was clamping down on his balls. The promise of saving his company was almost as appealing as eliminating Laura. It meant he would have a future, *and* access to untold numbers of young women in scanty outfits.

"Okay, supposing for just a minute that I buy into this crazy scheme, and I'm not saying I will, how much would it cost me?"

"Fifty thousand dollars."

"Jesus Christ, that's — "

"A pittance when compared to the estate that you will inherit."

"Hey, she's no millionaire."

"True, but the condo is paid off. How much is it worth?"

"After the sharks get their cut, maybe a mil. Depends on the market."

"A very nice piece of collateral for you, not to mention you keeping your business."

Steven waved the waitress off when she came to ask about a refill.

"Look," said Steven. "I'm not gonna say another word until I know if you're taping me."

"I expect no less."

"That means you got to strip in front of me."

"Not a problem." Alex drained his glass, rose and ambled toward the restroom, with Steven a step behind. They crowded into a stall, where Steven examined Alex's chest, back and attaché case. Once he was satisfied that Alex wasn't wearing a wire, they returned to the table. Steven said, "Okay, I admit, I like the idea. But what if you get arrested and you finger me?"

"For one thing, there is no evidence linking us. There's no paper trail. We share no business connections. No one can link you to me or to the death."

"That sounds good."

"Once the Medical Examiner files his report you'll make ten monthly payments that total fifty thousand. Each payment will be a different amount, but the total will come to the sum we agreed upon."

"You'll want cash, I'm sure."

"Cash is always best." Alex explained how Steven was to deliver his payments. The payment plan was as ingenious as the accidental death angle. Steven had to admit, this company had worked out all the kinks; they were pros, no doubt about it. Although he thought it was a good plan, Steven was still doubtful.

"I still don't know about this. It's so…drastic. I'll need some time to mull it over."

"Of course. You have twenty-four hours to give me your answer."

"*Twenty-four hours?* My trial doesn't come up for two months!"

"Waiting a week, a month, will not change your mind. You knew the moment you heard our proposal that it was the best course for you to take." Alex understood that the best salesmen warned that an offer was only good for a limited time. After that, it was gone forever. Take the once in a lifetime deal now or live with regret your whole life.

"I'm not saying it isn't appealing. But look at it from my angle. I mean, I can't research your prospectus. I can't contact other clients to see if they're satisfied."

"We have been in the business for seventy years. Look at the Hoffa affair. That was perfectly executed."

"Hoffa was a mob hit, wasn't it?"

Alex shook his head. "The wife. She retired to Italy."

Steven looked at him in awe.

"Be at home tomorrow at exactly…" Alex looked at his watch, a Rolex knockoff. "Six-fifteen in the evening. I will say that World Wide Delivery has a package to deliver. If you accept our offer, say that you agree to accept the package. If not, say you are not taking delivery of any packages."

"Agree to accept the package, I agree to the job."

"Correct. You will receive final instructions at that time."

"I don't know…"

"Everything will be explained at the appropriate time. Be at home at the appointed hour with your answer."

Alex stood, dropped a twenty dollar bill on the table, picked up his attaché case and walked out without looking back, confident he had made his first contract. He told himself he had to research that line about Hoffa's widow. The improvisational statement had been brilliant, but next time he would be sure his facts were correct. Good story telling was all about the truth.

THIRTEEN

Returning from the high school to the Department of Health, Nicholas entered the data for the students' lung function into his computer. He divided the students into two cohorts: those who lived or attended school near Ground Zero on 9/11, and those who were far away at the time. His computer program rendered a pair of bell-shaped graphs representing lung function, typical for a human population. An overwhelming majority clustered within two standard deviations of the mean at the peak of the curve. A few athletic types with large lung volumes occupied the right side of the curve. The kids with asthma or other pulmonary diseases trailed on the lower left.

Nicholas overlaid the data from the students who had been close to the toxic plume at Ground Zero with those who had not. The curve representing the non-exposed students was shifted to the right. *Very far to the right.* The lung compliance of the lower Manhattan students was shifted to the left. Their lung capacity was degraded compared to the control group.

He called Libby, his supervisor, and told her his initial findings were disturbing, could she look at them. When she came to his office a few minutes later he showed her the two bell curves.

"I see what you mean," Libby said. She was a dark haired woman with a face lovely enough to need no makeup. Libby leaned over the desk, placing her hand casually on Nicholas's shoulder as if for balance. He could smell her perfume. It was delicate and understated. He stole a glance at her, saw a button on her blouse casually open, revealing the smooth, creamy skin and the curve of her breasts.

He focused his eyes on the computer screen. "The lung compliance of the study group is reduced compared with the control." He looked into her face. "We should try and sample the students who have graduated and gone off to college."

"They're out of our jurisdiction."

"We could bring them in when they come home on their summer break."

"No. We will limit the study to the current student body."

Knowing it would be futile to continue the argument, he said, "I think we can assume many of the students will become symptomatic in the near future. If they haven't become sick already."

Libby stood up, letting go of his shoulder. "The data doesn't prove that their lungs are permanently damaged. These subjects are young. Their lung performance may improve over time."

"Come on, you don't really believe that."

"Why not? It's only been two years since the Twin Towers fell. There's no predicting its course in subjects that were only marginally exposed."

"Marginal? Half those kids went to school within a mile of Ground Zero! The other half all live in the same zip code. And look at the medical reports of the firemen and police who stayed at the site: their lungs are emphysematous, and they're in their prime!"

"There's no basis of comparison, the police and firemen worked directly at the site. The students weren't involved in the rescues or the demolition."

Nicholas gave her a printout of the data. "These are important findings. When will the DOH release them to the public?" He looked into her eyes, trying to determine her sincerity. He could see she was avoiding looking at him. She wrinkled her nose, a facial tic Nicholas assumed indicated anxiety. As in telling a lie.

"The decision to release information comes from the director. You know that, Nicholas. We'll have to wait and see."

"Yeah, right. Wait and see and bury the data, just like the city buried the remains at the site."

"Nicholas, don't go there." The anxiety in Libby's eyes turned to anger. She struggled to keep her temper. "We're bound by confidentiality laws, you know that. There are Homeland Security issues. We all took that loyalty oath, remember that."

"Like I had *a choice?*"Nicholas's voice cracked from the strain. "Like the fucking FBI gave me an *option* when I swore to keep my work confidential or face incarceration in some gulag for who knows how many years? You mean *that* oath?"

Libby's anger expired, replaced by sorrow. "Don't be a martyr, Nicholas, the world has seen too many martyrs. Just submit your data and go home to your family."

She walked out of his office, leaving Nicholas to marvel yet again at the efficiency of the Federal Bureau of Investigation. At how they came to New York twenty-four hours after the planes destroyed the two towers and made everyone at the Department of Health swear a blood oath of secrecy.

He remembered thinking, *now that's government at its most efficient.*

Planning to work on the student data at home, as he did with countless studies in the past, he used his thumbnail drive to transfer the pulmonary function files from his desktop to his laptop. Then he put his laptop in his bag, locked his desk and left the office.

As he waited for the elevator, he thought about Stanley's last heart attack. About his ten days on the respirator in the Intensive Care Unit; Fran terrified of losing her husband; Nicholas feeling helpless because he couldn't contribute anything to his friend's care.

He imagined his teenage daughter in the same condition. The image terrified him. She had to be warned. All of the students needed to be warned. But he knew leaking the data from his field work would cost him his job. Probably his freedom as well. The hole he'd dug was getting deeper and darker and there was no way out. He had never felt so helpless. So defeated. He could almost taste the damp earth in his mouth.

Nicholas was approaching the security desk on his way out of the Department of Health when the security guard held up a hand for him to stop. Puzzled, Nicholas approached the guard, who sat on an elevated seat behind a high desk. Banks of video monitors showed interior and exterior views of the building.

"Lemme see your bag," the guard said.

"Why?"

"'Cause I said so." The guard, tall and burly, held out a thick hand, his face as serious as a corpse.

"But I've been going out of this building for eight years. Nobody's ever —"

"The bag, or I search *you.*"

Stifling an urge to curse the man, Nick placed the battered old leather attaché on the guard's desk and watched while the frowning authority figure rifled through it. Nicholas noticed that the guard was wearing a sidearm.

When had they started carrying guns?

He watched the guard pull out his laptop computer.

"That's mine," said Nicholas.

"No computers go out of the building without your department head's written permission."

"But it's my *personal* computer."

"No laptops go out without authorization. Period." The guard pointed to the elevators.

Nicholas felt a fury boiling up inside. He was tempted to tell the guard to go fuck himself, but knew it would only get him sanctioned. If not suspended. He turned and returned to his office, where he locked his laptop away.

When he left the building after again submitting to a search of his bag, he asked himself, *When had paranoia taken over the mindset of the DOH?* It had been growing slowly. Inexorably. Until it became the norm.

Out in the street, he took out his phone and called Stanley. "You still want to meet for that drink?"

FOURTEEN

Nicholas entered Eammon's pub and settled into a seat beside his friend.

"What are you drinking?" asked Stanley, signaling to the waitress.

"I'll have a Jameson on the rocks," said Nicholas, glancing at the copy of The Post his friend had been reading. He saw the picture of Laura Metcalf-Reinhold promising her soon-to-be ex-husband would be sleeping in the street, and wondered if he would be in the same predicament before long.

"Great drink, Jameson's," said Stanley. "Maybe the Irish didn't invent whiskey, but they sure showed the world how to make it. Look at their Tullamore Dew, for Christ's sake. I mean, who else would name a whiskey after the morning dew?"

Stanley turned to the waitress and gave her their order. When the drinks were served, he took out a twenty dollar bill and put it on the bar, waving Nick's hand away. The two men sipped their drinks and waited for the relief it would bring.

"Tell me something, Stanley. What's it like, being a writer?"

"I've been in bar fights that left me with less bruises. The typical editor buys one new manuscript for every *thousand* that's sent to him. And even when your book is published, if you don't sell out the print run, no publisher will even look at your next manuscript."

"That sounds like a tough business."

"It is. But I get to do a lot of interesting research. Not as interesting as the stuff you're doing."

"My work? Oh, it's interesting all right." Nicholas took another sip and looked into his glass. Stanley waited for Nick to elaborate, but his friend kept quiet.

"You said something on the phone about testing high school students. What's that about?"

Nicholas looked around to see that no one was in earshot. "I want to test all the Stuyvesant students who were sent back to class a few weeks after nine-eleven, but it's two years since the exposure, and half of them are off in college. They're scattered all over the country. The DOH is limiting the study to the students who are still in school."

"And the results are...what?"

"Actually, the data is very compelling." Nicholas glanced around the bar once more to be sure no one could hear him. "The students who went to Stuyvesant or lived near Ground Zero have poorer lung function than students who were miles away and weren't exposed to the toxic plume. The exposed students don't seem to be symptomatic. Yet. But they should be followed closely, these findings are extremely troubling."

"The kids must be pissed as hell, knowing their lungs are at risk."

"That's the problem, the DOH won't release the data to individual students. As a public health agency we study whole populations, not individuals. It's maintained as *aggregate* data. Our study guidelines forbid us from releasing specific findings to individual test subjects."

"Typical government bull shit," said Stanley. "Hide the facts and hope you never get called to testify before a Congressional committee." He lapsed into a spasm of coughing. When it was over, he wiped his mouth and eyes with a handkerchief. "So what're you going to do about it?"

"I wish I knew. Violating public health disclosure laws gets you in a boatload of trouble as it is, but we were forced to sign a confidentiality agreement with the Feds right after 9/11. God knows what *they* will do to me if I cross them."

They sipped their drinks and contemplated their fates under the new federal rules of secrecy.

"You know what I think?" said Stanley, putting away his handkerchief. "It's not the crazy guys who flew the planes into the Trade Center that have me thoroughly pissed off. I *expect* scumbags like that to kill people."

"Who then?"

"It's the guys in high places who knew we were breathing poison and lied through their teeth. I expected them to look out for me; that's their *job*. That's what they're *paid* to do."

As Nicholas studied his friend's face, he felt the depression's claws grabbing his heart and squeezing it. The constriction was like steel bands choking off his blood supply.

"I should have got you the proper equipment," said Nicholas.

"That's a load of crap! You told me what to do. You explained about how a TB mask would protect me from the asbestos and the other shit in the air."

"I guess I did say something."

"Sure you did! But the fricking mayor *and* the governor were on the news saying the air was safe. They even told us not to wear our masks when the president came through, it looked bad on the nightly news. And don't forget EP-A-hole Christie Whitman saying the air wasn't toxic. It wasn't *your* fault I worked without any real protection, my friend. No way, no how."

"Wasn't it?" said Nicholas, draining the last of his drink. "I had access to the proper masks and gowns. I could have brought you a box of them, personal delivery."

Stanley put down his empty glass. "You were busy with your own shit, I remember. You came home ten, eleven o'clock at night for weeks; Beth was worried to death about you." Stanley coughed and spat into a paper napkin.

As Nicholas stood to leave, Stanley put his hand on his friend's shoulder. "Believe me, I know what I'm talking about, I've seen it too many times on the job. Ya gotta get your head on straight or this guilt trip will land you in worse shape than me!"

FIFTEEN

When Beth arrived home from work, she saw Chrissie's backpack on the floor at the base of the stairs. Walking up the steps of their duplex apartment, she heard hip hop music filtering out from behind her daughter's closed bedroom door and wondered if her friend Lucas was up there with her.

She knocked on the door, heard Chrissie yell, "It's not locked!"

She found her daughter on the bed reading a magazine with an erotic cartoon on the cover. Chrissie was tall and slim and lovely, with a face out of a Dutch masters painting. Beth hoped her daughter didn't spoil her natural beauty with a tattoo to her neck. Or god forbid, a nose ring.

"How was your day?" Beth asked.

"Murrow sucks. How was yours?"

"Actually, I had a very funny experience. One of the classes had a sub. A student ordered some Chinese take-out on his cell phone. He got the teacher to give him a pass for the bathroom, went down to the front door to pick up the food, and then he came back and sat with his buddies in the back eating lunch. *In class!*"

Chrissie's mouth fell open. "Mom, that's crazy! How did *you* get involved?"

"I was in the teacher's lounge when the sub came in in tears. She wanted to run out of the school and never come back because the students didn't respect her. I calmed her down, and then I picked the two boys out of their class and walked them to the Dean's office. The Dean wanted the kids to apologize to the sub, in writing, but he had to wait…"

"Wait? For what?"

"For the sub to stop crying and fix her makeup."

As the two women laughed over the episode, Nicholas poked his head into the bedroom. "What's so funny?" he asked.

Beth and Chrissie looked at each other and burst into another round of laughter.

While Beth was cooking dinner the doorbell rang. Chrissie yelled, "I got it!" just as Nicholas started to rise from his leather chair. The girl hurried to the door. A young man in a black T-shirt and jeans with hair as long as Chrissie's stood in the doorway, not coming in.

"I'm going out for dinner!" Chrissie announced, grabbing backpack.

"Wait a minute, aren't you going to introduce me?" Nicholas said, rising from his chair.

"Maybe next time," said Chrissie, hurrying out the door.

"That was Lucas Waterman," said Beth from the kitchen. "Let's eat on the terrace, it's a lovely evening."

"Okay." Nicholas carried plates of food outside, where Beth joined him. The evening sun was settling over the shoulders of the city. The southern tip of Manhattan was beginning to show lights in the windows and headlights in the traffic. The empty space in the skyline didn't seem quite so strange anymore. They were finally getting used to seeing the city without the Twin Towers.

When Beth asked Nicholas what was happening at work, he told her he was studying student lung function.

"Why ever are you doing that?"

He told her how he was comparing students who had been in class near Ground Zero with students far from the plume, and that the study group had somewhat reduced lung function.

Beth set down her knife and fork. "How much is 'somewhat', Nicholas?"

"On the average? Ten to fifteen percent."

"Oh my god! Chrissie has had a cough sometimes in the morning. Does that mean our daughter — "

"No, not at all, don't get hysterical on me. Chrissie went to middle school in Brooklyn. She was nowhere near ground zero."

"*Hysterical?* You're talking about our daughter's *lungs*, for god's sake! The wind blew that crap across the East River right into our neighborhood for weeks!"

"I haven't tested students from our neighborhood."

"But you will. Won't you?"

"I don't know, my supervisor doesn't give me the big picture. I suppose it depends on what we find in the first cohort of students." He wanted to reassure her, but kept silent, feeling the undertow of despair pulling him down. If his daughter's lungs *were* damaged, then so were his own. And his wife's. And all of his neighborhood in the Brooklyn Heights section.

Beth poured herself a glass of wine and waited to hear more, but her husband kept silent. She kept looking for signs that he would crack out of the shell he'd withdrawn into, but nothing ever changed. He spent more and more time alone in his study.

"Nicholas, I know I've been busy this semester. The debate team finishes this week. And I'm almost finished grading term papers." She watched for a sign of acceptance, but her husband's face was impassive. "Fran called and asked if we wanted to go out to the Brooklyn Museum with her and Stanley. They have a dance band in two weeks next Friday."

"I'll see."

Rising from her chair, she stepped close to her husband. "It would be sweet to go out with them, Stanley's been in such a funk, with his disability and all."

When Nicholas shrugged, neither agreeing nor refusing, Beth's voice turned hard. "Nicholas, we can't go on with you locking yourself up with guilt. I can't take it, and it isn't doing Chrissie any good, either."

"So what are you saying?" Nicholas's anger rose, replacing the depression. "You want me to leave? You want to split up? Is that it?"

"No, of course I don't *want* us to separate. I just want you to get past this guilt that's eating you up."

"I'm sorry. I don't see how things are going to change. You can't undo the past."

Beth picked up her plate and walked to the kitchen, saying, "Well, I hope for all our sakes you figure something out. It's no fun being married to a man of stone."

Seeking refuge in his tiny office, Nicholas booted up his computer, planning to check his email. He wished he had his laptop so he could look over the student data once more, but the god damned security guard had made him leave it at the office.

Suddenly he realized he'd put the file on his thumbnail drive in order to transfer it to the laptop. Pulling out his key ring, he transferred the data to his desktop, gave it an innocent sounding file name, and saved it. Opening the file, he realized this simple act was a violation of Homeland Security. Just looking at it outside the office could result in his termination. Or worse.

He smiled as he looked over the bell curves, pleased with himself at the small act of rebellion.

SIXTEEN

Alex sat at his desk, needle and thread in hand, sewing the name *Henry* onto the brown UPS shirt. He was particularly pleased with his fake ID. It wouldn't hold up under close scrutiny, but was good enough for a casual passerby.

The night porter in Laura Metcalf's building usually went out for coffee before his shift ended at six. The doorman came on at seven, sharp. Where would a criminal be without punctual people?

As for the client, Laura never changed her routine. He had followed her on the subway to her job. Watched her on her lunch break: one martini, never a second, and a salad with strips of chicken. Sometimes she had the salmon.

After work she usually went out for a drink with the girls. On Fridays it could be the girls or some guy with broad shoulders and a strong jaw. She always chose the body building types with slick hair and bulging biceps. Well, she knew what she liked.

To be sure that Steven had followed instructions to be far away at the time of the 'accident', Alex called the office from a payphone the day before and asked to speak to Mr. Reinhold. The receptionist informed him that Mr. Reinhold was out of town for five days and asked would he like to leave a message. Alex declined the offer.

Feeling better about his financial situation, he told the landlord he was expecting a royalty check for a foreign rights sale and would catch up on the rent in a few weeks. The landlord was used to the chaotic income of a writer, although he complained loudly enough for the neighbors to hear about it. Alex assured him that soon his payments would be as regular as clockwork, allowing himself use of a cliché since he was talking to an illiterate.

Now he stood at the bathroom mirror applying cocoa-colored makeup to his face, neck, and the backs of his hands, leaving the palms untouched, having studied the color tones of African-Americans on the subway. His dark brown eyes and dark eyelashes blended in with the disguise; the wig with dreadlocks, a perfect finishing touch.

It was five am, time to get in the car. He wanted to leave plenty of time to cross the Brooklyn Bridge into Manhattan. Although he expected very little traffic, you never knew when a broken down vehicle would slow the bridge traffic to a crawl.

He poured a small amount of liquid laundry soap into a reusable perfume bottle and dropped it in his jacket pocket. He picked up the fake UPS package and left the apartment. Driving over the East River, the lights of Manhattan beckoning him, he felt as if he owned the town. Like he was on top of the world. And why not? He had a business model that was a sure fire success. Where was the competition, for god's sake? *Lawyers?* They were a bunch of baby seals mewling for their mothers. He, Alex Germaine, was the real man on the scene.

He parked on East 23rd Street across from Laura Metcalf's apartment building. It was a no parking, tow-away zone from eight to ten am, but he would be long gone before eight. He squeezed in between a beat-up van and a worn out taxi.

As a police car cruised by, Alex kept his eyes focused on the street ahead. The cops threw a glance his way and kept on rolling. In a minute they were around the corner and out of sight.

Alex felt a brief twinge of fear, thinking the cops might have noted his license plate. But the street was dark, and with his car parked sandwiched between two cars, it would be impossible to read the plate from a vehicle passing in the street.

He waited patiently. Confidently. The street was quiet, with no pedestrians. The cops wouldn't be coming back, it was the end of their shift, and they loved their routines.

He sipped a cup of coffee and glanced at his watch, saw it was just six. He looked up to see the light come on in her bedroom window and a slender figure pass behind the sheer curtains.

As he sat waiting in the car, Alex felt a surge of power run through him, as if he could electrify the whole block with a touch of his finger. It was more intense than the joy he felt when his first book was published and he saw a copy of it on a shelf in Murder In Print.

He'd autographed a copy of his book, and then a dozen more, and then more copies at other stores around Manhattan. The reviews had been good, the sales, credible. But each succeeding book had received weaker reviews and brought in lower sales numbers. The last book was universally panned and sold only a few hundred copies. The rest of the print run was pulped.

Alex regretted that his new story would go unwritten and unread, it was such a masterful tale. And that it was a *true crime story* made it all the more impressive. Nonetheless he reveled in his new role of master criminal. The writers in the MWI would eat their hearts out if they knew that one of their own was living the dream. What's more, he was providing a valuable social service. Well, publishing his story was one satisfaction he would have to sacrifice for the sake of his work.

He recalled the day he received the return-receipt letter from his wife's attorney with the final divorce decree. 'Mental cruelty.' What a joke. She had tortured him with her indifference. Crucified him with derision. She held no respect for his writing or his sexual prowess.

If only he had thought of the murder business years ago, Donna could have been his first victim. A practice run. Somehow he would have worked out an unbeatable alibi. Well, it wasn't too late to redress an old wrong, the ex still lived in New York.

Standing in front of her dressing room mirror, Laura Metcalf hooked the black pearls around her neck and ran her fingers lovingly over the dark glistening surfaces. Her killer pearls. No common white pearls for her, black pearls spoke of mystery. And danger.

Her first client of the day was a mega-millionaire flying in to New York in his private jet. If he liked one of the new pieces in the gallery — liked *her* — maybe he'd fly them both to Paris. Or Rome. She could finally get away from this city and those horrid tabloids, the stinking paparazzi stalking her with their telephoto lenses. She brushed a bit of lint off her silk shirt and turned out the bathroom light.

When Alex saw the bathroom light go out, he stepped out of the car and approached the lobby, all of his senses charged and ready. A guy in a pinstripe suit held the door for him. As Alex entered the building and started up the stairs, he could already hear her scream.

SEVENTEEN

Returning to his apartment elated and energized by his first murder, Alex washed away the makeup in the shower. After dressing he poured himself a double shot of scotch and reflected on the brilliant success of the killing machine he had become. He peered into the pure amber liquid, admiring the craftsmanship that went into its distilling. Having forsworn alcohol for the week leading up to the murder, his pleasure was double as he inhaled the liquor's sweet perfume.

Alex reflected on the common myth that there was no such thing as a 'perfect murder.' Actually, killers eluded discovery all the time. *Solving the murder* was the unusual event. Feeling a kinship to a long line of professional killers, Alex imagined joining a secret society of professional assassins. Of trading stories with his comrades about his successful kills as he flew around the globe eliminating obnoxious mates.

Half way through the whiskey he decided to celebrate the launch of his new career. He would eat dinner at a good restaurant and hire an escort for an after-dinner massage. The kind she did with her tongue and her tits.

That evening Alex had dinner at a Russian restaurant on the boardwalk in Brighton Beach. The owner, a stooped, balding man with a cop's eyes, greeted Alex by name, walked him to a table in the back and recommended a bottle of Pinot Grigio. "You come celebrate a new book, Mister Germaine?" said the owner.

"Not this time, Mike. I've made some investments and they're doing very well."

"You are vury smart man. You write books, invest wisely. Vury smart."

The owner made way for the waiter, a handsome young fellow dressed in black, his dark hair slicked back, muscles bulging beneath his knit shirt. He took Alex's order for fried clams, Caesar salad, and stuffed tuna.

Alex savored each course, while the owner stood by the bar greeting new customers. An old Russian folk song played from the sound system. Across the boardwalk the gray-green Atlantic rolled its shoulders and rubbed up against the strand.

Over dessert of stuffed pears with sorbet, Alex glanced at the door.

A tall blonde with hair falling onto bare shoulders walked in. Her short tight skirt, webbed stockings and high heels announced her time-honored profession. She glanced around the room, catching the owner's eye. He frowned and started to walk toward her.

"Over here," said Alex, raising a glass of wine.

The woman smiled and brushed past the owner, who bowed and welcomed her once he realized she had been invited. At Alex's table she bent forward, revealing a sumptuous bosom. "You must be Alex," she said in a throaty voice. "I'm Crystal."

The young waiter hurriedly pulled out the chair for her. She thanked him, eyeing his muscular arms and chest, then she turned her attention back to Alex.

"I'm not late, am I?" she said, knowing she was right on time.

"No, my dear. Would you like some wine?"

"Please!" She held out a hand to the waiter, who quickly supplied a glass. "Do you live nearby?" she said.

"My apartment is three blocks away." He glanced down at her stiletto shoes. "Think you can make it that far on foot?"

"If I have a problem you can pick me up in your arms and carry me." She sipped her wine, leaving a deep red lipstick stain on the glass. Alex couldn't wait to lick the deep scarlet from her lips.

After paying the bill, Alex led her out of the restaurant, his arm around her narrow waist. As they walked he dropped his hand to her bottom and squeezed, eliciting a little squeal from Crystal. Then he pressed his fingers into the crack between her buttocks. He couldn't wait to pull her panties down and violate her front and back.

He supposed she would want him to pay extra for tying her up.

EIGHTEEN

Riding the subway to his morning assignment at another high school in Manhattan, Nicholas glanced at the headlines, finding nothing of interest. He turned to the obituaries for a distraction and let his eyes wander over the entries. He noted that several photographs of the deceased were taken years before the person died. Decades, in some instances, and wondered why the surviving relatives didn't post a current picture. He guessed they wanted to remember the striking beauty they first courted and wed.

He read the obituary for Laura Metcalf-Reinhold, a wealthy young woman who slipped and fell on the stairs of her apartment building. He recognized her face, having seen it on the front page of The Post when he had a drink with Stanley. She'd been on the television news as well. The arrogant young woman's divorce story had been trumpeted for weeks, there was no way to miss it.

Slipped and fell to her death. She was probably drunk or high. Or both.

As an epidemiologist with the Department of Health, Nicholas knew that falls were a common cause of accidental death. Since there was no disease involved, her death offered no medical interest to him, so he went on to read about a journalist who succumbed to pancreatic cancer after a "heroic one year struggle." *One year.* That was a pretty good survival time, most pancreatic cancer patients died in three to six months, it was a nasty, rapidly fatal cancer that spit in the eye of all the chemotherapy regimens.

At the high school he found the students much the same as his previous study. Some were surly and suspicious, others compliant and questioning. One young girl wanted to know what she should study to prepare herself for medical school. He told her not to focus exclusively on the hard sciences, but to study people in communities; it was in communities that they acquired many of their diseases.

Returning to the DOH, he generated another set of graphs, with less disturbing results. Only the students who lived near Ground Zero had diminished lung function, though the decrease was not as great as the students in his first study. He didn't bother arguing with Libby over the information, it was obvious the city didn't want the public to know how much they were effected by the air pollution from 9/11.

In the lobby leaving work he suffered another search of his briefcase from the same deadpan security guard. Arriving home, he found Chrissie in her room with the door closed. *Why did she have to be so totally antisocial?* He knocked and stuck his head in the door. "Where's your mom?"

Chrissie reminded him Beth was staying late for parent-teacher conferences. As he turned to go she yelled at him to close the door. Nicholas cursed softly under his breath as he trudged down the stairs.

He reheated a plate in the microwave and ate the food without tasting it. He washed the dishes and finally settled into his comfortable chair with a book about cholera just as Beth came through the door. She told him she was tired beyond all endurance and began ascending the stairs.

After reading the paper, Nicholas went upstairs. He found Beth sitting up in bed reading.

"Don't forget, we agreed to go to the dance at the Brooklyn Museum with Stanley and Fran tomorrow night." She snapped off her reading light and snuggled down in the bed.

"Oh, yes, I forgot." Stepping down the hall to their tiny office to check his email, he found Chrissie typing away.

"Why aren't you using your laptop?" he asked.

"I loaned it to Lucas, his hard drive crashed." She punched the send command on her email as Nicholas approached the desk.

"Well be sure not to open any emails you don't know who the sender is."

"Gee, like this is my first time using a computer."

As she got up to leave, he wanted to stop and talk to her about his study of the high school students' pulmonary function. But he knew it would end up in an argument, like all the other 'chats' he tried to have with her. She already believed he was responsible for every ill and misfortune that befell her, there was no point broaching the delicate subject. Besides, she would broadcast it to all her friends, and then he would really be in trouble.

Losing interest in his own email, he bid his daughter good-night and retired to bed, accepting Chrissie's harsh judgment of him. That he failed to protect her and all her friends during those terrible days. More than anything else, he hated that she was the one meting out his punishment.

NINETEEN

Alex skipped up the broad marble steps of the New York Supreme Court Matrimonial Division. At ten in the morning, the June sun was already high above the city's shoulders and heating the streets. He was confident that he had a sound business plan with no competition, and that he had the skills needed to grow the business.

Life was glorious.

Settling into his favorite spot in the courtroom, he dismissed the first couple in the divorce court for lack of financial resources. The next couple was financially secure, but they were as amicable as Quakers. Disgusting. They even agreed to shared custody of the children without a harsh word or accusation. Total losers.

He watched a curvaceous, red-haired beauty walk into the courtroom. Meredith Hamilton was decked out like a countess, with diamonds on her fingers and diamonds dangling from her ears. *Who wears diamonds to a divorce proceeding?* Meredith assessed the room as though deciding if the chef was good enough for her patronage. Her lawyer, a sleek, oiled gentleman in a perfectly cut suit, opal cuff links and pearl tiepin, escorted Meredith to a seat, his hand lightly touching the small of her back.

A moment later the husband came in, saw his wife, and sneered. Forest Hamilton was a large man, thickly built, with meaty hands and broad shoulders. His long gray hair pinned back in a ponytail made him look like a fading rock star; the sleeves of his black sports coat were pulled up as if he were going to wash dishes. Or strangle his wife by her long, lovely neck.

Alex quietly moved up to a row behind the husband and took out his yellow legal pad as the judge began hearing Meredith's testimony. When her lawyer asked her to describe the terrible, continuing abuse she'd suffered at her husband's hands, Forest's lawyer leapt up and accused him of leading his own witness. *"Why don't you testify for her?"* he yelled, then demanded a sidebar with the judge.

The judge told him there were no sidebars in family court. "Everything here is on the record," he said. "Let's get on with it."

Meredith described physical and mental abuse in vivid detail, naming days and times for specific injuries. Her husband's lawyer objected, asking how anybody could possibly remember dates and times with so much precision. In response her lawyer entered the wife's diary into evidence, as well as photos documenting the injuries. Every harsh word and sharp blow was described in a neat hand.

The testimony was deadly.

When the judge called for a recess, Alex heard Forest tell his lawyer, "I don't understand why the judge is even listening to her lies. She claims she's sterile because of *my* venereal disease? She gave *me* the clap. I'm lucky not to have fricking AIDS!"

"I should be able to quash that argument. But I have to tell you, the bruises and the diary are hard to dispute."

"The bruises are from when she attacked *me!* I have scars all over my body!"

"But you have no proof. That was your fatal mistake, my friend. She has hospital records with photos of where you hit her. You have nothing to counter them."

"I didn't hit her one time she didn't deserve it." Forest turned to look at his wife. "Merry was planning this from the beginning, Carl. Don't you see? *I was set up!* Her family's blue blood but they've got no money. Bunch of starving aristocrats. The bitch was out to rob me from the get-go."

"Well if we don't come up with some damages on your part, I'm afraid the judge is going to give her a healthy piece of your property."

"If she takes my art she gets my immortal soul. Carl, you've got to stop her!"

"I've got a few motions left to file. It's not time to panic."

Alex felt that the warring divorcees were evenly matched, presenting him with a tough choice. Both had much to lose, and both were supremely selfish. Given an even match, Alex's inclination was to kill the woman, they were easier to subdue. And more enjoyable to kill. But that was no way to run a business. He had to be coldly objective in his evaluation of potential clients, add up the pros and cons, and make a rational decision.

When the court crier called the case back from recess, Forest's lawyer stood to request a motion. "Your honor, this woman has a long, sordid history of sexual liaisons that have been widely reported in the press. Our medical expert believes that her alleged infertility is due to the multiple abortions she has undergone over the years prior to marrying my client. We ask that the court order a laparoscopic examination of Mrs. Hamilton's uterus. It is our contention that the scarring will be shown to have resulted from the abortions, *not* venereal disease."

"Your honor!" Meredith's attorney leapt to his feet. "*Our* medical expert is prepared to testify that the scarring of my client's uterus directly resulted from a sexually transmitted disease she contracted from her husband!"

Before Forest's lawyer could reply, the judge shut both lawyers down. He ruled that Forest's medical expert could perform a noninvasive examination of Mrs. Hamilton, such as an ultrasound, but there would be no invasive tests that could put her at risk of injury or infection. After that he would let the dueling experts fight it out. With a crack of the gavel the judge called for the next case.

Forest blew out of the courtroom like a threatening storm, Alex following at a safe distance with the intent of interviewing the man. When Forest hailed a cab, Alex flagged down the next one, telling the cabbie, "Follow that car," a delightful command that could never be a cliché.

"What are you, a private eye of something?" asked the cabbie, turning on the meter and pulling into traffic.

"No, a crime writer."

"Is that a fact." Forest's cabbie came to a stop at the red light.

"Don't lose him!" Alex cried, watching in horror as Forest's cab pulled father ahead and was nearly out of sight.

TWENTY

"I want you to step on it as soon as the light turns!" Alex told the cabbie, searching for Forrest's taxi in the traffic far ahead.

"Hey, I get a ticket and lose my license, how'm I gonna put food on the table? I got three kids, and that's just by my *first* wife."

Alex pulled out his wallet and shoved a twenty dollar bill at the driver. "This is your tip. Don't lose him."

"Twenty bucks don't buy what it used to," said the cabbie, leaning forward and looking up at the street light. When it finally turned green, an old lady pushing a cart laden with bulging plastic bags slowly inched across the street in front of him. Alex cursed her as the drivers behind him leaned on their horns. Finally the old lady was out of the way; the cabbie gunned the engine and shot forward.

"Hey, you said you're a writer. I got a million stories I could tell you. All the crazy things I've seen, you couldn't make 'em up. Me and you should get together, you could help me write some stories."

"Sure, I'll help you, just don't lose that cab!"

Now weaving through traffic like a Grand Prix driver, Alex's cab caught up with Forrest's just as it pulled over and his quarry stepped out. After taking the cabbie's card and promising to give him a call 'soon,' Alex followed Forest into a pub. He watched the bedeviled husband settle at the end of the bar and order a drink. Alex sat beside him and ordered a scotch on the rocks, it being a hot day. He looked up, listened to a local reporter on the television blabbing about a widower who'd lost his wife to a drunk driver.

"That guy doesn't know how good he's got it," Alex said loud enough for Forest to hear. "She would have dragged him through a divorce in the end."

Forest put down his drink and turned to Alex. "Sounds like you've been through it."

"Me and every man I know. Take this friend of mine. He had a classic Jaguar. It was the love of his life."

"What was it, an XKE?"

"You know your cars. No, it was a Mark Two. A touring car, like that

Inspector Morse drives, on the TV series? Burled walnut dash, premium leather, and a sweet sultry exhaust note that plucked your heart strings. She got it in the settlement. Bitch couldn't even drive a stick."

"I'd kill somebody tries to take a car like that away from me," said Forest.

"That's just what he did. Got the car back, too." Alex looked slyly at his companion.

Chuckling, Forest held up his glass and toasted the classic car lover. "I'm afraid my wife is going to get the Audi," he said. "I love that car. Bought it new and treated it like a baby."

"You're divorcing?" said Alex. Forest glumly nodded his head. Alex pointed to a table away from the bar. They picked up their drinks and settled into a quiet spot.

"Dennis Harley," Alex said, shaking his companion's hand in a strong grip, suggesting confidence and power.

"Forest Hamilton. Yeah, I'm right in the middle, and is she ever busting my balls."

"Do they ever do it any other way?"

"Right on." The two men clinked glasses again.

Alex listened as Forest told his sad story. When he was done, Alex told Forest the fates must have meant for them to meet, this was his lucky day. He ran through his pitch, pointing out the advantages of staging an accidental death and the minimal risks attached. He confided that the man who retrieved his classic Jaguar had been one of his clients. Alex finished with a reminder of how much Forest stood to lose when the judge made a final ruling. "Your art is part of your soul, my friend. *You can't let her get it.*"

At first, Forest expressed horror and doubt at the proposal. But soon his eyes looked past Alex as he envisioned a life of freedom from his wife. A paradise of independence and financial success where he was once again the master of his fate and the sole owner of his work.

"How do I know you're not playing me? That you're not working for my wife? Have you got a list of satisfied customers you can refer me to?"

Alex leaned closer. "You are right to be skeptical. And cautious. All of our customers react the same. But then they see where their best interests lie, and they hire us."

Alex offered to let the man search him for a wire in the bathroom.

Reassured by the offer, Forest voiced concerns about being an obvious suspect. Alex assured him there would not be a serious investigation because the death would be ruled an accident. On top of that, they would plan it for a time when Forest was far away from the scene with a solid alibi.

Alex finished by explaining that there was no money due until after the Medical Examiner's ruling, and how the ten cash payments would not raise suspicion, even if an insurance investigator or a private detective decided to nose around. He finished by saying that Forest had twenty-four hours to come to a decision. When the potential client balked, Alex told him, "In your heart you know this is your one chance for freedom and financial security. And remember, you pay nothing until you have the Medical Examiner's report of accidental death."

"Twenty-four hours to decide," said Forest. "That's not a lot of time."

"Great men act quickly." He told Forest when he would call to confirm the deal and left the pub, confident he had secured another client.

Now all he had to do was study the target and find where Meredith Hamilton was most vulnerable.

TWENTY-ONE

Once Forest Hamilton agreed to the contract, Alex decided that before killing Meredith Hamilton he needed to study the most common causes of accidental deaths. He realized that as long as he stuck to mimicking an accident that was a common cause of death, he was sure to avoid a police investigation. An unusual, rare type of accident might tickle someone's curiosity.

Going online for information, he was not surprised to learn that motor vehicle accidents were one of the leading causes of inadvertent death. But he was surprised to learn that hitting a deer on the road was almost as common an auto accident as drunk driving, at least in rural areas. Alex didn't think that he could engineer a deer accident in one of the five New York boroughs. But rollovers in SUV's' were still not uncommon occurrences, despite the manufacturers' touting their new 'anti-roll' systems. That was a promising idea, until he remembered Meredith Hamilton drove an Audi.

Slips and falls were the second leading cause of death. Laura Metcalf's fall on the stairwell had worked well, the spilled laundry soap an especially good piece of verisimilitude. Deciding to pursue a variant on the same slip-and-fall technique, he looked over his newspaper clippings and Internet printouts, studying Meredith's hobbies and habits. He saw that she enjoyed solitary rides on her horse Mayflower through a suburban woodland.

Solitary rides on a horse. Now there was opportunity knocking on his door. He went to the public library and read about head injuries due to falls. They looked easy enough to mimic, he just had to deliver the blow with sufficient force to produce a 'contra coup type injury'. That was where the brain not only hit the skull at the point of impact, but also bounced back against the opposite side, doubling the amount of damage.

Bleeding from torn blood vessels contributed to the swelling of the brain and led to coma. With coma, the tongue fell back into the mouth, blocking the windpipe. The coma suppressed the gag reflex, and the victim asphyxiated on his own tongue.

Her own tongue, the instrument of death: what a delicious irony for a nagging wife. It was worthy of the finest writers. His research into fatal accidents was proving to be more entertaining now that he had made the transition from writing about murder to the real McCoy.

A fatal blow to the head was just the thing for Meredith Hamilton. The only part left to determine was how to impose the fatal blow so that it looked exactly like an accident.

He downloaded directions to the riding stable where Meredith boarded her horse, then drove out to the stables to study the lay of the land. As soon as he walked through the quiet, secluded riding trail that Meredith favored, a plan leapt into his mind. It was simple, devilish and *brutal.* A fitting act for an accomplished, professional killer.

Returning to the city, Alex bought a book on home repair and studied soldering. Confident he could master the craft, he purchased the necessary materials from a hobby supply store. After that he searched on Craig's List for a cheap set of old golf clubs and bought them from a guy who needed money because he was, no surprise, going through a divorce.

The finishing touch: a lucky horseshoe purchased on Atlantic Ave from a used furniture shop trying to pass for an antique emporium.

In his apartment he selected a driving iron and practiced his golf swing. He was rusty, but the swing was adequate. Next he soldered the horseshoe to the head of the club. He tested it by swinging the horseshoe against various pillows, and even a sandbag. The soldering held, as he knew it would. The blow left a satisfying depression in the sandbag.

Once he was satisfied with his plan, he went to a payphone, called Forest and told him to be out of town and highly visible the following week. He could expect a heartbreaking phone call in the middle of his trip.

TWENTY-TWO

Alex stood behind a copse of trees watching the trail. The old golf bag stuffed with clubs leaned against a thick tree, green with new Spring foliage. Any moment Meredith would come sauntering by on her mare, Mayflower. She always rode at the same time three days a week, and she always rode alone.

Hearing the *clop, clop* of the horse's hooves on packed dirt, he took a sling shot out of the bag and loaded a sharp-edged stone into the thick rubber sling. Pulling the elastic band back taut and sighting along the slingshot, Alex watched as rider and horse came into view.

It wasn't Meredith! Some guy in an English riding outfit was riding a gray stallion. His polished leather boots came up to his knees and made him look ridiculous. Alex had a momentary urge to kill the guy just for being such a fop.

He ducked deeper into the trees and held his breath. The horse paused in its stride and looked around, perhaps smelling the intruder or hearing the rustle of the leaves. The rider clicked his tongue, snapped a whip across the horse's flank, and passed on.

The minutes dragged on. A cloud of flies buzzed around his face, alighting on his hair. He brushed them off, cursing softly. The warm June sun beat on his head and shoulders, making him sweat. He rubbed his hands on his pants, wanting them to be dry for the action.

Hearing the *clop, clop* of another horse approaching, he pulled down a branch and peered along the trail. It was Meredith, head held high, rocking rhythmically in the saddle. Alex couldn't help but note the look of pleasure on her face as she straddled the horse with her long legs and bobbed up and down. He wouldn't mind strapping her into his saddle and making her rock.

When horse and rider passed in front of him, Alex stepped out from the trees and let loose with the slingshot. The horse whinnied and reared up on her hind legs. Meredith cried out as she fought for balance, then tumbled backwards and fell to the ground as the horse bolted and galloped madly away.

While the dazed rider slowly pushed herself up onto her hands and knees, Alex ripped off her helmet and tossed it aside. She looked up at him from her position on all fours, her long red hair half covering her face. Fear overcame confusion. As her mouth opened in protest, Alex drew back his golf club in his best golf pro stance and swung the club with all his strength.

The horseshoe soldered to the head of the club struck Meredith on the side of the head with a terrible *crack!* Meredith crumpled face down in the dirt, one arm pinned beneath her body. With her free hand she clawed feebly at the dirt.

Pulling on latex gloves, Alex grabbed Meredith by her free arm and roughly turned her over onto her back. Her unfocused eyes seemed to be staring into eternity. Knowing that suffocation was a common cause of death in victims of head trauma, he straddled her shoulders with his knees, squeezed her nose shut with one hand and covered her mouth firmly with the other.

Struggling to breathe, she stared up at him, panic flooding her mind. She kicked with her legs, bucking and trying to throw him off. He felt a surge of desire as he forced her down into the dirt. Starving for oxygen, in less than a minute her limbs weakened and her eyes rolled up in her head. He gave her a full three minutes before removing his hands and feeling for a pulse. There was none. He stood up, leaving her on her back, her tongue the apparent cause of death.

Shoving the golf club back into the bag, he broke off a branch and brushed away the footsteps he had left in the trail. He hefted the bag onto his shoulder and strode away. As he walked through the wood he recalled the feeling of a panicked Meredith bucking beneath him, eyes wild with terror. The triumph of his raw animal conquest had aroused him even more than his killing Laura Metcalf.

He wished there had been time to violate her on the ground, but another rider might have come along the trail. He could have dragged her deeper into the woods, but that wouldn't have been consistent with his accidental death scenario. Perhaps some future contract would provide him the opportunity to satisfy his other passion.

As he threw the golf bag in the trunk of his car and drove away, Alex could almost taste the double scotch and soda waiting for him at home. He took a special satisfaction in having again avoided any alcohol in the days before the job was completed. He was in complete control of his life; the master of his fate; the ruler of his victims.

He steered the car along the Long Island Expressway back to Brooklyn. When he entered the borough he took out his cell phone and hit the speed dial for the escort service, telling the honey-tongued receptionist to send him a girl with leather straps and a whip.

"Certainly, sir. Would you prefer blonde, brunette, or redhead?"

Alex recalled Meredith's red hair falling over her face as she struggled on her hands and knees. "Redhead, long," he told the escort service. Asked if he would prefer to be the recipient or the giver, he told her, "I'll hold the whip." Then as an afterthought he added, "Any chance she could bring a saddle?"

When the girl arrived at his apartment, he was pleased that she was young, with a layer of baby fat that begged to be squeezed and slapped. He grabbed her long red hair cascading onto her shoulders, bent her head back and kissed her deep and hard, then he pulled her to the bed by her hair.

As he ripped off her clothes she said, "I get extra for the whip. And you only use it on my butt. Okay?"

"Of course, my dear, I'm a regular customer." Turning her onto her hands and knees, he grabbed a thick leather strap to fasten a bridle for her mouth before taking up the whip.

TWENTY-THREE

The salsa band laid down a hot rhythm and the crowd of dancers swayed and spun, so packed together, it was hard to tell the couples from the solo dancers. The high marble walls of the Brooklyn Art Museum's great hall were bathed in colored lights pulsing in time to the music.

Nicholas held his hands up as if he were shaking a pair of congas, while Beth danced toward him, swaying provocatively, a blissful smile on her face. Through the crowd he saw Stanley moving his hips a bit and smiling, while Fran spun and kicked up her heels.

As the song ended, the singer, a sexy Hispanic woman in tight black jeans and a skimpy top, told the crowd, "*Brooklyn! You are shaking up the joint tonight!*" The crowd whistled and cheered as the band started up another number.

Nicholas led Beth from the dance floor to where Stanley and Fran were listening.

"You're cutting up the floor," said Nicholas.

"I can still move my hips, anyway," said Stanley. "The air is a little close, let's grab a beer."

On the edge of the room they bought beers for the men, white wine for the women. As they stood listening to the music and looking at the crowd, Fran said, "I saw your Avanti in the parking lot tonight. Did you finish fixing it?"

"Nicholas is never finished with that car," said Beth. "It always needs a new this or a rebuilt that, and the part ends up on the kitchen table on a pile of newspapers."

"Classic cars require a lot of maintenance," said Nicholas. "But, yeah, I finished rebuilding the carburetor and she's running real good."

"You shouldn't complain, Beth, you bought it for him. Remember?" said Stanley.

"I don't know what possessed me. I inherited his mother's old diamond engagement ring, and it had this rather ugly emerald cut, so I sold it and Nicholas bought the classic car he always wanted."

"That's love, brother," said Stanley, clinking his beer bottle with Nick's.

"Ah, she never liked the ring, it was too gaudy. She never liked my mother, either."

"It was more like *your* mother never liked *me*," said Beth.

"Mothers and sons," said Fran. "When Freud talked about penis envy, he was talking about mothers and sons."

Nicholas was ready for another dance when his beeper went off. He saw it was from the DOH, and had a 9-1-1 suffix: *emergency*. With a sinking feeling that he was finally going to be punished for his sins, he took out his cell phone and called the number.

"This is Doctor Andreas."

"Nicholas, it's Libby."

"Libby? You beeped me to an emergency. What's happened?"

"Do you know anything about a student blog called 'School Drool'?"

"Never heard of it."

"Well today they published an article online that refers to *our* study of student lung performance. Nicholas, they even quote from the statistics for the school you've studied. That could only come from *your* database."

Nick gripped the phone tightly, unwilling to accept the implications of Libby's statement. How could a student group gain access to his report, unless... *Chrissie!* She had been using his computer the other night. Who knows how long she'd been opening his files and studying them. The files were password protected; she must have watched him log in one time and kept the password.

"It sounds like someone has hacked into the DOH computers," said Nicholas.

"Our I.T. people are looking into that. Nicholas, did you take the study home? Do you have hard copies anywhere other than at the DOH?"

"Of course not. I have no reason to bring my work home."

There was a long silence on the phone. Finally Libby said, "I hope that's true, Nicholas, for your sake. I would hate to lose you. Unauthorized release of departmental information is a serious offense. Losing your job would be the least of your worries."

"What do you mean 'the least'? What are you saying, Libby?"

"You know who runs the show around here. Public health data related to Nine-Eleven is covered under the Homeland Security Act. It's out of my hands. I can't protect you."

As soon as Libby hung up, Nicholas called his daughter's cell phone, but got only her answering message. She was probably blocking calls from him. "Call me, Chrissie. Tonight, it's important."

Cursing, he realized he had to get home right away and erase the data from his home computer.

"I have to go home," he told Beth. When she asked if it was about work, he told her he'd explain everything later. He hurried to the car, Beth agreeing to ride back with Stanley and Fran. The Avanti's lusty V8 growled and the tires screeched as Nicholas tore out of the museum parking lot and drove for home. He pushed through some yellow lights and a few that just turned red, finally roaring into the parking garage. He backed into his corner space until the bumper hit the old tire leaning against the back wall, then hurried to his apartment, not bothering to put on the nylon car cover.

Nicholas went to his computer, erased the file containing the high school data, then emptied the computer trash bin. Knowing that an erased file could still be recovered given the proper software, he ran a disk cleanup program, hoping it would scramble the erased file. Finally, he imported a large video file from one of the free webs sites, thinking that writing a lot of data to the hard drive would overwrite the illicit file.

He was about to erase the file from his thumbnail drive when it occurred to him that his computer at work would have recorded the command to transfer the data to the portable drive. That was going to be a problem. He decided to leave the thumbnail drive alone, for now. As long as he could get the portable drive back to his desk, he could claim it never left the department.

Nicholas typed an online search for *School Drool*. The high school web site was plastered with angry statements, accusations and demands for redress. He printed an article titled STATE SHOULD APPOINT SPECIAL PROSCEUCTOR TO INDICT MAYOR FOR INVOLUNTARY 9/11 MANSLAUGHTER. The article, written by Lucas Waterman, contained some of the statistical data from Nicholas's Department Of Health study. Data Waterman could only have received from Chrissie. She must have given him a copy.

Shutting down his computer, Nicholas worried that the Feds had already hacked into his home computer and found the incriminating file. He suspected that he'd be spending his days in solitary confinement somewhere in a Federal lockup. Still, Libby could have waited until he showed up for work the following morning to tell him. Was her call meant to give him time to remove the files before the Feds came for his computer? He hoped so.

It was a sliver of hope. Not much, but it was all he had. When he heard Beth coming into the apartment with Stanley and Fran, Nicholas felt as trapped as a victim under a pile of rubble. As much as he feared he would be arrested and taken away, he was doubly afraid for his daughter. The foolish girl was the one who released the data to the public. She would no doubt be picked up as well. A prolonged stay in the solitary confinement of a Federal prison for terrorists would break her. She would never survive.

TWENTY-FOUR

After erasing the incriminating file from his computer, Nicholas went downstairs, finding Beth and Fran in the kitchen. Stanley was out on the terrace looking at the night. The moon was hanging in a low sky. Lights from Manhattan reflected off low clouds, obscuring all but the brightest stars. He glanced over at Stanley, who inhaled the fumes from a hot toddy.

"Nothing like a shot of Jameson's to open up the lungs," said Stanley. He took a sip of the whiskey-laced tea.

"It's mainly the diuretic effect of the alcohol," said Nicholas. "You pee away the water on your lungs."

"Don't spoil the magic, pal. Leave me my illusions."

Fran and Beth brought snacks out onto the terrace and poured themselves white wine. They put out corn chips and salsa in bowls, olives, cheese, and sliced tomatoes from the local Farmer's Market.

Stanley popped an olive in his mouth. "Was a time I'd pick Fran up on the dance floor and lift her above my head. Remember that, honey?"

"You were a regular Gene Kelly. I loved it."

"Yeah. No more of that. The good times are gone...Long gone." He took another sip of his tea.

Fran leaned close to Stanley and gently stroked the back of his head. "You're still the best looking guy in the joint." She kissed his cheek, then stole a glance at Beth, who forced a smile of encouragement.

When Beth asked what the call from work had been about that made him rush home, Nicholas told them that a student web site had published information about lung disease among students who had lived or studied near Ground Zero. "They quoted some statistics that haven't been released to the public. I had that data on my home computer. It was password protected, but..."

"You think Chrissie took it?" asked Fran.

"I wouldn't put it past her."

"I don't think our daughter — "

"She's a *teenager*, for Christ's sake," Nicholas said. "She doesn't think things through, she acts on her feelings."

"Of course. Not like you, you're a responsible, rational adult," said Beth.

"Hold on you two," said Fran. "Nicholas. Is your job in jeopardy?"

"My job…My freedom…"

"Those Feds don't play," Stanley agreed. "All the Trade Center information is covered under the Homeland Security Act. You erased the files on your PC and scrubbed the disc, didn't you?"

Nicholas confirmed that was the first thing he did when they returned home. "I tried calling Chrissie but it went to voice message. I need to find her and get her to tell me what the hell she was thinking. She could be in trouble, too."

"Don't be hard on her, dear," Beth said. "If it was Chrissie, she was only doing what she thought was right."

"Meaning *I* never did, is that it?"

"No, of course not. But she's not a city employee. She doesn't feel bound by the same restrictions you do."

"Restrictions?" asked Fran.

Nicholas explained that shortly after 9/11 the FBI came to the Department of Health and made everyone sign a gag order. The threat of punishment for leaking information was loud and clear.

"I should have made you wear the proper respiratory gear from day one," said Nicholas. "We should have made everyone wear them. That's what this is really about. Liability. Lawsuits. Big bucks."

"The EPA certified the air was okay," said Stanley. "It wasn't *your* job to check the air."

"*But I knew better.* Light bulbs contain lead; computers contain heavy metals; the buildings used asbestos for insulation. If I'd explained to Stanley the way those small particulates diffuse through the bronchioles and work their way into the lung parenchyma…"

Stanley gripped Nicholas's shoulder, saying, "I keep telling you, my friend, you can't look back and beat yourself up, it's deadly. You have to accept we're all human, we all make mistakes, and move on."

Nicholas couldn't understand how Stanley could be so forgiving. The man's life was slipping away with every breath, and he never said a critical word about how Nicholas had let him down. It was a mystery how Stanley could forgive his own executioner.

TWENTY-FIVE

It was well past midnight when Nicholas heard Chrissie returning home. He hurried downstairs. When she saw him, Chrissie told her father she didn't want to hear about how late it was, she was a big girl, and besides, it was Friday night.

"You stole a file from my computer, didn't you? A confidential file from work."

"What are you talking about?"

Nicholas threw the printout from the SCHOOL DROOL on the dining room table and stabbed it with his finger. "That night you were using my computer to send your email. You said your laptop was not working. You were sending the file out to your *journalist* friend, Lucas. *Weren't you?"*

Beth came downstairs, having heard the yelling. She looked from Nicholas to her daughter, worried for both of them, but especially for her husband.

Seeing that for a change her mother was not immediately coming to her aid, Chrissie pointed to the student paper. "You had your chance, *dad!* Half the students from Stuyvesant in two-thousand one are sick because *you* sent them back to school a month after the towers fell!"

"My department had nothing to do with that decision; that was between the Board of Education and the Mayor."

"That's *bullshit!* Everybody says it was somebody *else's* responsibility! You could have said something! You could have talked to the newspapers. The TV news. But you didn't!"

"Dear," Beth said, going to her daughter. "What your father is telling you is that he will probably lose his job over what you did. He may even face criminal charges."

"Secrets and lies, that's all the government cares about. I care about the *truth!*"

"Oh, so it's okay if I go to prison for the rest of my life as long as *you* get the truth, is that it?"

When Chrissie didn't respond to his comment, Nicholas realized she was in no mood to listen. But even if his words would be wasted, he felt he had to make one thing clear to her.

"Chrissie. If I have to be punished for what I did or didn't do after nine-eleven, I can live with that. But you don't realize, I'm not the only one in danger here. When the FBI traces the leak to your email account, they'll take *you* away, too."

Chrissie's stubborn anger melted away as fear rose inside her. *"Mom!"* she called out, going to her mother for support. Beth put her arms around her daughter. They both fought back tears as Nicholas looked on, helpless to protect his daughter or himself. Bringing the files home had put his daughter in danger; it was another in a long list of his fuckups.

He didn't bother looking around him for rope, he was too deep to ever get out of the hole he'd dug.

Sitting up in bed unable to sleep, Nicholas took up the Times and tried to read the front page, but he couldn't follow the story, his mind was whirling like a Dervish, imagining all sorts of frightening scenarios: being locked up; being held incognito. There were no limits to what the Feds could do to him.

He turned in desperation to the obits, always a calming section of the paper. Was it his imagination or were there more deaths listed than usual? When his eyes fell on a photo of Meredith Hamilton, it triggered a memory: some kind of quote from the front page of the Daily News, he'd seen it at the newsstand. What was it? Oh, yes, it had been her husband Forest speaking. "*She takes my art, she takes my immortal soul!*"

The high profile divorce had been on the TV news as well. The husband was a successful artist who was fighting his wife over custody not of any children, but of his art, which was worth a cool million, or so the pundits proclaimed.

He glanced down at his sleeping wife, imagining the ugly scene that could erupt if she finally left him. How much of his silent brooding could a woman take? Watching her sleeping peacefully, he wished to god he could forget what he'd done and move on. But how? How do sleep when the noose was tightening around his neck?

TWENTY-SIX

Seated at a computer in the cool, air conditioned Brooklyn Public Library at Grand Army Plaza, Alex typed in the name 'Vincent Solomira' in the search box. Over fifty articles about the fellow he'd observed in Family Court the day before popped up on the screen. Alex chose an article describing the "boy wonder of ice cream."

The story from the New York Post described how Little Vinnie Solomira, a poor son of Italian immigrants, developed a soft ice cream in his mother's kitchen. "My mom loved to cook desserts, her sweets were *incredible!"* the story quoted. "And her homemade frozen creama was the best. It was a cross between ice cream, sour cream and yogurt. I decided to adapt it for the masses, and Vinnie's Icy Creama was born."

After selling his Italian Creama to restaurants and caterers, Vinnie turned the business into a franchise. That was where he struck gold.

Alex found numerous articles that told of a loyal wife, Jewel, who worked for years in her husband's kitchen making the ice cream while raising their two daughters. Later articles talked about Vinnie's girlfriends — exotic dancers and aspiring actresses, in sharp contrast to the aging wife, who was described as "a Saint" and "a jewel." Now Vinnie's high-powered lawyers were threatening to sever the marriage without leaving her a thin dime.

Alex left the library with a strong suspicion that the wife would be the better client. In the courtroom Vinnie had shown himself to be a cocky philanderer confident of victory. The only sticking point was, Jewel had appeared weak and depressed in court. That suggested she might not have the nerve to make the deal. But she had the most to lose, and Alex had learned early on that greed could turn a weak woman into a screaming Mimi.

Alex followed Jewel Solomira when she came out of the Frixlander Insurance Corporation, where she'd taken a job as a temporary secretary. She walked with her shoulders pulled together, head bowed, weary and miserable. For the third time he followed her to a bar on Pacific Street. She was trying to drink her troubles away. Alex had a better solution.

Seated at the end of the bar, Jewel took a cigarette from a pack in her purse and rummaged for matches. Then she cursed, remembering the new ban on smoking in bars the mayor had enacted.

"Terrible thing when a customer can't enjoy a smoke with his drink," said a voice beside her. She looked at Alex, saw his piercing eyes and confident air.

"It sure is. I got my rights, same as anybody else." She set her purse down on the bar and glanced at the worn attaché case in Alex's hand.

"May I, missus, uh, Solomira, isn't it?"

Jewel shrugged and made room for him beside her. She tilted her head and looked at him. "Do I know you?"

"No, but I know you. I'm an attorney. I saw you and your husband in family court the other day. Nasty bit of legal hucksterism on the part of your ex's lawyer."

"I should've got me a smarter lawyer. Are you smart?"

"I've pulled off a few surprises in my day. But I wouldn't want to represent you in this case, I'd be playing a losing hand. The judge is against you."

"*You saw that, didn't you?* He sides with Vinnie every time. *Bastard.*"

"These cases usually go to the one who leaves the judge with the most generous gift."

"What, he bribed the judge?"

Alex nodded his head. "

"My lawyer didn't say nothin' about a payoff! Can I still slip him something?"

"I'm afraid it's too late, your husband's lawyer has already sealed the deal. Judge Trigaboff goes for five large."

"Fuck a duck, am I screwed." She took a long pull on her drink. "I haven't got the bread to pay off a judge, anyway. I'm squeezing pennies trying to make my lawyer's payments as it is."

"A good legal defense never comes cheap." Alex signaled to the bartender, ordered another drink for Jewel and a single malt scotch for himself.

Jewel picked up the second glass as soon as it arrived. She stared into the amber liquid as if it foretold a grim future. Alex studied her face. He saw despair. Resignation. And smoldering rage. The rage would be his entrée to her soul.

"It's fortuitous I ran into you. I work for an organization that has the solution to your problem."

"Oh, yeah? What's that, victim's services?"

"In a manner of speaking." Alex looked around the bar. "Why don't we find a quiet spot and have a chat."

Jewel shrugged. Alex picked up their drinks and led her to a secluded table in the back. He began by explaining that his company offered a unique service that was guaranteed. There was no payment until the service was successfully completed. And payments could be made in ten monthly installments, with no interest.

"What're you gonna do, fit him for cement shoes and drop him in the East River?"

Alex picked up his drink, winked at her, and took a sip. "Something just as permanent, but much safer for you." He was pleased to see a hint of pleasure in her eyes as he explained his company's methods and proven track record.

Jewel Solomira choked on her drink when she realized Alex wasn't kidding. "Wait a second. You don't really mean you'd kill my husband, do you? Really whack him, like on the Sopranos or something?"

"We prefer to say that we would provide a permanent elimination of your problem." He assured her that in every case the Medical Examiner ruled that the victims suffered accidental deaths. Leaning closer, he added, "With no suspicion of foul play, there is no police investigation. You keep the ice cream business, which you thoroughly deserve. *And you won't have to worry your girls will one day be calling his bimbo girlfriend mother.*"

The promise of never seeing his daughters being hugged by one of Vinnie's young girlfriends with big tits was a compelling argument. Jewel felt a sudden surge of hope that her troubles might be over. She imagined what life without Vinnie would be: no fights over money. *No lawyer fees!* She could move back in the house. It would be just her and the girls. She could even afford a nanny to help out.

The fact that she would be responsible for her husband's death meant nothing to her. After all, he'd been torturing her ever since they were married. He'd hit her and ridiculed her in front of his family. He'd even made fun of her in front of the girls. That was cruel in the extreme.

She was a good mother. She loved her daughters. Just because she made the same peanut butter and jelly sandwich every day for school didn't mean she didn't care; it was just she put all her mental energy into helping with Vinnie's company. And then he went and kicked her out of the business and brought in the bimbo with the big tits, the creep.

The more Jewel listened to Alex's proposal, the more it made sense to her, as long as she could be assured that the cops wouldn't keep her up all night nagging her with questions. She was sure they wouldn't give her anything to drink in the police station. Nothing with alcohol, anyway.

"Look," she said. "Supposing...Just supposing that I *might* be interested in what you told me, from a maybe-couldn't-hurt-to-imagine point of view. How can I be sure, I mean, really sure, that the cops won't arrest me and keep me in jail for, like, forever?"

"As I told you, our company has a long standing expertise in creating scenarios that perfectly mimic accidental death. We have never had a case where a subject was ruled to have been killed. No homicide, no arrest."

"Yeah, but how can I be *sure* it'll work the same with my husband?"

He told Jewel some of the facts he had learned about Vinnie: where he worked, his girlfriend's name, the license plate number of his car, his favorite bar. "He operates a Sea Shark twenty-eight that he launches out of the Sheepshead Bay harbor. Dock Number Seven. Black hull, white interior with leather seats. Twin engines delivering three-hundred horsepower."

"Wow. You really know your stuff."

"Thorough research is the key to our success. Now, drowning is the third most common type of accident, after automobile accidents and slips and falls. It would be an easy thing to arrange for his drowning out in the middle of the Sound."

"But he'll have a life jacket."

"A life jacket will not save him."

"He has a radio. And a cell phone. He could call for help."

"We will incapacitate the radio before he goes out on the water. As to the cell phone, what plan is he on?"

"Z-Mobile."

"We'll find a zone in the sound that his plan doesn't reach." Alex took out a pad and jotted a quick note, adding, "The boat is stored in his driveway beside the garage. Correct?"

"That's right. He's got three fricking classic cars; thinks he's a regular Jay Leno."

Jewel stuck a finger in her drink and licked it playfully. "I know for a fact Vinnie sometimes takes his girlfriend out in the boat. Any chance you could kill both o' them?"

"I'm afraid the contract is for one spouse only."

"Too bad," said Jewell, who drained her glass and held it out to Alex for a refill, her sad eyes now twinkling with merriment. "Still and all, I'll get the house and the business. All she'll get is the clap."

TWENTY-SEVEN

With a black captain's cap, charcoal black mustache and hair, and an earring in one ear, Alex went into a marine supply store in Bay Ridge. The young man behind the counter ignored him, his eyes stuck on a handheld video game. The sounds coming from the game were not crashes or gunshots, they sounded like a woman moaning.

Alex considered: *A handheld video sex game: a digital approach to the old porno magazine. Brilliant!*

He bought a pair of drain plugs, having learned that Vinnie Solomira's Sea Shark took a lever-actuated plug. Back at home, he cut one of them open and studied the mechanism. The lever drove down a thimble-shaped metal plunger inside the rubber casing, expanding the rubber. He discovered that the lever screwed into the thimble. Some forceful turns with locking pliers soon loosened the thimble and had it removed. He sealed the rubber again with Krazy Glue, and felt the plug. It was as wimpy as an old man's prick. He didn't think it would stay in place more than a few minutes. That might not get the boat far enough out into the Sound. There was only one thing to do: test it on a real boat.

The sign in the Toms River marina on the Jersey shore read: *BOAT RENTALS – DAY, WEEK, MONTHLY.* Alex concluded from the fractured grammar the owner had not read *Eats, Shoots and Leaves.* He showed the proprietor a quality fake ID, purchased from an ex con he knew.

Some of the boats in the marina were anchored along a jetty; others were on stands waiting to go on a trailer. He found a Sea Shark that was considerably smaller than Vinnie Solomira's, but took the same size drain plug, something he'd checked in the company parts catalogue . He rented a trailer along with the boat.

He took a month-long contract, since he wasn't sure what day Vinnie would go out in the boat. A slow moving lad helped him attach the trailer to his car bumper. Once the trailer's brake lights were hooked up, he drove to a public access point a few miles from the marina where his subject launched his boat.

Before backing the trailer down to the water, Alex replaced the regular drain plug with the doctored one. Then he launched the boat, parked the car, and motored out into the bay.

As the boat rode the peaks and troughs of the swells, he put flippers on his feet and a scuba mask on his head, ready to jump in the water and replace the doctored plug at a moment's notice.

For a half hour the boat ran smoothly, the shore not far off his starboard bow. Then he noticed a trickle of water in the bottom of the boat. As soon as he cut the motor, water began running in. Chuckling, he pulled the scuba mask over his face and dropped into the water. Sure enough, the doctored plug had fallen out. He forced the original, functional plug into the drain, climbed back into the boat, and restarted the engine.

Motoring happily toward shore, the sun low over the cityscape, Alex knew that his only worry was if Vinnie brought his girlfriend with him on the boat. A double drowning was more likely to trigger a criminal investigation than a solo event. Worst case scenario, he could always call for help for them on his cell, an unregistered pay-by-the-minute phone, and take out Vinnie another day.

As he chewed on the problem facing him, Alex treated it like another plot twist in one of his novels. He had painted himself in a corner many times in the past and always found a way to get out of it. He was confident he would solve this little imbroglio in time.

Dressed in his sailor's cap, black T-shirt and cut-away jeans, Alex sat in his car watching Vinnie Solomira hitching up the boat to his pickup truck. The fool had no idea Alex had replaced the drain plug with a doctored one that wouldn't last long out on the open Sound. It was a lead-gray Saturday morning in June. Thick clouds concealed the sun, threatening rain. That was good: the weather forecast would discourage other boater's, making the kill easier.

When he spotted the girlfriend coming out of the house carrying a straw bag and a beach chair, Alex felt only a twinge of anxiety. If they went out on the water together, Alex had decided he would act the Good Samaritan when their boat began taking on water and call in their location for them, deferring the murder to another time and place.

The girlfriend was dressed in a bikini and a clinging robe that showed off her full breasts, ample ass, and pinched waist. She dropped the deck chair in the bed of the truck, looked up at the leaden sky. Her face sank.

The two exchanged words, Vinnie throwing his arms out as if to say, *I can't control the fricking weather.* The girlfriend pulled her robe tightly closed, turned and went back into the house, leaving Vinnie to go fishing alone.

Chuckling with delight, Alex put his car in gear and beat Vinnie to the marina, the poor schmuck having to pull his boat on a trailer. Once in the marina, Alex walked to his own boat, gassed up and ready to go. He ran the boat out into the bay and headed for a spot that would give him a good view of Vinnie and his boat.

Binoculars at the ready, Alex watched with satisfaction as Vinnie cast off his lines, fired up the big engines, popped a can of beer and roared out of the bay, cutting deep furrows in the ocean surface as he passed the end of the pier with the sign reading NO WAKE ZONE.

Following Vinnie's boat out into the Long Island Sound, Alex waited for the doctored plug to fail. The wait gave him time to reflect on life and the taking of it, and on the timeless watery grave that awaits all sailors. *In time the sea will claim its own.* A simple truth for an age that has lost its bearings.

TWENTY-EIGHT

Following Vinnie's boat from a discreet distance, Alex cast his line onto the water with a long, deep sea fishing. He left all the bait in a plastic jug, wresting with a fish would be a dangerous distraction. With his sailor's cap and black T-shirt, Alex looked all the world like an old salt who had been fishing the oceans of the world his whole life.

Alex watched as Vinnie cut the motor and began to prepare his rod and reel. The leaden sky, threatening rain, had kept most of the fishermen on shore. Even better, Vinnie had chosen a quiet spot with no other boats nearby.

Through his binoculars, Alex watched Vinnie patiently baiting his line. The fellow took a long pull on a can of beer — a positive sign. He cast his rod and settled into a leather chair, the beer beside him. After several minutes, Vinnie suddenly started, but not because there was a tug on his fishing line. He looked down at his feet. Then he bent down to look more closely.

Alex smiled. The fool had realized he was taking on water. Alex rolled that phrase over in his mind: *taking on water.* A classic phrase for a classic scenario. He waited to see how long before the fool realized he was in serious shit.

First, Vinnie tried the radio on the boat. He tried it a long time, but the damn thing didn't work. No amount of twisting the dial changing channels worked, Alex had loosened a wire and disabled it while the boat was parked at home beside the garage. The frustrated fellow threw the radio hand piece down and took out his cell phone. He punched in three numbers, nine-one-one, no doubt, and held the phone to his ear. Then he pulled the phone away and looked into the face, trying to read the digital screen. Vinnie dialed two more times, then threw the phone down in disgust. That was when he saw Alex's boat. Vinnie began wildly waving both arms in the air.

Alex gave a wave back. He took his time reeling in his line and securing the rod. Finally he motored slowly over to Vinnie, giving the stricken boat plenty of time to take on more water. When he was within shouting distance, he put his motor into neutral and called out, "Having a spot of trouble, are you?"

"The fucking boat is sinking, and I can't get any reception on my fucking cell! Do you believe my luck?"

"Good thing for you I came along!" Alex looked around them, saw no other boats close enough to catch their attention. "Not many boats out this morning!" he called.

"The weatherman called for rain!" Vinnie yelled.

"Did he?" Alex looked up at the gray sky as if surprised by the threatening clouds. He was enjoying toying with the soon-to-be-dead man almost as much as he enjoyed stalking and striking the wives. Although it wasn't sexual, the thrill was still exhilarating.

The two boats rose and fell in the growing swells, harbinger of more severe weather on the way. "I didn't bother with the weather channel this morning!" called Alex. "I guess I'm just a cockeyed optimist."

"Me, too. Listen, I'm gonna be knee deep in water in a minute! You want to come along side and help me stow my things?"

"I don't want to get too close if you don't' mind, my little boat gets tossed around in a chop like this. Your boat is so heavy, I'm afraid it will come down hard on mine and smash it to pieces. Then we'd both be in the drink." Alex was especially pleased with his use of nautical words, like 'chop' and 'drink.'

"Yeah, so what should I do?"

"I'll come as close as I dare. You throw your bag over to me, then pop in the water and swim over. It's just a couple of strokes to my boat."

"Jesus, Christ, this water is fucking *cold!*"

"Don't be squeamish, you'll only be in the water a few seconds. I have a blanket I'll throw over you once you're on board."

Vinnie looked down at his feet, saw the water was over his ankles and still coming in. Realizing he had no choice but to do as the Good Samaritan instructed, he said, "Yeah, all right, but come a lot closer, will you?"

Alex motored slowly to within ten yards of Vinnie's boat. Nick swung his nylon bag back and heaved it over. It landed on the gunwale of Alex's boat and rolled in.

"Good throw!" called Alex. "Now come on over!"

Vinnie put his legs over the side of the boat. The rolling waves were starting to come close to the rim of the hull. He hesitated, looked at

Alex, who waved him to come on. With a loud curse Vinnie dropped into the water. Even with the orange life jacked, the cresting waves broke over his head, forcing him to close his eyes and hold his breath.

Vinnie doggie-paddled toward Alex. Just as he came within inches of the little boat, a fresh wave broke over his head. While his face was submerged, Alex reached over the side, grabbed Vinnie's head in both hands and forced him down into the water.

The panicking figure dug his fingers into the backs of his attacker's hands trying to pry them from his head, but Alex had anticipated this and worn heavy leather gloves. The victim's clawing failed to loosen Alex's grip.

A fresh wave washed over Alex's arms. The rhythm was sensual, like a woman lifting him up in swells of ecstasy. Soon Vinnie's hands weakened. His fingers opened in surrender. His arms fell away and floated on the surface of the water, his body undulating with the sea like a jellyfish.

Alex released Vinnie's head. The bobbing figure remained face down in the water, arms spread in front, head lolling with each cresting wave. Alex let the body drift away from the boat. He put the engine in gear and motored back toward the marina, thrilling to the rising and falling of the boat. He threw back his head and laughed out load. There was no joy like the joy of squeezing out a life with your own hands.

As he pointed the bow toward shore, he began to sing, "Shiver me timbers, I'm sailing away!"

TWENTY-NINE

Once he had the boat out of the water and safely stowed, Alex returned home, where he poured himself a double shot of scotch. He wasn't drinking the cheap stuff anymore, that was for losers. He was buying Glenlivet by the case, that's what successful entrepreneurs drank.

The thrill of the kill still reverberated in his mind. It was better than sex. The thought struck him that the greatest thrill for a man would be to combine murder and sex in one act. It was so obvious, he couldn't understand why he had never given it a try. Well, he would rectify that one day. He pledged to figure a way to make one of his kills a sexually satisfying one without leaving any DNA evidence behind.

He called the escort service and asked for a girl who was well endowed. "I want to drown in her flesh," he told the service. After making the arrangements, he went over that phrase: *drown in her flesh,* and began to imagine how he could take that to new heights of passion.

The girl arrived right on time. She was East European, he didn't know from where exactly, with long dark hair, full breasts and hips, and long, lean legs set off by tight Capri pants. Alex explained he wanted her to soak in the tub before they had sex. He led her into the bath, turned on cold water and slowly undressed her while the tub filled. Then he told her to step into the tub.

As her foot entered the water, the girl said, "Why so cold? I catch my death in water so cold!"

"You'll get used to it. It's just like going for a dip in the ocean."

"I can't swim!" she complained, folding her arms across her chest as she stood in the tub.

"You'll do plenty of stroking soon enough," he told her. He offered her an extra hundred dollars, pointing out he was a regular with the girl's service and always tipped well. When he placed two fifties on the sink, she slowly crouched down in the tub and finally immersed herself in the cold water.

He watched as her skin became pale, goose bumps rising all over her body and her nipples growing hard. When her teeth began to chatter and her lips were turning blue, he decided she was ready. He led her out of the bath to the bedroom and had her lie on her back with one arm dangling down to the floor. "Leave your mouth and eyes open, but don't make a sound, and don't move a muscle. Understand?"

"You want me to play dead? Why you not say so?" she said, smiling now that she understood the game. She let her jaw drop, rolled her eyes up into her head so only the whites showed, and went completely limp. Her breathing became so shallow, it seemed as if she wasn't taking in a single breath.

Looking at the corpse-like figure, Alex felt an arousal like nothing he had ever known before. He began by kissing her cold blue lips.

THIRTY

As Nicholas held up his ID tag entering the Department of Health building, the security guard put up his hand to stop. It was the same guard who had made him return his laptop to his the week before.

"Lemme see your ID."

"Why?"

The guard glared at the physician. Nicholas gave his ID to the guard, who inspected it closely, then handed it back without a word of explanation.

Walking to the elevator, he looked back, saw the guard had picked up the phone to speak to someone, and felt a rising sense of fear. What awaited him upstairs? The FBI? The NYPD?

Am I paranoid or is this it? He rode to his floor, sweat now trickling down his sides, his heart thrumming in his chest.

As he passed Libby's office, he saw two men he didn't recognize talking to her. One guy, short and round with a shaved head, was doing the talking; a second one, tall and trim, stared at Libby as if measuring her for a coffin. They were wearing white shirts, dark suits and sour looks on their faces. They looked like Feds, not medical types. Libby looked up and saw Nick, but made no sign of recognition as he passed by.

Here it comes, he thought, reaching his office. Inside, he dropped his old leather bag on the desk, removed the thumbnail from his key ring and dropped it into his desk drawer. He settled into his chair and was reaching to the computer to boot it up when he noticed something odd. *His chair was lower than where he liked it.* Had someone been in his office? It had been locked when he arrived, and he was sure he'd locked it when he left the night before.

Booting up the computer, he wondered how he could tell if any file had been opened after he'd left the night before. It would be obvious if a file had been modified, the date and time of the change would be next to the file name. But what if someone had merely opened it?

I bet Manny could tell me. He called his friend in the IT section and asked if he was busy.

"Hah! *Busy?* You have any idea how much juggling we have to do to keep these old computers even *functioning?* Not to mention our interface with the hospitals that send us microbiological data every morning from their labs, and the syndromic surveillance input from the emergency rooms."

"I know you're swamped. It's just, if you could come take a quick look at my computer, I'm sure it'll only take you five minutes. What do you say?"

"If I come right over, will you let me take the Avanti out to the Palisades Expressway and open her up?"

"As long as you keep it under a hundred."

"Deal. I'll be right down."

Manny arrived minutes later. A five-foot elf with a Charlie Chan goatee, thinning hair on top and a pony tail behind, he settled into a chair, adjusted the height, and asked Nicholas what was the problem.

"It's not a problem, per se." Nick explained that he had a feeling someone had been accessing his files behind his back. He explained how his chair was at a different height than when he left it the night before.

"The cleaning crew mess with it?"

"Garbage was full, dust on the floor when I came in."

"Hmm. There's a lot of rumors going around about the Feds monitoring our work, but they can do that easy from a remote location, there's no need to break into your office."

"Can you determine if somebody *did* access my computer?"

"Should be no problem." Manny entered a command, calling up a window that looked like hieroglyphics. He quickly typed in commands, zipped through files, and finally arrived at a table filled with numbers and arcane commands.

Leaning forward and scrutinizing the screen, he said, "No surprise, you've got a spy ware program installed that monitors every keystroke."

"Shit! Is that legal?"

"Management's claimed the right to monitor their employee's computer use for years. The courts pretty much side with them."

"So if I saved a file to an external drive, like a thumbnail, it would record that. Right?"

"Naturally. *Everything* you do is monitored by the spy program."

"Shit."

"What's the problem?"

"I can't tell you specifics, Manny, I wish I could, but I don't want you being pulled into this thing. Let's just say, somebody doesn't like the way I save my data." Nicholas thought about what to do next. "Can you tell how long the program's been in my computer?

Manny's fingers danced across the keyboard. "They've been tracking your computer use for over a year."

"Who is *they?*"

His friend shook his head sadly. "We're supposed to safeguard the DOH computers from hackers and spy ware, but the Feds can come in and load all kinds of crap, and if I don't search the hard drive of a computer, it stays in the background. Spying."

"But if their spy ware program lets them know everything I do, why break into my office?"

"Who knows. Maybe they were looking for more than data on your computer."

By the time that Manny left, Nicholas was certain that the intruder had come looking for his thumbnail drive. Since it wasn't in the office, the inference would be that he had taken it out of the building. That inference would be his undoing.

He looked around the office searching for a place he could stash the thumbnail drive so he could claim it had never left the room. The wall cabinet above his desk was packed with journals, books and computer printouts. Stuck to the side of the cabinet was a funny, handmade tie Chrissie had made for him when she was in kindergarten. It was an outlandish, misshapen piece of purple fabric, hand sewn with huge, uneven stitches that spelled D-A-D. He loved it.

Nicholas took the thumbnail drive from his desk and hung it on the nail holding the tie up *behind the ugly tie.* As long as the interloper hadn't looked behind the tie—and why in hell would he?—it might just be enough to save him from arrest.

After all, he was in the habit of backing up *all* of his files on a flash drive himself, since the department's server crashed just about once a week. Saving the student file was no different than any other computer task he took on. There was no proof he'd taken the drive home, *so long as the Feds hadn't hacked into his home computer.*

As he settled in to work at his desk, Nick felt the noose tightening around his throat. It was the end of everything; a descent into a new hell that held a million unknown terrors.

He was inputting the data from the last group of high school he had tested when he heard a knock on the open door. The two guys in white shirts and dark suits were standing in his doorway.

"Come to the conference room," said the short guy with no hair. They didn't look like they wanted to talk about an outbreak of hepatitis.

THIRTY-ONE

Approaching the conference room, Nicholas vowed to stay calm and admit nothing. The two men gestured for him to take a seat. Libby was not in the room. A bad sign.

"Mister Andreas," began the short, bald one.

"*Doctor* Andreas."

"Okay, *Doctor* Andreas." He pulled a file from an envelope and placed it in front of Nick. It was a copy of the School Drool issue that featured the report on student lung performance.

"We know that the student who wrote this is friends with your daughter, Christina. We know that your daughter has access to your personal computer. And we have reason to believe that you violated city, state and federal regulations regarding removing confidential files from the Department of Health."

"Do you have any proof that's what I did?" said Nicholas.

"We ask the question, not you," the tall, athletic type said in a deadpan voice, his eyes, equally dead. Nick knew from the bulge under his arm that he had a weapon. No doubt he had handcuffs as well.

"That's fine. But I just think I should know what exactly the problem is that you're asking me to address."

The first man said, "Don't waste our time denying you took the files home with you, we know you downloaded them to your portable drive."

"I copy all my files as a backup, the DOH servers crash almost every day."

"And you take your work home with you to work on it as a matter of routine. Isn't that so?"

"I wouldn't call it 'routine,' but, yes, on occasion, I take work home. But my home computer is password protected. Working at home is within the regulations of the Department of Health so long as the information is protected from hacking."

"But not information related to studies of Ground Zero," said the first agent. "All of that material is restricted to DOH computers. You signed a statement acknowledging that fact. Did you not?"

"I suppose," said Nicholas, recalling the hated loyalty oath. As he found his fear giving way to fury at the two gun-toting agents from what agency, he didn't even know, he struggled to hold his anger in check. *Keep it cool,* he kept telling himself. *Tell them as little as possible, since anything I say will be used to bury me.*

"Do you deny working on the Ground Zero study at home?"

Nicholas suddenly saw a glimmer of hope. If the Feds acknowledged knowing the file had been on his home computer, they would have to admit hacking into his private computer. Maybe that was legal, maybe not, but there was a chance they wouldn't want to admit it. Not yet, anyway.

"Do you have evidence that I took those files home?"

"Just answer the question," said the second agent. "*Did you take the files home?*"

Here was the corner that had him in the trap. If he lied to the Feds and they had proof the file had been loaded into his home computer, he was a dead man, lying to a Federal officer was itself a crime. If he told the truth, he was equally dead and buried.

Looking into the second man's eyes, Nick said in a calm voice, "No, I did not work on any Ground Zero files at home." It was just barely a truthful statement. He *did* take the files home and load them into his computer, but he hadn't *opened* them and looked at them. If they didn't ask him a more specific question about the files…

The two agents leaned in toward each other and conferred. With a promise that they would be speaking to him again soon, the two agents walked out, leaving the door open and Nicholas bathed in sweat.

Returning to his office, Nick told himself he'd dodged a bullet, at least for now. But then a terrible thought came to him. Chrissie had opened the files on his computer. Opened them and emailed them to her friend, Lucas. There was sure to be an electronic trail the Feds could follow.

He had just implicated his daughter in the crime! His fear welled up and threatened to overcome him. In trying to save himself from prison, his statement, "I didn't open the files at home," had thrown his daughter into the hands of the Feds. The implication was more terrifying than his having to spend the rest of his life in solitary confinement.

How could he possibly live with himself if they took his Chrissie away because of his testimony?

THIRTY-TWO

A few moments after the Feds left, Libby came into Nick's office and handed him a thick folder. "I have a new assignment for you. I want you to evaluate the vaccination programs in our extended care facilities for the coming season. That will require a review of their influenza rates from last year."

He searched her face for a sign of his fate, but there was none. Her face was a mask, her voice a flat command.

"What is the study question?"

"The DOH wants to see a decrease in flu cases this winter. After reviewing the incidence of disease among the facilities for the previous season, you will visit the long term care facilities to assess their vaccine programs and their infection control practices.

"But it's only the middle of June. The flu season won't start for months."

"Which gives you plenty of time to summarize their past performances and to visit every one in Brooklyn. I have other practitioners visiting the other boroughs."

"What about the pulmonary function studies? I'm not finished collecting the data."

"Someone else will pick that up. You'll work with the nursing homes."

"This is about the student blog, isn't it?"

"I don't have anything to do with that, Nick. Those decisions come from way higher up the food chain."

He stepped closer to her. A head taller, he stood over her trying not to be threatening, but wanting to force her to believe him. "I didn't leak the data. You believe me, don't you?"

Libby took a step backward toward the door. Her face showed the strain of pressure from her own boss as well as the pressure from the Feds. Start telling a public servant she might be in trouble with the law and she gets very uptight. He knew that, as much as Libby wanted to protect him, she could do nothing to stop the investigation into his role in the leak.

"Look, Libby," he said, matching her steps. "Now that a scraggly school paper has told the public we have the report, don't you think the public has a right to the full data? Shouldn't the department release a summary of our findings?"

"We've been through this before, Nick. The data can be easily misinterpreted. We don't want to alarm the public." She was in the doorway now.

"Christ. The Feds are running the department, aren't they?" he said. *"They're* dictating city health policy to *us."* He was so close he could almost feel her trembling. "Has somebody been in my office, using my computer? I found some stuff on my desk was rearranged when I came in this morning."

Libby wrinkled her nose. "That's probably just the cleaning lady. I find my things moved around all the time." She stepped into the hall, the harsh overhead light showing her pale, fearful face. "Don't make things any worse, Nicholas. Do your job, forget about the student data, and hope for the best."

She turned and walked hurriedly down hall. Nick shut the door and sat in his chair. He cursed the department for taking him off the study. Through his curses a rising tide of anger began to lift him from his long bout of depression. If he was going to go down for his crimes, he was going to go like a man: fighting. Cursing the gods and the fates and the Feds. And he was going to make damn sure all of New York learned what total fuckups the health authorities had been on 9/11.

A new idea made him break out in a laugh. He was a fuckup, okay, true, but he wasn't the *biggest* fuckup. The Mayor and the EPA Chairwoman and OSHA fucked up *way* more than he had. For some inexplicable reason, that thought made him laugh out loud.

THIRTY-THREE

On his morning subway ride to yet another nursing home on his list, Nicholas was reading the headlines when an article caught his eye: a drowning on Long Island Sound. Somebody named Vinnie Solomira. His body was found floating in the sound, his fishing boat was upside down and submerged, with only the bow sticking up out of the water.

The authorities found no evidence of foul play. They assumed the boat had tipped over, the weather had been threatening, with six foot waves and strong winds. Solomira was known to be a heavy drinker, so alcohol was high on the list of possible explanations awaiting toxicology results.

Nicholas didn't find the drowning particularly interesting from a medical standpoint, fishermen and swimmers drowned all the time in the waters around New York City. What caught Nicholas's eye and got his mind engaged was the perfunctory mention that *Vinnie Solomira was in the midst of a knock-down, drag-out divorce.* He was the founder of a successful restaurant business of which his wife was demanding half the ownership since, according to her lawyer, it was her hard work that made Vinnie a success.

Another spouse in a contested divorce in an accidental death. What was it about these bitter divorces that made people accident-prone? Were they drunk or stoned? Were they so angry and upset they didn't look where they were going? Did the stress of potentially losing everything throw them into a depression? There were studies suggesting that up to a third of all accidental deaths were really unrecognized suicides.

The coincidences were intriguing from the standpoint of epidemiology. Assuming that bitter divorces were a risk factor for unexpected death, what was the mechanism that increased their relative risk of dying? What was the unseen hand of mental disease at work making them vulnerable to a deadly outcome?

He tucked the paper in his briefcase as he arrived at the nursing home and prepared to go to work.

If the Brooklyn Family Courthouse on Schermerhorn had air conditioning, you couldn't tell it by the air, which hung in heavy layers. Bunting from the recent Fourth of July festivities hung from the railing along the second floor stair landing overlooking the lobby. The marble floors and walls were cool, but the air in the corridors was hot and humid. Alex wished he didn't have to wear the suit.

The judge had called a recess, and the weary lawyers, unwilling to remove their suit jackets for fear of antagonizing the judge, fanned themselves with briefs and chugged bottled water.

An anorexic woman in a faded housedress, high heel sandals and lips that would benefit from lipstick, wiped her neck with a handkerchief and leaned toward her lawyer. "Zach is probably up north in the cabin screwing some fifteen-year old."

"Let's hope so, Gillian. If your husband doesn't appear we can ask for a summary judgment."

"I don't care about the money. I just wanna be sure he doesn't get custody of the kids. He wants to put Tommy in an asylum!"

She looked over at her husband's lawyer, a stout fellow with a florid face that seemed to radiate heat like an overworked stove. The lawyer glanced at his watch, a worried look on his face.

The doors to the courtroom were flung open and a tall, barrel-chested man with thick black hair stalked down the aisle between the seats. Though he wore a size forty-eight long shirt and a size twelve shoe, he moved quickly, his footsteps light on the marble floor.

Zachariah Thorne approached his overheated lawyer and spoke quietly in the man's ear. Thorne looked cool and confident, as if he were a minute late to a golf date and not a court case. They had just settled into their seat when the judge returned and the court crier announced that court was in session.

Zach's lawyer presented depositions from a police report, arguing that Gillian Thorne had been stopped for driving under the influence. He followed that by depositions from a bartender and two patrons of a local pub who swore that Mrs. Thorne frequently imbibed more than a few mixed drinks.

The lawyer followed with the coup de grace. He held up timed and dated photographs of Gillian with her children in the back seat. "As you can see your honor, the children are *without their seatbelts.*" He added that the wife was "unemployed and probably unemployable, as well as an unsafe and uncaring mother."

"That's a damned lie!" cried Gillian, jumping up from her seat. The judge pointed a warning finger at her lawyer, who grabbed his client's arm and pulled her back down to earth.

"Gillian, I told you, you'll just antagonize the judge if you keep speaking up."

She opened her mouth to speak, looked past her lawyer to see Zach was smiling at her, and decided to keep quiet.

Her lawyer stood. "I object to this characterization of my client, your honor! The subjective observations of a few barflies hardly amount to a psychiatric evaluation. Rear seatbelts are not required in New York at this time." The lawyer added that his client had a new employment, which she was to begin the following day. "This woman is a loving and dedicated mother who has spent years caring for her special needs son."

"Who belongs in a facility under the care of professionals!" declared Zach's lawyer.

Gillian's lawyer presented a deposition. "This is from the psychiatrist caring for their son Tommy, your honor. It states that removing the son, who suffers from schizophrenia, and placing him in an institution, as Zachariah Thorne has repeatedly stated he wishes to do, would be detrimental to his mental health."

The two lawyers wrangled for several minutes until the judge ordered them to submit professional evaluations, after which he would interview the child in chambers. Then he set a date for another hearing.

Leaving the courtroom, Gillian kept asking her lawyer if she was going to lose her son. The layer assured her that she had a shot at her being awarded custody of both the children.

"A *shot?* I can't go with a *shot*! Tommy needs to know he won't be taken away. *I* need to know!"

Watching Gillian Thorne stand in front of the courthouse with a frightened look on her face, Alex decided that, much as he would like to put the wretched woman out of her misery, business was business, she was clearly the better prospect.

THIRTY-FOUR

Alex followed Gillian Thorne and her lawyer down the courthouse steps. The smell of honey roasted peanuts and chicken shish kebobs from a street vendor drifted in the warm September air. A derelict picked through trash, his rusting shopping card overflowing with bottles and cans.

Alex heard Mrs. Thorne loudly complain, "He doesn't care about the kids. He never takes them upstate to the cabin anymore. He goes up there with his Wall Street buddies and drinks and watches porno movies."

Alex's ears perked up when he heard the words 'Wall Street buddies' and 'cabin upstate.' Even if it was a modest structure, it was a sign of a healthy income.

Mumbling and miserable, Gillian left the lawyer and made her way to a Greek restaurant on Court Street. She sat at the counter and ordered a cup of coffee. When it arrived she glanced around the room, then surreptitiously removed a flask from her purse and poured a shot of whiskey into the cup.

Looking over the cup as she sipped it, Gillian caught sight of Alex in his pinstripe suit and weathered leather attaché case. When he approached her she said, "Weren't you in the courtroom just now?"

"Yes, that's right." He flashed a warm smile, held out a hand. He held her hand in a warm, comforting embrace. "I'm so sorry that your attorney is having difficulty with your case."

"If you're trying to get me to switch lawyers, I can't afford to go shopping around for somebody else, I'm stuck with the one I got."

"Oh no, my dear, it's nothing like that. Nothing at all. May I join you?"

"It's a free country."

He settled into the stool beside her, laid his attaché case next to him, and saw her eyes focus on the bag. She was already convinced that he was an attorney.

"Let's move to a booth. I'll buy you dinner and a drink, it's the cocktail hour, and over dessert I'll tell you how I can solve all of your problems, including making sure that you keep sole custody of your children."

Gillian had no faith that this strange lawyer could help her case, but she never turned down a free drink and a meal. She followed him to a booth at the back, where she ordered the most expensive entrée on the menu and a Makers Mark Manhattan, up.

While they waited for their meal, Alex asked Gillian to tell him more about her marriage. She explained that she had married while in college. Zachariah had been a grad student in business school, she, an art major. "I wanted to work with a curator at The Met. I love restoration work. It's not an easy field to get work in. Mainly I worked at secretary jobs. I *hate* being a secretary."

"I'm so sorry to hear that your son has been having some psychiatric problems. Tell me about that."

She told him that Tommy had been diagnosed bipolar while in high school. It had been a struggle to get him through school, but she hoped he would be better in college.

"What happened to him?"

"I got him enrolled at the City University, but he couldn't focus. He walked around the city instead of going to class. His father wouldn't admit that our son even had a problem. He only cared about making deals and clawing his way up the Wall Street ladder."

"Men are often less nurturing than the women."

"Egomaniac is more like it," she said. "He's

so fucking competitive. I mean, when the kids were little he played Shoots N' Ladders with them like it was high stakes poker."

"That *is* insensitive," said Alex.

"Now I'm trying to get Tommy into a half-way house for troubled youth, but it's expensive. Zach has tons of money, but the cheap bastard won't put out a dime. Not a *dime!* I'd like to strangle him!" She took a long pull on her drink.

At these words, Alex put down his cup of coffee, leaned forward and placed his hand gently over hers. "You said you'd like to 'strangle him.' Well, that is just the topic I want to discuss with you."

She held her glass in midair, afraid to believe that this guy was serious.

After explaining to Gillian that his company had been in the eradication business for decades, with an unbroken string of successful operations, Alex went through the advantages of using his services, the easy financial terms, and the clear negatives barreling down on her if she let the divorce proceedings continue on their course. Gillian's objections were weak and half-hearted; she was eager to take up the offer. The only thing holding her back was the risk she would be apprehended.

Alex closed the deal by pointing out the risk of letting Zach gain full custody of their children. "With his Neanderthal approach to psychological problem, your son could end up in a terrible state. Who knows what he would do? To himself. To others. You owe it to your children to keep them out of that monster's clutches."

Gillian's maternal instincts overcame her timidity. She accepted his offer. As a sweetener, the image of her hated husband in a coffin brought her enormous satisfaction.

Alex told her to be at home at exactly six pm to receive a call that would confirm the contract. "Not five before six; not five minutes after six," he told her. He believed that insisting upon a rigid schedule impressed potential clients that his organization was business-like. "Oh, one more thing. What kind of car does your husband drive?"

"A two-thousand Explorer. It's three years old, but the bastard's too cheap to buy a new one. Why?"

"Just part of our research. Be ready for my call tomorrow, at six."

He left with the joy of a new contract before him. A new problem to puzzle over and solve. A new twist on an old and classic theme.

THIRTY-FIVE

At home that evening Alex went online to review the common causes of motor vehicle accidents, focusing on the ones that were most likely to produce a death. In court the wife had mentioned that Zach liked to drive upstate to his cabin. That would mean long stretches of empty highway. If he failed to use his seat belt, and if his SUV happened to roll over at high speed, the odds of his dying were exceedingly high. Arranging an accident was the most promising approach for this case.

The Department of Transportation had a treasure trove of information about rollovers of SUVs. So did the auto insurance agencies. A rapid swerve across a lane, as to avoid a deer in the road, was one cause of the rollovers. Another was a blown tire, with the front tire being the most likely to produce a rollover. The newer models were coming equipped with stability control programs that reduced the risk of rolling over, but cheapskate Zach Thorne had an older model.

One salient fact leaped out at him: drivers and passengers who failed to wear their seat belts were ten times more likely to die in a rollover. *Ten times.* Alex had a hunch the egomaniac Thorne was too cocky to bother buckling up. At the same time Alex had to learn how to reliably engineer a fatal tire blowout. He suspected that heating the tire sidewall to a very high temperature would weaken it enough to cause it to rupture once the tire pressure increased from the heat generated by miles on the road.

He studied the tire manufacturing processes. Even with their advances in construction, they were still susceptible to heat. *Especially if they were under-inflated.* That had been a major factor in those shredding tires and the spate of roll-overs ten years ago.

Under inflate the tire and weaken it with heat were all it would take to blow the tire. Easy. But how much heat? He decided to experiment on his own car. He would under-inflate and weaken a tire with heat. A *rear* tire in this case. That would produce less instability and less likelihood he would lose control of the car. And he would drive it at a moderate speed to see if the thing blew.

Meditating on his project, Alex mused, *Let us sing the praises of the scientific method, the key to a successful business.*

When Nicholas arrived home from work, he found Beth on the terrace watering the flowers while Chrissie lay out on a beach recliner in a tank top and shorts reading The Onion and laughing out loud. Flower pots with trailing vines and blood-red flowers hung along the railing, while flowers with thick green leaves and bursts of pink petal filled flower boxes.

After greeting his wife he said to Chrissie, "Did you put on sun block?"

She hid her face behind the paper. "Don't start in about my getting skin cancer, I'll be dead from lung cancer long before *that* ever happens."

"All right," said Nicholas. "Since you're convinced that all the students are sick, would you be willing to go for tests of your pulmonary function?"

"Who's gonna do the test—*you?"*

"The department has pulmonary technicians. But you can go to a private pulmonologist if you prefer."

Chrissie got up, stepped to the door to the living room. "This is fucking great. First you said I was never in danger; *now* you want to show me that I'm really dying. Thanks a lot, *dad!"* She slammed the door closed behind her.

Nicholas looked at Beth. "I'm trying to reach her," he said.

"I know you are dear. But you forget, children sharpen their teeth on their parents' bones." She carried the watering can into the kitchen to refill it. Coming back out to the terrace to water the rose bush, she told Nick it was too hot to cook and suggested they order sushi.

"Okay. I'll get the menu. You want tuna or salmon?"

"Both. And order some for Chrissie." Beth continued watering, perplexed at Nick's new attitude. Was something changed? She dared not put too much into one exchange, but still, he had reached out to his daughter. It was a sign of *something*, she just didn't know of what.

In bed that night, Nicholas sat reading the obits, while Beth graded student papers.

"You have a gruesome idea about bedtime reading, you know that?" she said.

"I guess." He wanted to see if the paper offered any more information about Vinnie Solomira's drowning on Long Island Sound. It only referred to the "tragic death by drowning while following his beloved sport of fishing." Nick had no doubt the man had been drinking, that's what sport fishermen do out on the Sound.

Of course no obituary was going to write that the deceased was a heavy drinker or a careless sportsman, it was submitted by the family. Gossip was under the purview of the tabloids, which he never read. He thought the Metro section of The Times must have something on the guy. If not he could always do a search online.

"Have you put the papers out for recycling this week?" he asked.

"That's your job."

"Sexist wench." He got up from the bed, went downstairs to the kitchen and dug through the pile of newspapers beneath the butcher-block table. Sitting on the floor, he found the article he wanted. Sure enough, there was a picture of Jewel Solomira trying to fight her way past her husband in the entrance to a restaurant.

He remembered somebody else in a pending divorce case that died unexpectedly. A rich woman, thrown from her horse. What had the headlines said? Something about a socialite killed by her beloved mare in tragic accident. Meredith somebody or other. Another one of those high-profile divorce cases that the local TV news was always blaring about.

Coincidence. But it nagged at him. There was that other obituary of a rich divorcee who fell to her death down some apartment stairs. He recalled the first rule of epidemiology: *There are no coincidences in nature, only unrecognized vectors of disease.*

The early days of an epidemic always followed the same pattern: the first handful of cases were ignored. Then the bodies mount until the spike in cases catches the attention of an epidemiologist, who searches for a connection among the cases, and the outbreak investigation is underway.

But what mechanism could produce an outbreak of accidental deaths? If the deaths *were* connected somehow, it would probably be by some underlying psychological state. Depression, maybe. Or extreme anxiety.

Tired, he returned to bed and dropped the paper on the floor along with the rest of the others.

"Leaving it for the maid, are you?" said Beth, who always piled her papers and magazines neatly on a bedside table.

"I want to save them, I found something interesting," he said and turned out his reading light. As he settled back into bed, he wondered how he could get hold of New York's death statistics in order to make sense of it all.

THIRTY-SIX

Alex set the hair curler on maximum heat, waited a few moments, then pressed the curler against the side wall of the driver's side rear tire. He had parked his car in the basement parking garage of his building. His new business model allowed him to buy a used Ford Escort and to rent a parking space in his building's garage.

He checked his watch and kept the curler in place for one full minute. When he withdrew it he noted a discoloration on the side wall, but no ballooning. He pressed the end of a screw driver against the spot on the side wall, feeling for weakening. It seemed no less strong than other places on the tire.

He went to another section of the tire and applied the curler for two full minutes. This produced a more pronounced discoloration and a slight softening of the area, but no bulge. He thought that he should see a definite weakening if he was going to guarantee a blowout.

Pressing the curler against the side wall of the tire on the other side of the car, he held it for three full minutes. That produced a definite softening and pouching of the wall. Satisfied, he put the curler away, waited a few moments, then pressed on the softened area. It was difficult to measure the degree of weakening. He would have to take the car out for a road test.

He lowered the pressure on both rear tires by ten pounds, which would further weaken them at highway speed. He stepped back and studied the tires. They looked a little low, but radials always looked low, he reminded himself. He lowered the pressure on the front tires so they would look symmetrical with the rear.

Satisfied with his preparations, he opened the garage door and drove out. It was mid-morning. Traffic shouldn't be too heavy on the FDR Drive. He decided to drive up into Westchester County, give the tires time to heat up, and see what happened.

The ragged teeth of the city passed by as he crossed the Whitestone Bridge. He was twenty-five miles outside the city driving at a moderate speed and nothing happened to the tires. It was looking like he would have to go back to the parking garage and apply more heat.

He watched the signs for an exit that would allow him to turn around. He was passing a sign for gas and lodging and considering getting off when the car suddenly lurched to the side. He let out a curse and wrestled the wheel as the car hurtled toward the wall of stone just past the narrow green shoulder.

Alex struggled to control the car as the bumper and side scraped the stone wall, making a hideous sound. He pulled on the steering wheel and guided the car onto the green strip, massaging the brake pedal and bringing the car to a stop.

He turned on his emergency flashers, shut down the engine and sat for a moment. His hands were shaking, but he was laughing with triumph. The heat treatment had worked, the tire had blown.

Stepping out, he saw that the tire he had heated for three minutes was flat. Had he treated the front tire, he doubted that he would have kept control of the car. But he had survived the test. The plan was set.

Grinning broadly, he opened the trunk and pulled out the spare tire and jack. As he worked, a State Police car passed by. The cop braked, pulled over and backed up. When he was abreast of Alex, Alex waved at him, the grin still on his face. The cop drove away wondering that a man could be so happy to be changing a tire.

THIRTY-SEVEN

At four AM on a Saturday morning, Alex entered Zachariah Thorne's garage, using the remote control that Gillian had given him. The guy had changed the locks on the house but hadn't thought to change the code on the garage door opener.

Closing the door behind him, Alex shone the pencil-thin light of a torch around the garage. It was bigger than a one-bedroom apartment in Manhattan. His light reflected off the full-sized sport utility vehicle. He studied the tires, which were enormous. They were much larger, and much thicker, than the tires on his own Ford. He realized he would have to apply more heat than he'd used on his own vehicle.

After lowering the pressure on all the tires by ten pounds, he plugged an extension cord into an outlet and set the hair curler to high. After waiting for it to reach its maximum temperature, he crawled under the front of the SUV. It was better to weaken the inner aspect of the tire; there was always the chance that Thorne would spot the bulge if he stopped to check the air pressure.

He pressed the curler against the inner side wall and checked his watch. He decided to go with six minutes, theorizing that the tire wall was bound to be twice as thick as his own.

He watched the second hand slowly twitch its way around the dial. The minute seemed to last an hour. The second minute felt even longer; the third, an eternity. By the start of the forth minute he was growing impatient.

As the sixth minute finally came to an end, Alex was about to crawl back out from under the car when he heard a rustling sound, followed by the sound of the bolt on a door being thrown.

Jesus Christ! Could that be Thorne? Now?

He turned off the tiny flashlight and brought his legs under the vehicle. He hadn't planned on Thorne getting up at four in the morning to drive to the Adirondacks. He must have stayed up all night and was planning on sleeping when he arrived upstate.

As the connecting door to the house opened, Alex felt a current of fear run through him. The extension cord was plugged into the wall, and it ran directly under the truck to where Alex was lying.

Alex heard a beep, followed by the sound of the rear hatch opening. Thorne had obviously used his remote. Lying on his back beneath the vehicle, Alex tried to predict which side Thorne was most likely to walk by to get to the rear hatch. The extension cord was on the passenger's side; the driver's side was closest to the door to the house. That was promising. Still, Thorne could easily walk by the passenger side, which would likely lead him to bend down and examine the cord.

Alex watched the heavy boots tramp across the cement floor along the driver's side. The truck dipped slightly as Thorne dropped something heavy in the back. Probably a cooler full of beer.

Once the hatch was closed, Alex watched helplessly as Thorne stepped toward the passenger side of the vehicle. He held his breath as the boots thudded on the cement floor, stopped at the rear passenger door. The door opened. Thorne dropped something light on the seat. Maps, maybe. Or a jacket for the mountain air.

Jesus Christ. What if Thorne got into the driver's seat and started off. He'd see Alex lying in the middle of the garage floor once the car had backed out!

The rear passenger door slammed shut, startling Alex. After the door was closed, the boots continued toward the front of the car without tripping over the electric cord. The idiot didn't even see the cord. Seconds later Thorne entered the house, leaving the door open. It was clear he was on the verge of leaving on his trip.

Alex rolled out from under the truck and coiled a short section of the extension cord in his hand. As he rose from his knees he pulled the cord from the socket. Then he stood and quietly stepped out of the garage, coiling more of the extension cord as he moved. Keeping to the shadows, with a silent praise for suburban shrubbery and the privacy they provided, he made his way to his car, ready to follow Zachariah Thorne to his doom.

THIRTY-EIGHT

An hour after slipping out of Zach Thorne's garage, Alex was following the man's SUV north on the New York Thruway, keeping his speed an even eighty miles per hour and Thorne's SUV a half mile ahead. The guy was riding the left lane, even when there were no cars to pass, his seat belt unfastened, as Alex observed when Thorne passed him outside his home.

Passing a sign warning of deer crossing the road, Alex chuckled at the thought of the guy running into a deer instead of rolling over from a blown tire. It was July, were the deer still mating? It would be criminal to collect a fee from the wife, but hey, he was a criminal, wasn't he? Alex visualized Thorne running head on into a big buck and, not wearing a seatbelt, being thrown through the front windshield.

He reflected on his good fortune, then reminded himself that a cunning man made his own luck. The little imbroglio in the garage and his quick thinking reinforced his sense of mastery over people and events. In books he had moved his characters like chess pieces, sending each one of them to their fate. Now he found the manipulation of real people infinitely more exciting.

Driving and thinking about his life, Alex reflected that as he continued to collect the monthly fees, he would have a cool million dollars stashed away after only twenty contracts were paid in full. That chunk of change would last a long time, especially in cities where the standard of living was low. A man could live like a king with that kind of grubstake. Prague was cheap, and prostitution was legal. Mexico had its attractions: everyone spoke English. He would have to research his retirement options carefully.

He had a passport and driver's license in another name, courtesy of an ex con he'd interviewed for a book and even helped find work. Making the break would be easy. Once he had his million dollars, Alex Germaine would disappear from the world, never to be seen again. Out of print, out of life. What could be more fitting?

As the ribbon of highway spooled out before him, Alex worried that he hadn't applied enough heat to Thorne's heavy truck tire to make it blow. He'd tried to estimate how much more heat the big SUV tire would require, but it was guesswork. There was nothing he could do about it this trip, the cabin in the woods would probably not have an outside electric outlet. If the tire held, Alex decided he would have to come up with a Plan B at the cabin. A shooting accident, perhaps, that sort of thing happened all the time. Fools from the city got drunk and mistook each other for a bear. Killing Thorne with a gun would be simple.

A sign foretold a rest stop three miles ahead. If Thorne stopped there to take a leak and get coffee, it would cool the tires a bit. That might reduce the chance of a blowout even more. Well, patience *was* the lubricant of satisfied desire. At the exit Thorne kept on barreling along in the left lane. Alex figured he had a mighty big bladder.

They climbed a long stretch of highway, with a third lane on the right for slow vehicles. Over the top, Alex enjoyed a spectacular view of misty mountaintops receding to the horizon, the sky above growing to a deep blue as the mist was burned away.

On the downward slope Thorne picked up speed. *Christ, the fool must be doing close to a hundred.* Alex let the distance grow between them.

Suddenly Thorne's vehicle jumped to the right. It veered back to the left onto the shoulder, the nose dropped and the vehicle began to roll. It rolled over too many times for Alex to count. Thorne's body flew out from the smashed front windshield, hit the pavement and bounced, then skittered across the tarmac, finally coming to rest on the gravel beside the road. The body lay in a twisted heap, the rag doll victim of a child's brutality.

Alex braked gently, passing the accident at a modest fifty miles an hour. Thorne wasn't moving: a good sign, but not proof of death. Could anybody survive such a horrific battering?

He drove on, keeping to the posted speed limit, and turned off at the first exit, some ten miles away. He reentered the highway going south, noted the mileage, and drove in a leisurely fashion back toward the scene.

At exactly nine miles along he saw the flashing lights of an ambulance and a State Trooper. The traffic, thin as it was, had slowed so the drivers could rubberneck along the scene. Alex did the same. He noted that the paramedics were chatting with the Trooper and making no effort to revive Thorne. For his part, the body was lying exactly where Alex had last seen it.

Alex had no doubt the man was dead.

Turning his attention to the road ahead, Alex, kept to a cautious seventy. His heart was light, his face radiant with happiness. *Is there any high as good as snuffing out a life?* If only he could combine sex with murder in one long exhilarating act; now *that* would be paradise.

He took out his cell phone and hit the speed dial for the escort service. "Hello, this is Alex Germaine. That's right, twenty-seven-o-five Shell Road, apartment 3-M. I want a girl for tonight, is Delilah available? She's *booked for a party?* Oh, well, send me a young Asian girl. I want her demure. A Comfort Girl. Good. Eight o'clock."

He turned off the phone, settled back in his seat, lowered the window to breathe in the fresh upstate air, and considered how he could render the call girl unconscious without leaving any marks or lasting damage to her brain. The last girl who had played dead was satisfying enough, but he wanted something more. Something really intoxicating.

Roofies might do the trick. But some of the girls took so many drugs, he wasn't sure what dose to give her. Besides, he had to be careful not to leave any evidence he had drugged her, those escort services had some tough guys on their payroll. He didn't want to have to face a mug with long arms and a short temper.

Life is a puzzle waiting to be solved. A little research; a few contacts among some of the made guys he knew from his research, he was sure this problem would be solved as easily as one of his killing.

THIRTY-NINE

On the subway ride to work on Monday morning, Nick skimmed the headlines, then went on to the lesser articles. His eye caught the story about a Zachariah Thorne, who died when his SUV rolled over on the New York Thruway. One of the front tires evidently had a weak spot. It was likely under inflated as well, since the three other tires were found to be ten pounds under the recommended filling pressure.

The weakened tire blew when the driver was barreling downhill at a high rate of speed. The State Policeman at the site estimated Thorne had been going close to a hundred miles per hour when his car flipped over. The man was thrown from the car, not having fastened his seatbelt.

Nicholas wasn't sure the death was relevant, until he saw a photo that showed the widow and the deceased's girlfriend arguing outside the funeral home over who would ride in the limousine to the gravesite. The deceased, a successful investment banker, had been in the middle of a hotly contentious divorce.

Here we go again. He recalled the restaurant guy who died at sea, the high society woman kicked to death by her horse, the whining woman with the philandering stud of a husband who fell down the stairs. And now the fellow in the SUV. *All in hotly contested divorces.*

What were the odds of four well-do-do divorcing spouses all suffering accidental deaths? Although he didn't know the crude rate of accidental death for this age group, he was sure that it was astronomically low. That was why insurance companies offered adults in their prime such low rates for accidental death coverage.

Nicholas realized he would have to get a handle on the numbers if he wanted to make sense of the deaths. He needed to know the rate of accidental deaths for adults in this age group. He also needed to know how many people were in divorce proceedings in a given period. Say, in a month; or in a quarter, that would give a larger, more statistically reliable number of cases. Then he could compare the *expected* mortality rate for this specific group with the *actual* one. If the difference was statistically significant...Well, he'd jump off that bridge when he came to it. He always followed the first rule of epidemiology: don't accept there is an outbreak until you have a case definition and data to support the theory.

Once again he recalled a study he read in medical school that argued as many as a third of all accidental deaths were really *unrecognized suicides.* The theory was that a depressed person suddenly encounters a situation that offers an escape from his despondent state and chooses to take it. He jumps in front of a subway train, but it's called an accident, since the deceased had no time to write a note, it was a spontaneous decision. Nicholas wondered if divorcees were subject to depression and suicidal thoughts.

Arriving at work, he put aside his curiosity about the accidental deaths and spent an unexciting morning calling more nursing homes, now addressed with their politically correct term 'Extended Care Facilities.' He asked them to describe their plan for vaccinating residents and employees, and requested a fax copy of their policy and procedure for influenza prevention. Several of the facilities had robust, imaginative programs. He was impressed.

"We expect to vaccinate one-hundred per cent of our clients and seventy-five per cent of our staff," said one Infection Control Nurse bursting with enthusiasm. Nicholas believed she might meet her goal, which was miles ahead of the acute care facilities.

Once he'd filled his quota of appointments, he found himself thinking again about those accidental deaths. He searched the Internet until he found a table posted by an association of insurance carriers that listed the incidence of accidental deaths for different age groups. It also listed the most common types of accidents. Not surprisingly, falls were the most prevalent, followed by motor vehicle accidents, accidental poisoning, and electrical shocks.

People die every day, and they got divorced every day. He theorized that the failure of a marriage brought on despair, and the despair eroded the will to live. Maybe anger turned within really did lead to death.

On his way to the first site visit of the day, Nick was relieved to leave the DOH and be out in the field, interviewing nursing home practitioners. It meant not having to look for signs on everyone's face at the office that his fate had been sealed. That his job was toast and his arrest was imminent.

FORTY

Nick had put the dinner dishes in the dishwasher and was scrubbing the pots, his apron wet and his arms covered with suds, when he heard Stanley and Fran come in.

"I'm in the kitchen!" he called.

Seeing his friend in suds up to his elbow, Stanley said, "I hear you do a mean job with a mop and bucket, too."

"Grab a beer from the fridge," said Nicholas. When his friend asked how things were going at work, he said, "The place is going down the crapper. Somebody is reading my computer files at work. I'm pretty sure they searched my office."

"Employers love to snoop on their employees, but entering your office puts it on a different level. What were they looking for?"

He explained how he was sure the investigators knew he'd transferred files of the Ground Zero study to his thumbnail drive, and that he'd tried to make it look like the portable drive never left his office. Then he described the interview at the DOH.

"The agents asked me if I took the files home with me."

"What did you tell them?"

"I prevaricated. I said I didn't *open* any of the Ground Zero files at home, which is true, technically. But if they hacked into my home computer, they know *somebody* opened the file and emailed it, which means…"

"They charge Chrissie along with you." Stanley slowly nodded his head, realizing the seriousness of the crime. "Who was it interviewed you, the FBI? CIA?"

"They didn't say, and I didn't think it would be smart to demand to see their IDs, my supervisor arranged for the meeting."

"Could be the city's anti-terrorist unit, those guys think they're some kind of super spies."

Nick rinsed the last pot and dried it with a towel. He poured some olive oil into the pan and began to rub it into the metal. "It's crazy, Stan. Thousands of New Yorkers could be dying from a wide range of diseases they contracted at Ground Zero, and the city *still* won't release the relevant data."

Stanley sipped his beer. "My friend, governments and businesses are all the same. When your company faces liability, it's C-Y-A time. Shred the documents and erase the emails."

Nicholas hung up his apron and took a beer from the fridge. He and Stanley stepped out onto the deck. The rose bush in the corner was filled with buds.

"I read something odd today in the paper," said Nicholas, settling into a lounge chair.

"What was that?" Stanley opened a folding deck chair.

Nick explained how the obituary of a man who died when his SUV rolled over caught his attention when he realized the fellow was facing a hotly contested divorce. "I remembered another divorcee suffering an accidental death the month before, and *another* case just like it the month before that. It sounds weird, but I have a sense it's too damned improbable."

"Instinct. Every good cop has it. It might send you on a wild goose chase, it might break a case wide open." Stanley sipped his beer, thinking about what he'd heard. "The guy in the SUV, was he worth a bundle?"

"He worked on Wall Street. Investment banker."

"Tell me about the others." Stanley sat back and half closed his eyes.

"Well, the fellow who drowned was being sued by his wife for half of his restaurant. Somebody named Solomira . . ."

"Vinnie Solomira? The Italian Ice Cream King? That guy was rolling in dough. His wife was looking to end up with chump change."

"And there was this Jackie Onassis type who was in protracted divorce proceedings. She was kicked by her horse. I forget her name."

"Meredith Hamilton. Very rich, very bitchy."

"You must study the society pages."

"I'm on disability. I read three, four newspapers a day."

Nicholas added an account of the trust fund gal working in an art gallery who fell down the stairs in her building. Stanley explained that Laura Metcalf had married her personal trainer, then found him screwing some exotic dancer. "The husband was going to lose his business. She was his only financial backer."

Stanley's eyes twinkled at the prospect of investigating a criminal conspiracy. "Tell me something. How come these deaths caught your eye? People die in accidents every day."

"Epidemiologists don't believe in coincidences. When we see a cluster of illnesses, we look for a common source. More often than not, we find it."

"Like, twenty people come down with diarrhea, you find out they all ate at the same restaurant and the cook didn't wash his hands after taking a dump."

"Exactly."

"So let's investigate these accidental deaths. You could—"

"No you don't Stanley Bezlin!"

Stanley froze, seeing the look of anger on his wife's face, who had been standing in the doorway to the terrace listening.

"What's the matter, honey?" said Stan in an innocent voice.

"What's the matter? You're on medical disability. You can't go running around looking into a bunch of deaths."

"But I'm just gonna make a few phone calls, and Nick is gonna crunch a few numbers, is all."

Standing over her husband, radiating anger and fear, Fran said in a trembling voice, *"You'll investigate them over my dead body!"*

FORTY-ONE

Fran sat down beside her husband on the terrace. The anger and fear had bled away, replaced by a tender sympathy. "Stanley. I understand, you miss being a cop. But Doctor Andreas has told you, you can't exert yourself. You can't go running after some perpetrator and put yourself back in the hospital."

"I'm only helping Nick follow his nose. There's no exertion there."

Seeing the look of doubt on Fran's face, Nick said, "We're not talking about knocking down doors and chasing down suspects. All we plan to do is collect some data and look over the numbers. That's all."

Fran shuddered, remembering the long days when Stanley had been on the ventilator. Nick came in every day to check on him and to speak to the doctor in charge of his case. The doctor had said Stanley had a fifty-fifty chance of getting off the breathing machine.

"All I'm gonna do is have some fun with a puzzle," Stanley said. Nick assured her that they were just playing around with some odd data, there would be no running around.

"Well, as long as you have Nick keeping an eye on you, I guess you can't get into too much trouble." She passed around a tray of roasted vegetables. "So, Doctor Andreas, how would you explain these couples settling their divorce in the morgue?"

"Well, there are some studies that suggest a lot of accidental deaths are really unrecognized suicides."

"You think they were depressed."

"It's possible."

Beth brought out a plate of sliced fruit. Fran spooned several slices onto Stanley's plate. "She makes me eat five servings a day," he said, taking a piece of fruit. "Lemme tell you something. When a bunch of people end up dead and there's money involved, it's not a mental problem, it's a conspiracy."

Nicholas picked up a slice of fruit. "I've got another problem. I don't know if the death rate for this group is significantly higher than you would expect in the larger population. Without knowing their expected mortality rate, I can't tell if this population's rate is too high."

"So we'll track it down." When Nicholas looked puzzled, Stanley explained, "Call up the Medical Examiner and find the names of all the accidental deaths in New York City this year. I'll hook up with a friend in the courts and get a list of people in divorce proceedings."

"I think we need to separate out the contested divorces, those are the ones most likely to result in psychological trauma."

"Good idea," said Stanley. "We look for the same names popping up on both lists, we have our pattern." He bit into a slice of mango. "I say the accidents were staged. Murder is always an appealing option when your back's to the wall. And if you hate your mate, the decision's a no-brainer."

"We'll have to cover all five boroughs," said Nicholas.

"Definitely."

"I'll call the ME tomorrow."

"I'll call around the courts, start getting the names."

Seeing that Fran was still worried, Beth smiled and said, "Every man needs a hobby."

Fran did not smile back. As she looked at her husband, she felt a deep well of fear come rushing up. The fear threatened to drown her.

Standing at the kitchen table, Nicholas looked from the diagram showing the power window motor to the object half disassembled on the table. He turned a gear on the motor, trying to determine why the motor failed to stop when the window reached the end of its run.

He was poking through the parts bag of the rebuild kit looking for something when he saw Beth standing in the dining room watching.

"Problem?" he asked.

"Please wash up before you come upstairs. I don't want you smelling of motor oil when you get into bed."

"Fine."

He found the part, held it up to the light, saw that she was still watching him. He put the part down.

"Do you really think Chrissie will be in trouble?" she said. "She's a teenager. Teenagers don't think about the consequences of their actions."

Nick put down the part he had been examining. "I suppose if anybody is charged it'll be me. I don't see what they'll get out of locking up a high school student beyond pissing off every kid in the city."

"That's right. The teachers would be angry, too. We have some clout, don't we?" She was putting on a brave face, but Nick could see she was scared to death. As he went to put his arms around her, she recoiled at first. But realizing he was keeping his oily, dirty hands off her and just hugging with his arms, she laid her head on his shoulder for a moment, savoring the safety of his arms.

Beth turned to leave. Stopped. Said over her shoulder, "Nick, I don't want you to think I don't worry about you as well. It's just…"

"Forget it. I'm a big boy, I can take care of myself. As long as I've got you behind me."

She smiled and went on upstairs, while Nicholas reached for the hand cleanser and began rubbing it between his fingers. The smell of petroleum products tickled his nose. It felt good.

FORTY-TWO

Nicholas was on his lunch break when he called the New York Medical Examiner's office and asked to speak with one of the coroners. After a long wait on hold without even music to assure him the other party hadn't hung up, he finally heard a hurried voice say, "Reed Kohlberg, here. Who's calling?"

"This is Doctor Andreas with the DOH. Listen, I'm looking into a cluster of accidental deaths in New York, beginning, say, January of this year. I need you to send me a list of all the deaths that were ruled accidental."

"Oh, yeah? What's it all about?" said Reed.

"The death rate appears to be higher than you'd find in this age group. I'm looking at the possibility that the deaths were not actually accidental."

There was a moment of silence. In an icy voice Reed said, "You realize, *doctor,* that our department has some expertise in this field. I hardly think that a *public health* physician would be in a position to challenge the diagnosis of a trained pathologist."

"I'm not doubting your conclusions as to the *cause* of death. I'm investigating the possibility that some of the deaths were unrecognized suicides."

"Oh, I see." The ME's voice softened. "Yeah, I read those sociological studies when I was in med school about spontaneous suicides being mistaken for accidental deaths. I thought the studies weren't altogether convincing."

Realizing he needed to placate the ME, Nicholas said, "I should have said from the start, I thought we would collaborate on this investigation. I have epidemiologic tools that I can bring to bear, and you have the tools of pathology. If we put our heads together we can settle this matter quickly. There could even be a paper in it for us."

"So, you're going to share your findings with this office before coming to any conclusion?"

"Definitely."

"And what dates do you want the data from?"

"The latest death was five days ago. August fifth."

"*Five days ago?* We won't have the toxicology report yet, we're backed up the wazoo."

"I appreciate that," said Nicholas. "We have people out on vacation as well. If you would just send me the names of the previous deaths..."

With a heavy sigh, the Medical Examiner agreed. "What's your email address?" After getting Nicholas's address, Reed added, "Be sure and send *all* your findings to me. I'll run them by my boss and let you know if *we* think they have any merit."

"I will, thanks very much. Oh, and I suppose I should give you a heads up on another theory a police detective friend of mine is entertaining. I don't give it any credence you understand, but he thinks the deaths could have been staged."

There was a long silence on the phone. "I haven't received any memos from One Police Plaza about a review of this department's findings."

"No, no, it's just my friend's speculation, there's no official investigation. I just wanted you to be aware of it is all."

The pathologist clicked off, leaving Nicholas feeling excited. For a moment he forgot his troubles with the department and the Feds. For a little while he could still be an epidemiologist following a hunch.

FORTY-THREE

It was three PM on the eighth of August. Although Atlantic City was bathed in heat and humidity, Alex was cool and dry in his air-conditioned hotel room. He adjusted the cowboy hat on his head, pulling the front down to conceal his eyes. He applied tincture of benzoin above his upper lip and to the handlebar mustache he'd bought at a theatrical supply store. Once the benzoin was dry, he pressed the fake mustache firmly onto his lip and held it for a full minute.

Taking his hand away, he wrinkled his lip. Smiled. Grimaced. The mustache followed his movements in a natural fashion, giving no sign it would come loose.

He put on a gold-colored necklace and a loose, gold-colored bracelet he'd bought from a guy in the street. The jewelry and clothes gave him a look of easy money and high rolling lifestyle. He was ready to walk the casino floor.

As he walked from his hotel room to the first casino on his route, he reflected once again that the divorce courts were indeed gold mines. When couples began to separate, it brought out the most violent emotions. Hatred. Rage. *Vengeance.* All the psychological states that can justify hurting the other. Divorce was the perfect soil for planting an act of murder.

Alex always knew that he was a first rate novelist, even if his sales never reflected his gift and the critics were too stupid to recognize his literary excellence. Now he realized that he was also a genius of crime. His criminal enterprise was infinitely more imaginative than a Dragon Tattoo book. It was a terrible shame that the public would never realize the depths of his intellect, but that was the price he had to pay for his brilliant mind. Even if he disguised his crimes in a work of fiction, the similarity of the crimes would alert the police. They would track him down and use his words against him. His triumph would of necessity only become known posthumously, like so many great writers of the past.

The façade of the Atlantic City Taj Mahal was a garish affair. Inside, the ringing of the gaming machines and the buzz of the players filled the long, low room. Multicolored blinking lights gave the place a festive look, although the smell of sweat and cigarette smoke took something away from the cheerful atmosphere.

He stopped at the bar and ordered a scotch and soda. Watched the barmaid go for his drink, her mini skirt revealing delicious thighs when she bent to hear an order over the noise of the casino. Alex wondered if she was wearing a thong. He longed to run his fingers up over her buttocks to find out.

Hadn't he read that the Playboy bunnies were making a comeback? They had been fetching morsels. Classy. Teasing. Great tits and asses. He loved the paradox: cuddly and sensuous; wicked, yet innocent. He sipped the scotch, savoring the drink and reflecting on his brilliance.

He checked his watch, saw it was time. Leaving a generous tip for the barmaid, he went to the poker machine and played quarter bets for a while. A waitress with deep bronze skin and glistening black hair offered him a second drink, but he declined. Had to keep a clear head, this was business.

Right on time, Steven Reinhold stepped up to a nearby slot machine, a tall plastic cup filled with coins in his hand. Alex turned away from Reinhold and watched him in the reflection on the face of the poker machine he was playing.

While he watched Reinhold play the machine, Alex cast his eyes about the room. Nobody was watching. There were video cameras in the ceiling; he had anticipated that. The cameras would show unrelated patrons making solitary bets, with no connection between them.

Alex rose, walked over to Steven. He watched the man put another quarter in the machine and pull the handle. "I believe my luck is due to change," said Alex in a soft voice just loud enough for Steven to hear.

Steven rose from his stool without looking at Alex and walked away, leaving the plastic cup in the well where the winning coins were meant to fall. Alex slid onto the barstool, looked down into the plastic cup. Beneath the silver coins were several five-hundred dollar chips. He reached into the cup for a silver dollar, fed the machine and played a hand. As the painted icons on the slot machine spun past the window, the gay music sang to him, promising riches that needed no luck to win, but only patience and confidence.

Alex continued playing at a leisurely pace for a half hour until the silver dollars were gone. He rose nonchalantly, plastic cup in hand, and made his way to the cashier's window, where he cashed in the ten five hundred dollar chips. Five thousand dollars. A good number. Seven more and Reinhold's debt would be paid.

Pleased almost as much as when he'd carried out one of the killings, he went back to the bar and ordered another drink from the same barmaid. When she brought the scotch, Alex handed her a twenty dollar bill. "Keep the change," he said, touching his cowboy hat. She smiled at him. "What're you doing after your shift?" he asked. She told him she had to go home and take care of a sick child□ so her husband could go to work. On the police force.

The barmaid turned away from Alex and grimaced, thinking, *An old New Yorker in a cowboy outfit. Who was he trying to kid?*

Not discouraged, Alex was sure he could find a willing partner once his work was done, and he would make damn sure she was wearing a thong. Finishing his second drink, he went back to the same bank of poker machines, inserted a ten-dollar bill into the machine and began to play.

Five machines away on the opposite side of the bank of games, Forest Hamilton sat at a machine, a cup of coins in the recess of the machine. He played slowly, taking his time reading each hand, thinking about what cards he would draw.

Alex looked at his watch, collected the few dollars in the well of the machine and pocketed them, then he walked around the bank of poker machines, approached Hamilton, and quietly muttered the same comment that his luck was about to change. Without a word, Hamilton rose and walked away from his machine, allowing Alex to slip into his seat and take command of the plastic cup in the well.

He looked down into the cup and smiled to see another pile of five hundred dollar chips. And in a half hour Jewel Solomira would be seated at another machine waiting to make her payment.

FORTY-FOUR

Nicholas placed the electric motor for the power window, now rebuilt, into a cardboard box and set it on the floor. Rolling up the oily newspaper, he was pleased that no oil had leaking onto the surface. It was marble, it would clean up well, but he knew how much his wife valued a clean kitchen.

Beth was boiling noodles when they heard the front door buzzer sound. Nick went to the door and let Stanley and Fran in.

"I got the divorce data from the courts," said Stanley, waving a CD-ROM as he entered.

"How did you get it so quickly?"

"I told the court clerks I was calling for a task force on organized crime. Did you get the names of the accident victims?"

"Yes. They're on my desktop."

"Let's run the program," said Stanley. They went upstairs to load Stanley's software into Nicholas's computer. Using a program he 'borrowed' from the Anti-Terror Task Force, he entered the list of people who were in divorce proceedings. Then he opened the file from the Medical Examiner listing victims of accidental deaths and copied it into the other database.

"Okay," said Stanley. "Let's see how many names they have in common."

He pressed a command to 'Search & Signify,' waited a few seconds. "We got a hit," he said, pointing at a name from June that was highlighted in red. "Laura Metcalf-Reinhold. Died March twenty-fifth."

"I remember, she was a fall on a stairwell," said Nicholas. "Scroll down, see how many more there are."

"There's another name in May, then three in June and four in July, and three more in August," said Stanley.

"That's twelve," said Nicholas. "It's curious, there are no names in common *before* Laura Metcalf. That would make her the index case."

"The what?"

"The first one. In an outbreak we look for the first case that was the source of the epidemic. This isn't an infectious process, but we'll use the same case definition."

Stanley listed the common names in a new database, printed it out, and handed it to Nicholas.

Nicholas read over the names. "Twelve people in divorce proceedings who died by accident over four months." He looked at Stanley. "We need to determine if the numbers are within the range of statistical probability. If they were not, we have to ask if the deaths resulted from natural causes or other factors."

"My money's on murder. That's a natural *human* cause."

"Let's look at where the victims were living," said Nicholas. "That may suggest links among the cases." He listed the names by borough. Five were from Manhattan, four from Brooklyn, one from Queens and two from the Bronx. "They don't divorce on Staten Island?" he asked.

"It's a mellow place to live," said Stanley. "Remember, I only asked for *contested* divorces."

"We can drill down for more common characteristics," said Nicholas. He listed the names by gender. There were seven women and five men. "I'll have to compare the incidence of accidental deaths by gender in the larger population. It might be that women are more accident prone."

"Or the husbands are more ready to hire somebody to whack their wife."

Stanley was ready to look for a conspiracy, but Nicholas cautioned his friend that they had to study the cases more thoroughly before trying to draw any conclusions.

While the men were upstairs, Beth mixed Margarita's in the kitchen. She added frozen lime juice and tequila to a pitcher, then squeezed a fresh lime. "It's a good thing Nick finished working on his motor, the table was covered with dirty parts."

"Men and their toys. Stanley is the same way. Do you know what he's into now? *Wood carving*. He leaves wood chips and sawdust all over the spare bedroom."

"At least his mess isn't in the kitchen."

"I guess it's good to see Stanley enthusiastic about something," said Fran. "He was down for so long after the heart attack and the lung problems. I was worried sick for months."

"Nicholas has been in a funk, too. You know how he blames himself for Stanley's medical problems." Beth rolled the rims of two glasses in a plate of salt and poured the drinks. "It's funny, though, even with him being in trouble with the government over the student reporting the DOH material, Nicholas seems to be in better spirits."

"Maybe this investigation is as good for his mood as it is for Stanley's."

"Must be," said Beth. "After all, he *is* an outbreak investigator."

They carried their glasses into the living room. A few minutes later, Chrissie came in, threw her backpack on the floor and greeted the two women. "What're you girls drinking, margaritas?"

"We sure are," said Beth. "Would you like one?"

"Yummy."

Beth went into the kitchen and retrieved a glass. She poured another drink and handed it to her daughter. "You lick the salt before you drink it."

"*Mom!* Like I don't know how to drink a margarita?" Chrissie looked at Fran. "She still thinks I'm a child." She licked the rim of the glass and took a long, lugubrious drink.

Nicholas made a second copy of the names in common between the two lists. "We have to remember, these are crude numbers. To get a real world statistic, we'll use the number of people who were involved in divorce proceedings during the same period as the denominator."

"I gotcha. We divide the number of divorcees into the number of deaths."

"Correct. Then we compare *that* percentage with the mortality rate for the larger population of which they're subset."

"You mean, with the general population?"

"No," said Nick. "We have to match the groups. We compare adults in contested divorces with couples who are *not* getting divorced."

"Je'ez, Louise, where the hell do we get *that* information?"

"You'd be surprised how much data the city collects. I'm sure somebody's got an estimate of the number of married couples in New York City. We'll work out a crude mortality rate for them and compare it with the rate for the couples in contested divorces."

Nicholas fed the numbers in a calculator and did the calculation. As he scribbled the number on a pad of paper, Stanley told him, "You know,

Nick, this is gonna turn out to be a criminal organization killing people."

"That's one theory."

"It stands to reason some organization would take their murder for hire business to the divorce courts. I mean, who better to offer your services to than couples fighting like cats and dogs over their property? The opportunity is too good to pass up. This could have been going on for years. Decades, even."

"The data suggests the events began in July. I suppose we could go back a few years, once we have the current data set thoroughly analyzed."

"Yeah, you're right, let's stick to this year for now. Call me at home tomorrow when you get all the numbers punched in."

Stanley folded the list of the twelve accident victims and shook his head.

"What's the matter?" asked Nicholas.

"I'm thinking after I turn this over to my old lieutenant, there's gonna be cops serving search warrants, checking financials, examining phone logs. The whole shebang."

"Yeah, so?"

"So I won't be in on it."

"Perhaps you can get them to keep you informed as the investigation unfolds."

"That ain't gonna happen."

"Well, I'll tell you what," said Nick, getting up from the computer. "When the crime ring is broken, I'll see to it that the media knows who the cop is that started the investigation."

"That's okay, pal. As long as I can be there for the trail, I'll be happy." Stanley tucked the printout in his pocket. "I need a drink. Let's go tell the gals."

FORTY-FIVE

Coming down the stairs, the men found their wives and Chrissie in the living room drinking margaritas.

"How did the research go, dear?" asked Fran.

"We've got several names in common between the divorcees and the accidental deaths, but we need more information."

He explained how Nicholas was going to compare the odds of people in divorce dying in accidents with couples that were staying married.

Nick said, "It's really a simple epidemiologic question. We start with the larger population's mortality rate by accidental deaths and—"

He saw Chrissie pour fresh margaritas into three glasses, pick up one, lick the salt on the rim, and take a long sip. To Beth he said, "Since when do we allow our daughter to drink alcohol?"

Beth winked at Chrissie. "Since *today*!" She held out her glass and toasted her two companions. "Here's to mothers and daughters!"

"This is hardly the appropriate behavior to teach our daughter," said Nicholas.

"Yeah, like you never drank in high school!" said Chrissie. "Mom told me about you and your homeboys cutting school and drinking under the boardwalk!"

"That doesn't mean you have to do the same stupid things I did when I was your age."

"At least you had a future to look forward to. Our generation is gonna die from lung cancer, unless some freak blows up a nuclear bomb in Times Square first."

"This is not the time or place to discuss *that issue*," said Nick, a hard edge to his voice.

Chrissie shrugged and sipped her drink without answering.

Nick glared at Beth, looking for support, but she just held up her drink to her companions. "Here's to dads and their homeboys. May they all learn to leave the next generation to make their own mistakes!"

The women laughed and drank. Chrissie clinked glasses with her mother and with Fran and took a long pull on her margarita, taunting her father.

Stanley, having gone to the kitchen and opened a couple of beers, handed Nick a bottle and a glass. "Better the kids drink at home where you know they're safe. And not driving around Brooklyn."

A battle raged within Nicholas between criticizing his daughter and letting the matter drop. He saw that his wife and daughter were relaxed and enjoying each other's company. How often did that happen? He realized that continuing to argue would ruin the evening.

"Oh, what the hell," said Nicholas, taking the beer from Stanley and settling into his favorite chair.

Stanley picked up where Nicholas had left off, explaining they had found twelve accidental deaths among the list of couples in divorce proceedings.

"Do you really think the police will investigate a bunch of curious coincidences?" asked Beth.

Stanley explained that if their hunch is right and the death rate is too high, it will be enough to open a murder investigation.

"So you're sure it's murder?" said Fran.

Nick put forward his theory that depressed people are prone to committing spontaneous suicide, but their deaths were often misdiagnosed as accidental.

"People in divorce are *angry*, not depressed," said Stanley. "Say you're a wife that's gonna lose custody of your kids. Or the brownstone and the Lexus. Wouldn't *you* pay to have your husband whacked?"

"What does she do, put an ad in the Village Voice?" said Nicholas.

"I don't know. Maybe she goes to the local bookie. Maybe she puts out feelers and the mob finds her. There are lots of ways to hire a hit man."

"We'll need to determine the emotional state of the deceased spouses if we're going to do a thorough investigation. I would look for signs of depression."

"How can you do that?" said Chrissie. "They're dead!"

"The police can interview the surviving spouse. And the children. The co-workers. There are multiple sources of information about a person's emotional state prior to their death."

Stanley emptied his bottle of beer, set it on the coffee table. "You know, Nick, you work for a public health agency. You could interview the survivors."

"My supervisor would never go along with it. I'm in the dog house.

You know that."

"Why wouldn't she want to follow up what we've found? Aren't unexplained deaths right up their alley?"

Nicholas shrugged. "Better let the police handle it." He didn't want to talk anymore about the trouble he was facing. Not to mention the danger to his daughter. It was all too depressing. What was the point talking?

He got up to fetch another beer.

In bed later that night, Nicholas watched as Beth rubbed lotion on her arms. She handed him the bottle of lotion, dropped the straps of her nightgown and turned her back to him.

As Nicholas rubbed lotion over Beth's shoulders and back, he said, "You could have supported me over our daughter's melodrama about her health."

Beth took the lotion and rubbed a dollop into her leg. "Honestly, dear, can't you remember when you were her age and everything was a big deal? Every crisis was a major life event?"

"I was a lot calmer than that."

"That's one way to describe you."

"What the hell does that mean?"

Beth capped the lotion bottle and set it aside. "Haven't you been listening to anything I say? Don't you know by now that if you don't start *listening* to Chrissie, and stop judging her, and even more, stop judging *yourself*, you'll lose *everything* you hold dear?"

"Here we go again. You're thinking of walking out on me, aren't you?"

Beth's eyes grew sad and glistened with impending tears. "Nick, I don't want it to come to that. You know that. But the way you bury yourself in guilt and anger, it's hard for us to live with it." She wiped away a tear with a tissue. "All I'm saying is, I want you to try and come out of that shell you keep around yourself and hear what we're all telling you. Okay?"

She pulled up her strap, adjusted her nightgown, and settled into bed, not expecting her husband to respond to her, but hoping he would think about what she'd said.

Nicholas snapped on his reading light, picked up a copy of Hemmings Motor News, and tried to read, but he was unable to concentrate. Beth's words kept repeating in his mind. *Lose everything you hold dear.*

"Okay, I'll try to listen to our daughter and not lecture her. Okay?"

Beth reached up and kissed him on the cheek, then turned away and pulled the covers up to her

neck.

He felt that his efforts would in the end come to naught; that Chrissie would never forgive him his crimes. What was the point of reaching out to her when the girl had long since written his obituary?

FORTY-SIX

Nicholas sat at his desk in the Department of Health looking over the names of the divorcees who died from accidental deaths. Stanley had called to tell him that ten per cent of all divorces in New York City are contested, according to his source in the courts. That gave them a ballpark number to use for comparing the mortality rate of divorcees with couples who are staying married. He was jotting down some figures when he heard a tap on the door and saw Libby poke her head in the doorway.

"How are you coming with the Extended Care survey?" she said, coming into his office.

"I finished calling the facilities. I've got my first interviews scheduled for this afternoon."

"Good." She looked down at Nick's computer. "What's that you're working on?" She stepped closer, saw a two-by-two table on his computer screen. "Are you going to look at risk factors for influenza outbreaks?"

"No, it's, uh, just something I was curious about."

"Oh?" She read the caption below the table. "Accidental deaths..." She pulled back a stray wisp of hair and gave him a questioning look.

Nicholas explained that he'd been puzzled by a cluster of accidental deaths among people in contested divorces. "I want to determine if their death rate is significantly higher than you would expect in this population. I know the average accidental death rate among adult New Yorkers."

"And you want to compare that rate with the mortality among divorcees. Interesting epidemiologic question." She leaned in toward the computer screen, placing a hand on Nick's shoulder for balance. "Do you think the victims were accident prone?"

"I couldn't see how going through a divorce would make someone careless."

"Well, it's an awfully stressful event. You don't sleep, don't eat. Your adrenalin levels are high all the time from the anxiety…"

"That's no doubt the case. But I haven't found anything in the literature to support it." He had a strong suspicion that Libby had been through a divorce. She didn't wear a wedding ring, and the photos on her desk didn't show a mate or children.

"What about unrecognized suicides?" she said, standing up and taking her hand away from his shoulder. "Divorced people can grow awfully lonely. Have you thought of that?"

"That's pretty much where I'm going. If I were doing a real investigation, I would derive a psychological profile of the victims to determine if they were clinically depressed."

"What were their ethnicity and religion?"

"I didn't check that. Do you think it would be an important risk factor?"

"Some groups have an extremely low suicide rates. Orthodox Jews, for example. Let me see the data"

Nick called up the database, saying, "I used the mortality rate for couples in contested divorce. It's significantly different from the general population of married couples."

"Okay. Let's see the data."

Nicholas opened up a new statistical table. "The Office of Vital Statistics says there were one thousand, eight hundred fifty-two people involved in contested divorces during the period we're studying. That's twelve accidental deaths in around eighteen-hundred individuals." He entered the numbers in the table and selected a command. In seconds the computer compared the mortality rate for people in contested divorces with married people not undergoing a divorce.

	Accidental Deaths	**No Accidental Deaths**
Spouses in Contested Divorce	**12 (.006%)**	**1,840**
Spouses Not Divorcing	**480 (.0002%)**	**2,158,013**

P=.0001
Odds Ratio=28.9 (8.8-248.7)

"You can see right off that the percent of non-divorcing couples dying by accident is extremely low."

Libby picked up Nicholas's calculator and punched in some numbers. "They died at a rate of twenty-two deaths per hundred-thousand."

"New York is below the national average," said Nick. "I checked."

"Really? Who's has the highest rate?"

"The southern and mountain states. Guns and deer in the road."

Libby ran a new set of numbers on the calculator. "Let's see, the people in contested divorces died at a rate of…" She stared at the results. "This can't be right." She punched in the numbers a second time. "My god," she said, looking into Nick's eyes. "They died at a rate of six hundred fifty per hundred thousand."

"That's why the Odds Ratio predicts that the people in divorce are almost twenty-nine times more likely to die in an accident than non-divorcing spouses. Those deaths were *not* a random occurrence."

Libby looked puzzled. "Nick, this means there *is* an association between divorce and accidental deaths."

"*Contested divorce,*" he reminded her.

"Right. Contested divorce." She studied the Two-By-Two Table. "I suppose there could be a confounding variable."

"An unknown factor that causes angry divorces *and* accidental deaths?" said Nicholas. "I don't see how."

"Neither do I. But how can divorce be a risk factor for death? Are they *that* depressed that they jump out of a window or throw themselves under a train?"

"My friend, who's a cop, has a theory." He pointed his first finger at Libby, holding his other fingers and thumb tucked to mimic a gun.

Libby's face took on an anxious cast. "You mean…" When she saw Nick's look of cold conviction, she added, "You must realize, Nicholas, this sort of investigation could be dangerous."

"All I'm doing is crunching some numbers. My policeman neighbor is turning the whole thing over to the professionals."

"Good. Let the authorities investigate this matter, you have enough problems in your life already." She left him without elaborating on the threat from Homeland Security or the FBI or whoever it was investigating his activity. Nick wondered if she would tell him if she knew anything important about his case. He doubted it, she had sworn an oath of secrecy herself.

After Libby left, Nick called Stanley using his cell phone, he had doubts about the security of his office phone. If they hacked into his computer they would certainly hack into his office phone. He told Stanley how he analyzed the mortality rates, and that they were worse than he could have imagined. "The spouses in contested divorces were twenty-nine times more likely to die in an accident than those not in divorce. It's statistically impossible."

"I better hold on to my wife," said Stanley. He asked Nick to email him the statistics.

"I'll bring you a copy," said Nick, not wanting to put anything more in his email.

"Great. Your results will strengthen my hand when I talk to my old lieutenant. I'll take it to the precinct tomorrow."

Nicholas rang off. As much as he'd been excited by their discovery, he was glad that Stanley was taking the data to the police. They were equipped to investigate the deaths. And Stanley wasn't strong enough to go running after perpetrators. If he ended up back in the hospital, Fran would never forgive him. Nor would he ever forgive himself.

FORTY-SEVEN

As soon as the doorman went on a break, Alex let himself into the apartment building and walked up the stairs to the apartment of Dean Everett Hodges. Entering the apartment with a copy of the keys given him by the maligned and vengeful wife, Alex donned latex gloves and went into the bathroom. There he replaced the long screws attaching the grab bar on the wall in the shower with screw too short to bear any weight. Then he sprayed the surface of the tub with a nonstick vegetable oil that was invisible to the naked eye.

He looked up at the shower curtain, wondering if it was strong enough to hold a man's weight should Hodges grab it as he went down. Alex pulled down hard on the end of the curtain. It held for a few seconds, then ripped at the hole where the hook connected it to the bar. To be sure the curtain would fail, he opened every other ring and slipped the curtain out of the rings. The casual person entering the shower would be unlikely to notice.

The scenario set, Alex settled into a comfortable chair in the living room to wait. He recalled his successful interview with Victoria Hodges just ten days before. She had been seated alone on a stone bench in a little seating area off Fifty-Second Street, an iced cappuccino in one hand, a paperback novel (a *crime story!)* in the other.

He studied the tall, shapely blonde, appreciating the full lips, ample breasts, and long supple legs. She had just turned forty; her husband Dean was seventy-two.

Dressed in his lawyer outfit, Alex introduced himself as David Slater, attorney.

"You're not here to serve me more papers, are you?" she asked in alarm.

"Good heavens, no." He gave her a warm, reassuring smile. "I saw the proceedings in family court yesterday."

"You did? I didn't see you."

"We attorneys all look alike. I couldn't help but note that your case is not going well."

"Tell me about it. My lawyer says things aren't as bad as they seem, but

I can see the writing on the wall."

"May I?" he asked, looking at the seat beside her. She moved her hips a few inches, making room for him.

Victoria bowed her head and stirred her drink with a straw. When she sighed deeply, the rise of her breasts led Alex to reflect that, were he to offer his services to the husband, Victoria would make a heavenly corpse. But business demanded an objective assessment of the respective spouses, and Victoria definitely had the most to lose.

"I'm afraid your husband's case is exceedingly strong."

"*I know it!* It's all so unfair! I can't even get into the apartment to collect *my* things. Dean *gave* me all kinds of jewelry, but now he claims they were only a loan. *Who loans a woman diamonds?"*

"Unfortunately for you, the pre-nup stipulates that all articles of jewelry or art, excluding a wedding band, are the property of the husband should the wife violate the marriage agreement." He saw the pained expression on his face. "It was a cold, selfish contract," said Alex, his voice oozing compassion.

"I thought I'd stay with him till death us did part. I really did. But when he hit seventy he got prostate cancer and it's been gross-out city ever since."

"It must have been hard for you."

"I'll say. I don't care so much about the sex, but he dribbles and stinks up the bed. It's disgusting. I get nauseous from the smell."

"You have suffered greatly."

"Who could blame me for going outside the marriage for my needs? Old never-trust-anybody Dean hired a private detective. He got pictures. After that he changed the locks, left *one suitcase* of clothes with the doorman, and I was out on the street, like *that!"* She snapped her fingers in front of Alex's nose.

"A deeply selfish man," said Alex. He looked at her sad eyes and slumping shoulders. "You will doubtless be surprised to hear that I have the solution to all your problems."

He watched as a puzzled Victoria Hodges looked at him with curiosity and hope.

After making his pitch, even the cynical Alex was surprised when Victoria Hodges accepted his offer without taking the required twenty-four hours to make up her mind. Nor did she balk at the price or the method of payment.

"I love the casinos," she told him. "Could I make some of my payments at Los Vegas?"

"That's too far to travel," he said, wishing he could meet her there for a torrid weekend. But there was no consorting with the customers, no matter how deep the cleavage. Engaging in a personal relationship with the customers would be deadly.

When he told her that he wanted the accident to occur in the apartment, but the change of locks would make his entering it a problem, the wily woman confessed that she'd secretly made copies of the new keys by hiring their old housekeeper.

"I remembered that she had the keys of all her clients labeled on a big key ring in her bag. When she had her head buried in my toilet I sneaked the key out of her purse and had copies made."

"You haven't been back yet, have you?"

"No. I was afraid the doorman would dime on me. They have cameras *everywhere.*"

"I'll need the key."

Victoria removed the keys from her key ring and placed them in Alex's hand with a little squeeze, slowly sliding her fingers along his palm. She told him that Hodges maintained a strict schedule. He worked five days a week, arrived home at six, changed into his sweats and ran on the treadmill for thirty minutes. Then he watched the news, showered, got dressed again and went out to his favorite restaurant for dinner.

He was in bed by ten.

He instructed her to be out of town at the appointed time in a highly public place where witnesses can testify to your presence. Once Hodges was out of the way, she would inherit everything. Seeing the smile return to her lovely face, he reminded himself that he was indeed providing an important social service, spreading joy and harmony throughout the city.

As she walked away, her full hips rotating with the promise of a roller coaster ride in bed, Alex wished again that he could enjoy an intimate engagement with Victoria. Dead or alive, she was delicious.

FORTY-EIGHT

At 5:45 pm Alex rose from the armchair in Dean Hodges' living room and retired to the walk-in pantry, knowing that the victim would soon be home from work. At six he heard the lock in the front door turn. Punctual people were indeed the easiest to kill. A pair of footsteps clicked on the marble entranceway. The footsteps stopped in the living room, then went on to the bedroom, which was carpeted and quiet.

After a moment Alex heard the whirring sound of the treadmill, slow at first, then gradually picking up speed. He was pleased by the sound: a vigorous workout would guarantee a long hot shower.

Eventually he heard a *flap, flap* sound from bedroom to bath. Hodges was wearing old man's slippers. Alex crept out of the closet and tiptoed to the bathroom, where the door was ajar. He watched the naked Dean Hodges pull the shower curtain aside and, with steam billowing around his skinny, old man's body, lift his right foot and extend his leg over the rim of the tub.

Hodges lowered his right foot into the tub. As he raised his back foot, his right foot suddenly slipped out from under him, the spray of vegetable oil having made the surface slippery. The steel bar on the wall that he grabbed in desperation pulled out instantly. Hodges went down hard, striking his head on the rim of the tub with a hideous *crack*.

Dazed and in pain, he was looking stupidly at the wall where the grab bar had pulled loose when a stranger's face suddenly loomed over him in the mist. Through the steam the face had a ghoulish grin. Dean Hodges thought he must be dreaming. Or dead.

Before the stricken man knew what was happening, Alex aimed a narrow jet of hot water into the groggy man's face. When Hodges tried to block the water with his hands, Alex pinned the man's arms down with his knees and directed the victim's face toward the stream of water. Hodges closed his mouth to block the water, but it ran into his nostrils and down his windpipe. When he opened his mouth to cough, a fresh stream of water ran down his throat. Panic seized him as he felt the terrifying sensation of drowning.

The more Hodges gasped for breath, the more water entered his lungs.

Quickly his strength ebbed, his mind clouded over, his open mouth overflowed with water.

The ghoulish face hovering above him faded into darkness. The dying man's last thought was that he would never suck at a beautiful woman's breast again.

Alex carefully cleaned away the non-stick oil in Hodges' bathtub, replaced the long screws holding the grab bar, and re-snapped all the curtain rings he had released from the rings. Leaving the water running onto the dead man's body, Alex left the apartment and made his way home. In his apartment he poured himself a double shot of scotch and held the new crystal glass up to the light, admiring the golden color. He drank deeply, savoring the elixir as he congratulated himself on another perfect murder.

Bursting with energy, he called the escort service and asked this time for a girl built like a brick shithouse. "Natasha has an ample figure," the girl on the answering service assured him. "And she cries like a baby." He settled on the Russian girl and went to his safe in the closet.

From the safe Alex removed a vial, and studied the handwritten label: *GHB*. The dealer who sold him the drug assured Alex that it would induce unconsciousness for thirty minutes, minimum. A "super Roofie" he'd said, "with complete amnesia, and *no hangover.*"

Checking the drug's effects on a drug information web site, Alex was confident that the agent would meet his needs. The key was that when the girl awoke she wouldn't suffer the side effects that told her she'd been drugged. He broke the narrow throat of the glass ampoule and poured the liquid in a tall champagne glass, noting a small chip in the base of the goblet. He set the glass beside its twin on a tray, and placed a bottle of chilled champagne in a bucket of ice.

When Natasha rang to be buzzed into the building, Alex poured the sparkling wine. He met her with a kiss and a smile, settled her on the couch, and proffered the wine. She took it eagerly, cooing to Alex, "You are good man to give Natasha champagne. We will drink, and then you can make love to me until all bubbles are gone."

Alex sipped his wine and looked over Natasha's full, ripe figure, waiting for the drug to take effect. When she passed out, he stripped off her clothes and rubbed her down with ice, chilling her skin. Dragging her to the bedroom, he imagined she was newly dead and totally his to enjoy. He was a wild man from a primitive age, unbound by any law, untamed and free.

FORTY-NINE

Stanley found Nicholas in the basement garage installing the rebuilt motor for the power window. Resting on Nick's three-legged stool, a mechanic's best friend, he said, "Do you believe this shit? They're not gonna investigate the deaths."

"What"? Nick pulled his head out from the interior. "Why the hell not? Did you explain that these deaths couldn't have happened by chance? That there's got to be an agent behind it?"

"Sure I told him. My old lieutenant said that he couldn't launch an investigation as long as the ME ruled all the deaths were accidental. We don't have evidence a crime was committed."

"Finding evidence is their job! *They're* supposed to determine that a crime was committed."

"I think partly it's 'cause the deaths happened in different boroughs. One was on Long Island. He only has jurisdiction one borough."

"Three deaths in his own backyard and he won't investigate? What a load of crap." Nicholas put down a wrench and wiped his hands with a rag.

"Well, you know what it means," said Stanley, his look of anger changing into a look of humor. When Nicholas didn't pick up his meaning, Stanley said, "We gotta to it ourselves. You and me."

"Now hold on a minute." Nicholas dropped his tools in his tool bag and stowed it in the trunk. "I know you miss your police work, but if you think I'm going to help you run yourself into another heart attack..."

"I'm not talkin' about running after the perps. I just want us to nose around a little. Very low key."

"Out of the question. I'll lose my job and you'll end up back in the hospital."

"Oh yeah? Just take a look at this." He showed Nicholas an article in the latest Daily News about a Dean Hodges slipping and falling in his bathtub. His body was discovered by the building super.

"Let me guess," said Nicholas. "He was in the middle of a messy divorce."

"Very messy. He married a blonde like thirty years his junior with a body to die for. When he found her cheating on him he filed for divorce and invoked his pre-nup."

Nicholas tried to hold onto his objection, but Stanley patiently and methodically made his case. It was up to them to investigate the deaths or the killings would go on. Nobody else knew about them; nobody else cared.

Entering Nicholas's apartment, Stanley administered the coup de grace. "Besides, I'm going nuts sitting home doing nothing. You'll be saving my life helping me crack open this case."

Nick got a couple of beers from the fridge and placed them on the island separating the kitchen from the living room. "What exactly do you want us to do?"

"Nothing strenuous. We'll go to the scenes of the deaths and look around. Ask a few questions. Keep it simple."

Nicholas led his friend out onto the terrace and settled into a folding chair. "I suppose we could look into the first couple of cases."

"Laura Metcalf, the slip and fall on the stairwell."

"And Meredith Hamilton, the woman allegedly kicked to death by her horse."

Settling into a chair, Stanley said, "I bet you could come up with some public health reason to talk to the husband."

Nick considered the possibility. "I could say I'm studying the health effects of loss and grief. Depression is a recognized risk factor for accidental deaths."

"That's great! You talk to the husband, I'll check out the crime scene."

"If it *is* a crime," Nicholas reminded him. "And I don't want you walking up and down any stairs. Fran will kill me if you end up in the hospital again."

"She'll kill the both of us." Stanley took out his cell phone. "I'll ask Fran to come over. We'll tell them together."

"I'll get Beth, she's upstairs."

When the wives came out on the terrace, Stanley began his story. After he finished, Fran objected furiously, complaining that Stanley would drive himself into another health crisis. Nick argued it would be good for his friend's mood, and promised it would not involve any physical exertion. "We'd just be asking a few questions, is all."

"Yeah, we're keeping it simple," said Stanley. "And safe."

In the end, Fran accepted the plan. "You can play detective for a while, but I don't want you to exert yourself one bit!" She turned to Nicholas. "And I'm counting on *you* to keep Stanley under control. No running after suspects. No walking more than a block. No stairs. And only *one* drink a day!"

Beth added, "Stanley thinks this is an organized crime operation. Isn't this going to put both of you in danger?"

"I don't think so," said Nicholas, seeing the skeptical look on his wife's face. "I'm going to tell the surviving spouse that the Department of Health is studying the emotional after effects of loss. They'll have no idea we think the death was suspicious."

"Yeah, and I'm gonna quietly look over the scene. Nobody will even know I was there."

"I still don't like it," said Fran. "Nicholas is in trouble with his bosses already, and Stanley is barely able to walk three blocks without getting out of breath."

"My supervisor knows about this," Nicholas said. "She knows we're going to turn over whatever we find to the police. She's okay with it."

"And we're gonna be riding around in a car," said Stanley. "No exertion. No chasing perps. Honest."

Beth got up to start dinner, saying, "Well you both better keep a low profile. Fran and I don't want to end up widows."

Stanley winked at Nicholas, knowing they'd carried the day. But Fran looked anxious as she put on an apron and helped Beth in the kitchen. As much as she realized the investigation was doing great things for Stanley's mood, she was afraid it was doing bad things for his lungs.

FIFTY

Approaching the building where Laura Metcalf-Reinhold died, Nicholas showed the doorman his DOH identification and asked if Steven Reinhold was in. The doorman rang the apartment and spoke to Steven, saying there was a doctor from the Department of Health to see him.

When Steven expressed reluctance about talking to anyone, Nicholas told the doorman, "Tell him it's a five minute interview. Tell him it's about grief in the loss of a loved one. He'll feel better for talking to me."

The doorman passed on Nicholas's comments, nodded, hung up the phone and buzzed Nicholas in.

Once Nicholas was in the elevator, Stanley showed the doorman his gold shield, a three-quarter replica of the actual badge given him when he was put on permanent disability.

"I got a couple o' questions for you. If you don't mind, Mister…"

The doorman flashed a knowing smile. "Everyone calls me Gus. Come on back and have a seat. I been expecting you."

After explaining to Steven Reinhold that the Department of Health was studying 'grief reaction to loss of a spouse', Nicholas took out a questionnaire and settled into a chair. Steven fidgeted where he sat opposite Nick. "It's just a few questions, sir. Have you been feeling depressed since your wife's death?"

"I've been down in the dumps some of the time, sure, her dying just like that!" He snapped his fingers. "And on the stairs, of all things. It was *so* unexpected."

Nicholas made an entry on his form. "Have you had trouble sleeping? Have you been waking up in the middle of the night? Been troubled by nightmares?"

"Uh, yeah, the first couple of weeks I had trouble getting to sleep. I was so used to having her there beside me. You know, sleeping alone, that's like a foreign experience for me."

Nicholas recalled that Steven and his wife had been separated while the divorce proceedings unfolded.

"But now you sleep through the night?"

"Yeah, most nights I do pretty good."

Nicholas made more checks on his questionnaire.

"Had your wife shown signs of depression? Flat affect. Not eating. Withdrawn. Anything like that?"

"No. She was usually pretty chipper."

"She wasn't taking medications for depression or anxiety?"

"No, she was solid as a rock." Steven got up from his chair and walked to a bookshelf, where he adjusted a picture of Laura. "What's Laura's mood got to do with the accident?"

"There are studies that suggest depressed individuals are more likely to be involved in accidents. That's part of our research." Nicks wondered how he could get anything useful out of the man. "Were you the one who discovered the body?" When he saw this question surprised Reinhold, he added, "That kind of traumatic experience may contribute to feelings of despondence."

"No, I was out of town. I got a call in my hotel room from her sister. She was really freaking out. Listen, are we done here, 'cause I've got this appointment…"

"Just one more question. After your wife's death, have you seen a physician and been treated for any new disorders, such as high blood pressure, diabetes, kidney failure?"

"No."

"You haven't experienced chest pain or palpitations."

Steven tapped his chest. "Healthy as a horse."

Nicholas wanted to ask about the divorce, but saw no way to do it without arousing the man's suspicions. When Reinhold looked at his watch, Nick realized the interview was over.

Waiting for the elevator, Nick didn't see that he had gleaned anything useful from Steven Reinhold. The whole enterprise seemed a waste of time.

In a tiny room behind the lobby, Stanley sat on a beat up folding chair across from Gus, the doorman. He explained that he was following up the report on Laura Metcalf-Reinhold's death, and just had a couple of routine questions.

Gus opened a stainless steel thermos, poured a cup of coffee and offered it to Stanley.

"I'm supposed to stick with decaf," said Stanley, accepting a cup.

"Me, too," said Gus. "Bad ticker."

"Heart surgery?"

"Four bypasses."

"I've out on disability myself. Bad lungs, working at Ground Zero."

"You guys got screwed up the ass," said Gus, pouring himself a coffee. "What the Feds and the city did to you guys, it's a crime. All their heads should be on the chopping block."

"I'm with you," said Stanley.

"I say bring back the guillotine," said Gus, holding his mug up to toast. "And a hangman's noose for the governor!"

After enjoying the taste of the coffee, Stanley asked his new friend what he meant saying he'd been expecting somebody to come interview him.

"I knew there was something fishy about her dying on the stairs. Just 'cause the husband was out of town…Oh, he made a big deal about that, telling everyone he was in some fancy hotel and how he had to pay through the nose to change his return ticket. Phah!"

"You think he protested a little too much."

"Better believe it."

"I understand that Laura slipped on laundry soap that was spilled on the stairwell. The Medical Examiner put her death at around six in the morning. Is that right?"

"So they say."

"Did she always take the stairs? Was she some kind of workout nut?"

"Not that broad. The only workouts she ever got was in bed. With her hips."

"I gotcha." Stanley sipped his coffee.

"One thing confuses the hell out of me, though," said Gus, draining his cup.

"What's that?"

"How come a bunch of other people didn't slip on the stairs during the night?"

"How do you mean?"

"I mean, the laundry room closes at ten PM, so it stands to reason that somebody spilled the soap the night before Metcalf fell."

"That's logical."

"But see, if the soap was spilled before ten, a whole lotta people would have slipped and slided on those steps all night long, and I would have got an earful about it come morning. *But nobody said a word.*"

Gus wiped their cups with a towel and tucked his thermos away on a shelf. "There's one other thing that bothers me. Most people take their laundry downstairs in the elevator. Whoever heard 'a somebody carrying a bag of dirty clothes down the stairs?"

"Gus old buddy," Stanley said, handing back the coffee cup, "you'd make a hell of a detective."

FIFTY-ONE

On the subway ride back to Brooklyn, Stanley told Nick that the doorman thought it was suspicious somebody carried their laundry down the stairs when they had an elevator.

"Somebody could have forgotten their soap, gone back up and hurried down the stairs," said Nick.

"I don't buy it. With a loose cap on the jug? Besides, the laundry room was closed at ten PM. Nobody complained about liquid soap being on the stairs the night before Laura Metcalf died."

"That's very interesting." Nicholas told his friend what he learned in the interview, adding that he thought there had been nothing useful coming from it.

"You say he was in a hurry to get rid of you?"

"He said he had an appointment."

"If he had an appointment, how come we didn't see him go out through the lobby?"

Nick thought about it. "He probably has a car in the garage."

"He'd still go past the lobby to get to it. I scoped out the building layout."

As they talked, a stout Russian fellow with a clarinet came into the subway car and began to play a mournful tune.

"Duke Ellington," said Nicholas. "Imagine that?"

"The Russians love jazz," said Stanley, pulling out his wallet. "It's so damn melancholy." He dropped a single into the musician's cap. Nicholas matched it.

Nick told his friend that Laura Metcalf had shown no signs of depression before her death. Stanley said, "What woman kills herself on a stairwell? She's more likely jump off the roof. Or take a lot of pills."

Nicholas agreed.

Watching the musician collect his tips and pass on to the next car, Nicholas said, "I wonder who thought up this scheme."

"A slick operation like this, well thought out, well executed, it's gotta be the mob. Probably some young Turk with a little college behind him came up with the idea and they jumped at it."

The subway ran over the Manhattan Bridge, giving a view of the east river and the greater New York harbor. A cruise ship was heading out to sea. Nicholas recalled Beth's frequent suggestion that they take a long cruise. He had demurred, suffering from seasickness. She thought there must be medications for that; he was a doctor, after all. He'd never found the time.

As the subway began its decent into a tunnel, Nicholas wondered if a puddle of laundry soap spilled in the evening would still be wet and slippery the following morning.

Steven Reinhold paced back and forth in his living room. He didn't like the visit from the doctor. Why would the Department of Health come knocking on his door? Probably it was nothing; a stupid study that didn't mean anything.

If the guy was really a doctor. He could have been an undercover cop. But he didn't ask anything about the accident, just how he felt. That seemed legit.

He took out a leather folder with a wad of bills. It was so much money. Eight thousand dollars. More than enough to catch up on his account with the organization. Tomorrow when he went to the casino, he would pay the money and tell the guy about the interview. Let the pros deal with it.

Back in Brooklyn, Nicholas asked Stanley if he wanted to go for a ride in the Avanti, now that the carburetor was rebuilt. He led his friend to the parking garage, pulled off the car cover, opened the hood and made a last check of his work, noting the tension in the throttle return spring and the fluid motion of the choke. He reconnected the negative lead to the battery.

"That's smart," said Stanley. "You don't want anything sparking when you work on the fuel system."

"I keep a fire extinguisher in the trunk. It's required for the antique car shows."

Nicholas held out the key to Stanley, who eyed it with a look of doubt.

"You sure? It's your baby."

Nick got into the passenger seat, waiting while Stanley turned the key. The big V8 engine roared to life, the rumble amplified by the free-flow exhaust pipes and the bare walls of the underground garage.

"Man, that thing starts better than my car, and it's only five years old!"

"The three twenty-seven is one of the best engines Chevy ever made. It's the favorite block for hot rodders."

With a conspiratorial smile Stanley shifted into first and carefully drove out of the garage. Out on the street, he gave the pedal a little push and the rear tires screeched, throwing up smoke. He laughed with glee, easing off on the pedal and looking for an open road.

They took the Gowanus south toward Staten Island. "Head toward the Verrazano but don't take the exit," said Nick.

"I know the spot." Stanley roared south, weaving around cars, his two hands gripping the wheel in a race driver's embrace. At the Belt Parkway he went west, the Atlantic glinting off the driver's side. The Belt became a narrow road empty of traffic. Stanley downshifted as he approached the U-turn.

"Give her a little gas in the turn," Nick suggested.

In the middle of the U-turn the engine roared, breaking the rear wheels free. The car fish-tailed madly, Stanley fighting to keep control as the car spun a half circle. He eased off the throttle, the rear wheels regained their grip on the road, and the car shot back along the Belt. Stanley yelled with glee as he accelerated along the empty stretch of road. Nicholas was pleased to see his friend lighthearted as he tore up the roadway.

"Take Fourth Avenue back, the lights are timed," Nick told him. Stanley drove more carefully, not pushing the car as it wound through the streets, turning heads and raising smiles from old men and young.

Carefully driving down into the parking garage, Stanley said, "Ya know, I don't buy that soap on the stairwell. If we could prove it was a plant, it would go a long way to convincing m lieutenant to take the case."

"Why don't we conduct an experiment?"

"Like what?"

"I'll pour some laundry soap on the stairs in our building, let it sit overnight and check out how slippery it is in the morning."

"I get it. If the soap is dried, we'll know the detergent that killed Laura Metcalf had to have been put there that morning, before the laundry room opened." Stanley chuckled as Nick pulled the cover over the car.

"You public health people, you really are scientists, aren't you?"
"Absolutely."

FIFTY-TWO

Dr. Reed Kohlberg, of the New York City Medical Examiner's Office, was not surprised at the weight of the lungs he removed from the body of Dean Hodges. Swollen from the hot water, they were over ninety grams. The reddened, wrinkled face, neck and shoulders were consistent with long-term exposure to the hot water in the shower.

The detective who investigated Hodges's death told the ME that the building super had responded to a complaint of no hot water. He determined that the water heater was in good working order, but the hot water was running continuously up through the pipes. After knocking on several doors, he got a report from Hodge's neighbor that she heard the old man's shower had been running for an inordinate length of time.

The super knocked, entered with a spare key, and found the dead man in the tub beneath a stream of now tepid water.

The Medical Examiner's dissection of the scalp and skull revealed contusion of the occipital region of the brain and bruising of the skin. He suspected that the blow from the fall had probably stunned and not killed Hodges. In his stuporous state he had been unable to turn away from the stream of hot water and drowned.

The faint discolored regions on the dead man's upper arms could have been made from struggling to pull himself out of the tub. The ME was prepared to report the cause of death as accidental drowning caused by a fall that left the victim unconsciousness. But one fact not connected with the death itself made him consider an alternative scenario.

A few days before, a Dr. Nicholas Andreas from the DOH had called Kohlberg with a cockamamie idea that the accidental deaths of divorcees were not accidents at all, but the result of suicide, perhaps associated with depression. Even more ludicrous was the suggestion that the deaths had been due to murder. Supposedly, couples fighting over their estate were now shopping around for hit men.

With these new theories in mind, the ME realized that the bruises on Dean Hodges' arms could have been produced by someone holding the man down beneath the stream of water. Intrigued by Andreas's theory, he asked the detective who had examined the scene if Hodges had been in divorce proceedings. He had been, and the wife, a young hottie, faced losing everything due to a pre-nuptial agreement.

Dr. Kohlberg pulled off his latex gloves and went to his office. He made a note to himself to send a copy of his preliminary report to Andreas in the Department of Health. With a sigh, he realized he would now have to review all the previous cases of accidental death. And somehow he would have to separate out the ones who had been facing divorce.

Nicholas was in the kitchen pouring a small amount of liquid Tide into a cup when he heard the front door open and Chrissie come into the apartment.

"I hate work even more than I hate school!" She dropped her backpack on the floor, threw her MP3 player and earphones on the dining room table and stomped into the kitchen. She took a can of diet soda from the fridge and popped the can.

Nicholas dipped two fingers in the cup of liquid soap and rubbed them together, testing their slipperiness.

"Why are you checking out the laundry soap?"

"It's a science experiment. Like you used to do in school."

"God, I hated those experiments. They were so boring!"

Nicholas tried to remember what his wife had advised him: don't lecture; don't be the all-knowing father; listen, and don't judge. It was all he could do to bite his tongue and not tell her about the importance of school and a good science background.

He took out a short step stool from the front closet, a large piece of paper and the bottle of detergent. Both hands full, he asked Chrissie to open the front door for him.

As he stood in the hallway, he asked her to hold open the door to the stairwell.

"Why are you taking the stairs?"

"I'm pouring detergent on the steps," he said, entering the stairwell.

"That's real smart. You're asking people to slip and crack their heads." She followed him up the steps to the top of the stairwell, which opened onto the roof.

He poured a small amount of the soap onto a step close to the wall. Then he placed the step stool over the soap. He taped the piece of paper to the stool. The paper announced: CAUTION! SLIPPERY STEP.

"Dad, are you crazy? Somebody's gonna break their neck."

Nicholas smiled at her. "That's why I have the sign."

Following him back to the apartment, Chrissie said, "Does this have something to do with that investigation you're doing with Mister Bezlin?"

Nick explained about the suspicious death of the woman who fell on the stairs. "I'm trying to determine if the soap could have been left out all night and remain slippery enough to induce a fall."

"Do you even know what kind of soap it was?"

"Next time you go to the supermarket, read the labels on the laundry soap. They all have roughly the same ingredients. I don't think the drying time would be much different."

"Science. It's just full of useful information, isn't it?" As she followed him into the apartment she added, "So how come your science can't tell me how long before us students all die from lung cancer? Huh, *dad?*"

FIFTY-THREE

Finishing his morning coffee, Nicholas went out to the stairwell before leaving for work to examine the pool of laundry soap on the stairs. As he'd suspected, the soap was nearly dry and was no longer liquid. When he rubbed the goo between his fingers, it felt sticky, not slippery. It was nothing like the liquid described in the police report or by the doorman.

So the detergent in Laura Metcalf's stairs had been fresh. What's more, a resident on their way to the laundry room couldn't have dropped it, the laundry room wasn't open until eight in the morning. She had died around six

This death was no accident.

After cleaning up the soap, he knocked gently on Stanley's door, in case his friend was still sleeping. Stanley came to the door in his boxers and t-shirt. Nick told him about the dried soap.

"It still doesn't add up," said Nick. "How could the killer be sure that Laura would be the one who fell? How could he be sure somebody else didn't slip on his way down the stairs?"

"My friend, when we figure that out we'll break the case wide open. You want a cup of coffee? I got time for a quick brew before I see my doctor."

"Are you due for another PFT?"

"Yeah, same old same old. He's got me on a new drug. It isn't doing squat, but he wants to do another pulmonary function test anyway. Gotta pay the college tuition."

Nicholas had hoped the new medication would expand his friend's lung capacity, but deep down he suspected it would fail. He had gone with Stanley for the first several tests, alarmed at the weak inspiratory effort and the small volume of air his friend had been able to expel. Even worse, while Stanley was getting dressed the pulmonologist had shown Nick the biopsy report. It had been chilling. Thickening of the lining of the airways and loss of secretory function, diminished elasticity in the alveoli, the grape-like sacs that expanded with each breath, and loss of blood flow through the lungs. Most troubling of all, there were flecks of metal and strands of fiber embedded in the lung tissue.

Stanley, who stood six feet tall and weighed two-hundred, had the lung capacity of a medium sized dog. Reading the grim report, Nicholas felt as if his own heart had been damaged.

The casino was quiet as Alex walked into the area with the slot machines and poker games. Early arriving seniors were clutching coffee cups in one hand and cups of coins in the other.

Anticipating that Steven Reinhold would be short again, he made up his mind to read the deadbeat the riot act: pay up in full, or look over your shoulder every day until something really bad happens.

He spied the man at the poker machine, the telltale cup of chips in the well in front of him. Alex sat at a stool two machines away and played a cautious game. After a few moments Steven spied him and stopped dropping coins in the machine.

As Steven rose from his chair, Alex got up and stepped toward him, making the exchange smoothly. But instead of leaving, Steven slid onto the adjoining stool, raising waves of new irritation in Alex's mind.

"What are you doing hanging around?" Alex muttered in a harsh whisper.

"We have a problem!" Steven hissed.

"What happened? Have the cops been knocking on your door?"

"No. Not yet, anyway. I got a visit from a doctor in the Department of Health. Somebody named *Nicholas Andreas.* He was doing a survey. Some kind of study about grief when somebody dies. It creeped me out."

"Jesus H. Christ!" Alex took a breath, lowered his voice. "You wife's death is a statistic. It shows up in a city agency's database, they come up with some bullshit psycho mumbo-jumbo and conduct a survey. It doesn't mean a damn thing!"

"I don't know. I didn't like it."

"*Didn't like it?* What's not to like? Some city functionary fills out a form and puts your answers in a grid with a thousand others. It's meaningless!"

"Maybe so, but–"

"I'll check the guy out. Leave everything to us, you've got nothing to worry about."

Steven dropped a quarter into his machine and pressed the button to draw a hand. He drew a pair of threes and an ace.

Alex picked up the cup of chips in the well, stood and stepped behind Steven. "Are you caught up with the payment?"

"Yeah, this one catches me up." Steven discarded two cards, holding on to the ace.

"Don't get behind again," Alex growled. "We don't tolerate late payments." He watched Steven draw a Jack and a seven, losing his quarter. "Never keep a kicker," said Alex and walked away.

Alex didn't like the Department of Health coming around asking questions any more than Reinhold did. But he would be a fool to let Steven know about his concern. The idiot would get scared and stop making his payments. He might even do something really stupid, like flee the city. Or run his mouth.

Better to reassure him there was nothing to worry about and see if any of the other clients had been visited by some public health flunky. As he walked through the casino looking for the others, he began to feel a current of anxiety. Perhaps the doctor really *was* working with the police.

But why would the police go to all that trouble? They would have sent a pair of detectives and asked questions about the relationship. The alibi. The life insurance. Asking if they were depressed didn't sound like a police investigation. But still…

He continued feeling anxious as he collected the other payments, even though none of the other clients complained of a suspicious visit. Alex decided he had to find out exactly what this Dr. Nicholas Andreas was up to.

FIFTY-FOUR

From his online search, Alex learned that Dr. Nicholas Andreas was indeed a physician with the New York City Department of Health, that he was in the department of epidemiology, and that epidemiology was the study of epidemics. Outbreaks. TB and AIDS and influenza. In other words, a tired bureaucrat who filled out questionnaires and put the results on a meaningless graph.

Although Alex was satisfied that Andreas was a bona fide physician, he decided it made good business sense to verify that the doctor was not also working with the police.

The DOH's website posted lists of past and ongoing investigations, along with public health alerts and bulletins from the New York State DOH and from the CDC. An hour of searching uncovered no study of depression linked to the loss of a loved one. Perhaps the city didn't publicize its studies until they were completed.

Checking up on Dr. Andreas was going to require some serious subterfuge. The important thing was to not let an annoying distraction interfere with business. He had potential clients to interview, research on the victims-to-be, materials to buy. Alex took satisfaction knowing that his years of researching, writing, and polishing crime novels made him uniquely equipped to carry out the business of murder.

He was going to make damned sure that no pencil pusher interfered with his perfect plans.

At his desk, a second cup of coffee at hand, Nicholas looked over the list of remaining nursing homes. He had visited eighteen so far, with thirty-one to go. Opening a subway map to plan his day's appointments, he saw that one of the facilities was close to the home of one of the surviving spouses, Forest Hamilton. Nicholas called the nursing home and told them he would be there in an hour, giving him just enough time to stop and try to talk to Hamilton.

Arriving at the apartment building, Nick showed his ID badge to the concierge and asked if Hamilton was in. The concierge told him the painter usually slept until noon.

"I suppose I could come back later," said Nicholas. "Would you mind just ringing and see is he up and about?"

"Maybe you'll be lucky, doc," the concierge said, picking up the phone. "Sometimes Hamilton stays up all night working. Could be he hasn't gone to bed yet."

Minutes later Nicholas was standing in the doorway looking into the lined and weathered face of Forest Hamilton. Ushered inside, Nicholas held out his hand and felt his fingers squeezed to the point of pain in the artist's powerful grip. The fingers and sleeve of his faded denim shirt were stained with paint.

Hamilton led Nick through a large informal dining room and kitchen into a cavernous area with windows that ran from floor to ceiling. The southern exposure let in a soft October light. Canvases leaned against a blank wall in a haphazard array. The air smelled of kerosene and sweat.

"Doctor Andreas. How can I help you this day?"

"I'm sorry to interrupt your work."

"Not a problem, I was just cleaning up." He wiped his hands on a rag and dropped several brushes into a tall jar of solvent. "I'm a little curious why you would visit a humble painter such as myself. Is there a health problem with the building?"

"No, it's not about the building." Nicholas explained that he was conducting a survey of individuals who suffered an unexpected death in their family. "We're investigating the effect of sudden loss on physical and mental health."

"How very interesting," said Hamilton. "I've read that it's common to develop all kinds of symptoms during the grieving period. I always assumed they were psychosomatic."

"By no means. Studies have found diabetics developing uncontrolled glucose levels during the grieving period. Cardiac patients have a higher incidence of heart failure and heart attacks. There are many physical effects of loss that we're just beginning to understand."

He took out his questionnaire and went through the list of symptoms. Hamilton answered "No" to most of the physical ailments, while acknowledging a degree of sadness and a loss of appetite.

"I don't sleep well, but I've always been an insomniac. I've lost some of my fire to paint, but lucky for me, I have several unfinished projects that give me something to work on."

"Yes, that is lucky." Nicholas looked down at his questionnaire. "It must have been a terrible shock. Were you here in your studio when you got the news?"

"Here? No, I was out of town on a business trip. My business manager and I are negotiating for a show in Chicago. I was there when the terrible thing happened."

"I see."

"Why do you want to know where I was?"

"The literature of grief reports that emotional trauma is often greater when the family member is the one who discovers the, uh, deceased."

"Perfectly understandable."

Nicholas recalled a piece of advice from medical school. *When interviewing patients, use open-ended questions; they triggered unexpected information.*

"Tell me about your marriage."

Hamilton gave his questioner a guarded look. He picked up a pencil and doodled on a large pad. "We were like any other couple, I suppose. We loved each other. Sometimes we argued over something stupid, but we always managed to find a compromise somehow." He erased a line and redid it. "Why do you ask?"

"We're looking at whether or not a partner with a strong emotional bond to the deceased experiences more severe health effects."

"Ah. So I'm at risk of suffering a heart attack, something like that."

"Hopefully not."

Hamilton looked at his watch. "I want to help you, of course, but I've been up most of the night and I really must try and sleep."

"I understand." Nicholas rose, held out his hand. "I can't thank you enough for speaking to me." As he turned to go, he looked back at Hamilton. The lines on Hamilton's face were deeper. Was he anxious about the interview, or had it dredged up fresh feelings of loss? Nicholas had no idea.

On the way to his first nursing home appointment he reflected that Hamilton had been out of town when his wife died, *just as Steven Reinhold had been.* He wondered what were the odds of that happening. The mortality rate for the divorcees was already statistically improbable. Nicholas had a strong sense that this new coincidence was equally unlikely.

He was becoming more and more inclined to accept Stanley's theory that the deaths were criminal, not biological.

FIFTY-FIVE

Stanley parked his car in a dusty parking lot and walked to the office with the weathered sign reading WINSOME RIDING ACADEMY. Below the letters was the image of a woman on a horse jumping a barrier, an ecstatic look on her face. It seemed like a risky business for woman or man.

He showed his badge to the woman at the desk, who directed him to the stables. He stepped gingerly over the ground, remembering his occasional visits to the mounted police stables and the annoyance of having to clean the shit off his shoes.

The stables were a sun-bleached wooden structure with a galvanized roof. He thought it must get pretty noisy when it rained. The smell of hay, horses, urine and shit filled the air. It was a good earthy smell. A welcome change from the air conditioned, HEPA-filtered air of his apartment. Several horses stood in pens watching him as he walked by. Stanley winked at one of them.

A sheep dog came running into the stable yapping. When Stanley knelt down and held out his hand, the dog wagged his tail and sniffed the visitor's crotch, which made Stanley chuckle. The laughing brought on a coughing spell that left him dizzy. He reached for the side of a stall for support.

An old fellow in a black T-shirt, jeans and cowboy boots came ambling out of a pen, pitchfork in hand. His dark brown skin was weathered and lined.

"Howdy," the man called. "What can I do for ya?"

Stanley let go of the stall and extended his hand. "Stan Bezlin, NYPD."

"Dale Yardley." Dale wiped his hand on his jeans and shook Stanley's.

"I'd like to ask you some questions, if you can give me a minute." Stanley saw a guarded look in the man's eyes. "Is there some place we can sit and talk a bit?"

"What's it about?"

"Give me someplace to sit down and I'll tell you all about it."

With a shrug, Dale led Stanley to a little room at the back of the stable with two wobbly wooden chairs and a tiny desk. Pictures of horses and riders leaping over barriers filled the walls. Dale pulled two mugs from where they hung on the wall and poured coffee from an old Mr. Coffee machine. He offered Stanley milk and sugar and a battered leather chair.

Seeing Stanley read the names of the horses in the pictures, Dale said, "We used t' breed some fine race horses back in the day. Brought the owners some good money. Now we mainly get by boarding them for the fancy-pants in the city." He leaned back in his chair and sipped his coffee.

"You worked here a long time?"

"Goin' on fifty years."

"You must like your work."

"Pays the bills." Dale wiped his face with a red bandanna. "You didn't come all the way out here to ask me about my retirement plans."

"No, not for that. I have some questions about Meredith Hamilton's death."

"That right? Coroner said it was a accident."

"What do you think?"

"It ain't for me to second guess no doctor examines a corpse."

"Nobody asked you your opinion at the time?"

"Ha! Ask the opinion of an old stable hand? Not hardly."

"Well I'm asking for it now. What did you think when you heard how she died?"

Dale chewed on the question a moment. "T' tell you the truth, it kinda surprised me."

"Oh? Why's that?"

"First off, the horse the lady was riding. Mayflower? I never seen a gentler, more even-tempered animal in all my days."

"Can't any horse throw off a rider?"

"Sure they can. She could've been spooked by something that jumped out at her. But it would take something mighty scary to make *that* horse throw a rider."

"A loud noise do it?"

"Oh, sure. A canon going off. Or a bomb." He offered to top up Stanley's cup, but the guest declined.

"Dale, if this horse is so gentle, how do you explain the kick to the head?"

"I can't. 'Specially on account she was wearin' a helmet." Dale pulled a riding helmet off the wall and handed it to Stanley. The double straps looked secure enough to keep it on a rider's head, ever after taking a fall.

Dale drained the last of his coffee, cleaned the cup with a paper towel and hung it back on the wall. "And there's another thing I can't explain. Not more'n two days after the accident, the husband had that sweet mare put down. Vet called and told me he was comin' for her."

"That's unusual?"

"Sure it is. Throwin' a rider don't mean a horse is mean. *Or* dangerous. Accidents happen on lots a' horses, we don't put 'em down for it."

Stanley handed the helmet back and thanked Dale for his help. As he turned to go, he spotted a weathered picture of a black cowboy riding a bucking bronco, a crowd of black men, women and children cheering in the stands.

"That's my great uncle Desmond. He won a gold buckle that day." Dale gently touched the wooden frame. "Used to be a whole lotta black cowboys. They couldn't get into the white rodeos back then, so they made their own."

"Like the Negro baseball league."

"Same thing. First prize was a gold buckle."

Thanking Dale for his time, Stanley walked to the gate of Winsome Farm with a good feeling that the case was developing. His next step would be to visit a friend with a boat anchored at Sheepshead Bay. Stanley wanted to know how Vinnie Solomira drowned in the middle of the Long Island Sound.

About to step into his car, he stopped, struck by a new idea. Retracing his steps, he found Dale in the stables cleaning out a stall. "Say, Dale, when they come for a horse to put down, what do you do with the horseshoes the animal is wearing?

FIFTY-SIX

A bearded old man in dirty clothes, crooked dark glasses and a floppy hat shuffled along Court Street heading for the subway entrance. With the October sun just getting out of bed, shopkeepers ignored the old man as they pulled up their metal grates, preparing for another day.

Slowly making his way down to the subway platform, the old man stood in the shadows and watched Nick Andreas open the New York Times and glance at the headlines. Other men in suits and women in power outfits gathered along the platform.

The derelict shuffled along the wall of the subway, muttering to himself. As the subway train rumbled into the station, the homeless guy stopped to watch Nick fold his newspaper and tuck it into his briefcase. The old man studied the line of commuters as they shuffled into the subway cars. When the bells rang, the doors closed and the train lurched out of the station toward Manhattan. Removing his dark glasses, Alex Germaine watched the few exiting passengers ascend the stairs to the street, leaving the platform empty.

Having studied Andreas's movements for the past three days, Germaine surmised that the man was nothing more than a harmless public health bureaucrat, and not a police agent. Andreas hadn't reported to any police precinct. He had taken the train to the Department of Health and entered the building along with hundreds of other minions. Later he traveled to various nursing homes and spent one to two hours at each facility.

The one disturbing element was that Andreas had not gone to any public apartment buildings and interviewed private individuals. If he was in fact conducting a survey for the city about grief or loss or some such bullshit, why hadn't he gone to a single private residence? Why wasn't he interviewing more survivors?

Still, the interview had spooked Steven Reinhold. If the doctor went on to interview his other clients, there was no telling what they might blurt out. The man had to be stopped, no question about it. Alex thought a fall onto the tracks of an oncoming train would be an effective way to rid himself of the pesky Dr. Andreas. But if he pushed the doctor off the platform, there was the risk that some overzealous vigilante type would tackle and hold him for the police. Or an undercover cop could be passing the station and apprehend him before he could remove his derelict's disguise and make his getaway.

No, the subway station was not the place to eradicate this pest. Alex realized he would have to study the subject a little longer. Still, he was confident he would find the solution. Genius would untie the Gordian knot, it was only a matter of time.

Stanley walked out onto the dock at Vinnie's Marina in Sheepshead Bay and saw that his friend Billy was seated on the deck of his boat.

"Hey, Billy! How's the fishing?"

"Good to see you Stanley. Come aboard, I'll get you a beer."

"Thanks." Stanley stepped off the dock and settled into a plush leather chair. He took in a deep breath, as deep as his crippled lungs allowed, enjoying the smell of the sea and the sound of the gulls wheeling overhead as they waited for a fisherman to throw scraps over the side.

"You ought to make one more trip with me before it gets too cold," said Billy. "The tuna's all gone south, but there's still blues and sea bass. I spotted a flock of gulls dive bombing just the other day."

"I'd like that, Billy, but fighting for balance on the boat would wear me out. Besides, I'm on a case."

"I didn't know you were back on the force."

"I'm just doing a friend a favor." He explained that a man's motorboat had taken on water out on the Long Island Sound and sunk. The sole pilot had drowned. *With* a life vest on. "Or so the Medical Examiner thought."

"You think it was foul play?"

"I'm open to possibilities. The drain plug was missing. Is that a common event?"

Billy considered the problem. "How big a boat?"

"Twenty-eight feet."

"Brand?"

"Sea Shark."

"That's a fast boat. Cuts through the waves like a knife. The drain plug is spring loaded, like the do-dad you put in a champagne bottle after you pop it."

"Could you jimmy it so that it came loose from the vibration of the motor?"

"Sure. A good mechanic or a handy man could do it."

"But you couldn't time it so the boat stays dry until you're out pretty far, could you?"

"Ah, that's not as hard as you think. Small boats that lose their drain plug don't take on a whole lot of water as long as they're moving forward. The plug faces back, and believe it or not, they'll only let take in a trickle until they stop moving. Once they stop, the water rushes in."

"You're sure about this?"

"*Oh* yes. It's happened to me."

"Wouldn't the boat still stay afloat?"

"Are you kidding? The Shark is built for speed, period. With those double engines hanging off her rear, the stern would drop down, you'd have just the tip of the bow poking through the surface."

Stanley looked out at the Atlantic. He imagined a man alone in a small boat that was taking on water. Wearing a life jacket, it still seemed like a long shot the man would drown before being spotted. Although the weather had been threatening that day; not many boats out on the water.

He recalled the woman who had been kicked by her horse, and the woman who cracked her skull on a set of stairs. A man who drowned wearing a life jacket. All the deaths pointed to someone giving Mother Nature a kick. In the ass.

"Yeah," said Stanley. "I'm going fishing, too, only I'm hauling in a killer."

FIFTY-SEVEN

Nicholas was writing up a report on the Nursing Homes he'd visited the day before when his phone rang. "Doctor Andreas."

"Reed Kohlberg, here, at the ME's office."

"I'm glad you called. What did you think of the statistical analysis I emailed you?"

"I went over it with my supervisor. Didn't you say you're working on a theory of unrecognized suicide?"

"That was my original hypothesis. But so far my interviews with the survivors haven't uncovered any evidence that the victims were depressed prior to their accident."

"That's interesting," said Kohlberg.

"To tell you the truth, I'm actually considering a criminal conspiracy is behind the deaths."

"That's what I wanted to talk to you about. I found something troubling in a recent autopsy."

Nick sat forward, excited at the possibility that someone finally had found forensic evidence that would advance the investigation. "Tell me what you've found."

"The other day I did an autopsy on an elderly white male, a Dean Hodges. He drowned in his bathtub. He fell and hit his head, then he lay beneath the shower and took water into his lungs. I'm still waiting for the tox screen, so he could have been intoxicated."

"But you're thinking…"

"I'm thinking a slip and fall would be a plausible scenario except for two things. He had superficial bruises on the inner aspects of his upper arms, which he could have sustained flailing around the tub trying to get out."

"Or someone could have held him under the stream of water."

"Correct. The other thing that caught my attention was, the detective mentioned Hodges' wife was going to save a bundle on lawyer fees with her husband dead. The man was going through a nasty divorce, and she was evidently going to lose everything."

"Does this mean the Medical Examiner's office is going to reopen the other cases?"

There was a moment of silence.

"We haven't got that far. *Yet.* But off the record, when my report gets to the department chair, I'm confident he will order a review of the previous autopsies of all accidental deaths."

Delighted that he was getting support for his work, Nicholas thanked Kohlberg and hung up. He made a note about the bruises on Hodges' arms and added the man to his database. He wished he could call Stanley and report on the latest findings, but he didn't trust his office phone. For that matter, his cell could just as easily be tapped, the Feds were capable of anything. The new information would have to wait until he was home.

After leaving the marina, Stanley called up Eastern Mutual Insurance, identified himself and gave his badge number, and asked to speak to an adjustor. He explained that he was looking into the rollover death of a Zachary Thorne, giving the adjustor the date of the accident and the make of the vehicle. In minutes the insurance man had the information up on his screen.

"What department did you say you were with?" the adjustor asked.

"Homicide."

Excited at the prospect of canceling a life insurance policy that was about to pay out for accidental death, the agent said, "Then you think foul play was involved."

"I think a lotta things. Have you got photos of the tires?"

"Yes, sir. I have digital shots of the tire that blew and the others as well."

"I'm coming over there to look at them. Can you print me copies?"

"Certainly. I'll have them on my desk awaiting your arrival." The adjuster was grinning from ear to ear as he hung up the phone. He had a bad feeling about that MVA as soon as the police report came in; the rollover issue and the faulty tires had all been cleared up by the manufacturers. He put a hold on the payout request, punched the Send button on his computer, and leaned back, thinking about the praise he would earn when the boss found out he'd saved the company a cool million bucks.

Stanley clicked off his cell phone, confident that every one of the so-called accidents would turn out to be a murder. Giddy at the prospect of cracking a murder conspiracy, he drove toward the insurance company, window open, Tony Bennett on the radio, and all things right with the world. He hadn't felt this good since before 9/11.

Having learned from the DOH website that Dr. Nicholas Andreas worked in the Epidemiology Department, Alex called and asked to speak to the supervisor. When he heard a woman say, "This is Doctor Olivia Keppel speaking," Alex put on a vaguely English accent.

"Doctor Keppel? Jeff Kaplan here, New York Dispatch. I'm following up on a report that your department is investigating the, lemme see my notes, 'the health effects of mourning on husbands and wives who have lost a spouse.' Is that right?"

"Excuse me?" said Libby. "I'm not sure I'm following you. This is the Epidemiology Department. It sounds like you need to talk to the Mental Hygiene Division."

"Yeah, it sounded like that to me, too, but see, my editor gave me this number. He said a Doctor Nicholas Andreas was interviewing married men and women who recently suffered a death in the family."

Recalling the data that Nicholas had been 'curious' about, Libby felt a wave of anger. Could he really be such a loose cannon that he was investigating subjects without her authority? Without DOH approval? It didn't seem like him, but how else to explain this reporter's call? She cursed softly under her breath.

"What was that, doctor? I didn't hear you."

"Mister Kaplan, Doctor Andreas does work in this department, but we are not currently engaged in a study such as you described. Perhaps you have the wrong name."

"I don't know, my editor was pretty sure he had the right guy. He says the doc is going around with a questionnaire and everything."

"I will have to speak to Doctor Andreas and call you back. Where can I reach you?"

Alex gave her the number of his prepaid cell, which was not registered, then hung up. He felt that Keppel's swearing under her breath at his mention of the study could mean the whole thing *was* a police operation that no one was supposed to know about. She was pissed, no doubt about that. The whole situation was very strange. Very worrisome.

On his way to the divorce court in Queens, Alex was determined to find out once and for all if Andreas was legit or a police stooge. If the man was investigating murder and not mental health, Alex vowed that the Medical Examiner would soon be cutting up one very annoying city employee very soon.

FIFTY-EIGHT

Libby knocked on Nick's open door and stepped in.

"Nicholas. I need to talk to you." Her face was drawn; her mouth, taut; her eyes, on fire.

Dreading that he was about to be fired, Nick pulled out a chair for her, saying, "Is there a problem with my nursing home surveillance?"

Libby perched on the edge of the chair fighting to control her emotions. "I just got a call from a reporter. He asked me about some sort of study you're supposed to be conducting of surviving spouses. Is it true? Are you involved in some kind of investigation?"

Nick kept silent, feeling trapped in a corner. He couldn't lie to her, the truth would come out in the end, anyway. He silently cursed his decision to help Stanley with the investigation. It had been a fool's errand, and now he would pay the price

"Okay, I talked to two guys about grief. Just two. I was following up that improbably high mortality rate in divorcees I told you about."

"And you represented yourself as a DOH investigator?"

"Yes."

"I can't believe you would do such a thing. I can't..." She let her sentence trail off, not knowing how to express her surprise at his actions. "This is very troubling. I don't even know where to begin reprimanding you."

"But you knew I was looking into a cluster of suspicious deaths. I showed you the data."

"You never told me you were going to do field interviews!"

Nick shrugged. "Maybe I assumed you understood that would be part of my study." When he saw that Libby wasn't buying it, he added, "Studying mortality trends is our mandate. It's what we do."

"Yes, but the law and medical ethics require that any study of human subjects be vetted by a supervising committee. There are HIPA problems with you accessing confidential DOH information, invasion of privacy issues, unapproved use of city time. I mean, you were already in trouble up to your chin, and now *this?* Nick, what the hell were you thinking?"

Nicholas felt a gnawing sense of dread creep into his gut. But it wasn't the blowback from the city that worried him, that was peanuts compared with the threat he was now facing.

"Libby, it doesn't make sense, a reporter asking about my interview with a few surviving spouses.

"Why? Why doesn't it make sense?"

"Because the two husbands I talked to hired somebody to kill their wives! There's no way they would tell a reporter. The only person they would tell is the guy they paid to carry out the murders."

"Oh my god!" Libby rose from her chair and pressed a hand to the side of her face, stunned at the meaning of the phone call she'd received.

"What paper did he say he worked for?" asked Nick.

"He said it was the New York Dispatch."

"Never heard of it." Nick scribbled the name on a scratch pad, intending to show it to Stanley. He looked up at Libby. "Look, you can fire me, I'm not concerned about that. I'm concerned about who this person is that represented himself as a reporter."

"Nick, you've got to speak to the police about this. If something happened to you…" She put a hand on his shoulder. Her feelings for him overcame any obligations as a supervisor or city employees. The man she loved was in danger; nothing else mattered. "Promise me you'll call the police. You'll take care of yourself. Won't you?"

Nick stood and put his arms around her. He saw tears welling up in her eyes. Embarrassed, he put some space between them.

"I'm sorry I dragged you into this, Libby. I never expected it to come to this. I really didn't."

She released Nick and turned to go. "I know you didn't, Nick. I'll do what I can to cover your back. Not that I can do much, but I'll try." She stepped into the doorway, turned back to look at him one last time, then walked away, from what terrible consequences she was not quite sure.

FIFTY-NINE

Once Libby left his office, Nicholas picked up the phone and dialed Stanley's cell phone. He had no doubt the caller had been a member of the gang committing the murders, not a reporter. The same little voice that had noted the string of accidental deaths was loudly telling him to be careful. And afraid.

Getting Stanley on his cell, Nick related Libby's conversation with the alleged reporter who asked about his interview of the spouses. He pointed out that the two survivors would have no reason to call the press in response to an innocuous questionnaire from a public health official. "Do you think it was one of the killers calling?"

"It's possible. Very possible. I've never heard of this New York Dispatch." He paused before adding, "I want you to be careful, Nick. Watch your back. Keep away from isolated areas."

"I ride the subway to work, come home, shop in our neighborhood. You don't have to waste your time worrying about me."

"Hey. You've been worrying about my health ever since I went in the hospital last year. Now it's my turn." Stanley added that he needed a photo of Meredith Hamilton's head injury.

"You've been to the stable?"

"Yeah. The horse was mighty tame. Plus, the husband had it put down right after the accident."

"Getting rid of the evidence?"

"No doubt. I need to compare the size and shape of the head wound with Mayflower's shoe."

Stanley went on to tell Nick how he learned from his buddy at the marina that it would have been easy to doctor the plug on Vinnie Solomira's boat. "Take out the spring and it'll pop out from the engine vibrations."

"Wouldn't it take on water right away?"

"Not as long as it's moving forward. Kill the engine and the sea floods in."

"But if the man had a life jacket on, why would he drown?"

Stanley told him a swimmer alone out on the Sound could pass out from hypothermia. "But I think the killer was out there waiting for him. Probably held him underwater 'til he drowned."

"Christ, these people don't play around, do they?" He described Dr. Kohlberg's report about the suspicious death of Dean Hodges, an elderly man divorcing a young wife and leaving her penniless.

Stanley said he was heading over to the insurance company to check on the tires in the Zachary Thorne SUV rollover. Nick promised to get the complete files on all the victims from the Medical Examiner. "Good. I'll pass them on to my lieutenant once they agree to take on the investigation. And for Christ's sake, be careful!"

Hanging up, Nick considered how he would carry out his friend's advice to avoid isolated places and to watch his back. For the first time in his friendship with Stanley, he was glad the guy was a cop. With a gun.

Finally leaving his office, Nicholas considered telling Beth when he met her after work about the danger facing him. He had suggested they meet and walk across the Brooklyn Bridge together. An effort to connect, probably futile, but what the hell, he knew he had to do something or he would lose her.

There were so many threats all coming down on him at once, he didn't know which one was the most dangerous or which would hit him first. At the moment, losing his family felt more terrible than losing his life.

As he walked out of the DOH building and headed south, he saw Beth walking toward him. She gave him a wave and a disarming smile. He was relieved to see her.

"Nick, I'm so glad you asked me to meet you." She planted a kiss on his cheek. "I think it shows great promise."

He held her face in his hands. "Actually, I'm looking forward to spending time alone. With my wife." He kissed her tenderly on the lips.

They began walking toward the bridge. Beth told him she was pleased that he hadn't tried to lecture Chrissie the other night. "You listened. You really listened to her. I think that's great, Nick. Really I do."

"She'll never forgive me."

"Don't be silly, of course she'll forgive you. She'll grow up." She laid a hand on his chest as they walked along. "She just needs for you to grow up, too."

He looked down at her, puzzled.

"What I mean is, I hope you'll give up this superman sense that you were single-handedly responsible for every illness that's fallen on the first responders. I know you're an important guy, but you're not *that* important."

Nicholas looked at the Brooklyn Bridge as they approached the entrance. It was stoic and silent. It looked as if it would stand forever. Why couldn't he be like that?

SIXTY

Stanley Bezlin walked past the sign that said TIRES REPAIRED/ RETREAD/ REPLACED and into the dark recess of the tire shop. The concrete floor was slick with oil, and black dirt filled spaces between stacks of tires and machines.

Spotting a familiar face, he called out, "Hey! Tino! What's shakin'?"

A wiry Hispanic fellow who was freeing a tire from a rim looked up, grinned, put down the tool in his hand and walked toward Stanly.

"Hola, compadre. Long time no see." He wiped his hands on a filthy apron and took Stanley's in a strong grip. "Is this a social call, or you looking to trade up? Get some Kumo All Weathers for your car, maybe. They speed rated, man."

"That's a pricey brand for a little re-skin shop like yours."

"Don't judge a book by its cover, bro'. I can get you four brand new tires below wholesale. I buy right from the factory in Japan."

"It's all who you know," Stanley said. "Listen. I need some expert advice. You got a minute?"

"For you I got an hour. Come in the office."

Stanley joined Tino in a tiny room with a desk overflowing with papers, catalogues and industry magazines. "Someday I gotta get a secretary."

"She better be tiny if she's going to work in this place."

"If she got no meat, I don't want her." He settled into a creaking wooden chair, held out his hands in expectation.

"I'm investigating a guy whose SUV rolled. The front tire blew on the highway."

"What make?"

"Grand Cherokee."

"Michelin's. Those are good tires. Were they inflated the right pressure? Were they old? Worn out tread? What?"

Stanley showed his friend photos of the tires he'd picked up at the insurance agency. "The accident investigator told me the tires were only a year old. You can see they had plenty of tread. The one that blew had a weak spot on the sidewall. That's what popped the tire."

"That don't sound right. The tread didn't peel away?"

"No, the tread's still intact."

Tino pulled a catalogue down off a sagging shelf and thumbed through it. "Look. Here's the tire. See?"

"Yeah..."

"Most've the tires that blow do it because the tread separates from the steel belt. The whole layer peels away."

"Don't they ever have weak spots on the side wall?"

"Sure they do. And when you go to fill up at the air pump you see the bulge and you get it replaced."

Stanley studied the pictures of the tire. "What could cause a soft spot on the side?"

"Could be a defect, but I don't see them too much in this tire." Tino considered the problem. "If the tire was *over-inflated,* that could stress a defect. But if it was over-inflated, then the tread would be worn along the midline. There." He pointed to a band running along the middle of the tread.

"The tread is evenly worn," said Stanley.

"Did the tire scrape something, lose some the sidewall?"

"There's no evidence of that." Stanley pointed at the blown sidewall. "Could somebody *make* that happen?"

Tino said, "Maybe. Be easier to put a nail through the tread."

"That would produce a slow leak. I'm talking about a blow-out. You know, *Bam!* You lose control at high speed..."

"Sure, sure, I see where you're going. You put enough heat on that bad boy, could weaken the rubber, make it blow. You flip over, don't wear no seat belt 'cause you're mister macho, and like that, you dead."

Standing up, Stanley held out his hand. "I can't thank you enough, Tino."

"No big thing. Any time you got a problem you come to Tino. What you did for my brother that time he was in trouble, I never forget." Following Stanley out to the repair shop, he added, "You look pretty good for a guy had one foot in the grave last year. You all right?"

"The undertaker hasn't measured me for a box yet."

"Tha's good. We got too many goin' in the ground already from the dust. That poor nun worked at Ground Zero? They should make her a saint."

"Her and a thousand others," said Stanley, getting into his car.

SIXTY-ONE

Nick and Beth stepped onto the Brooklyn Bridge and walked leisurely among the joggers and the cyclists, enjoying the cool October air. Looking at his wife's face in the evening sun, he thought she'd never looked lovelier.

"Are you using a new makeup or something?"

"No, the same old junk," she said, smiling at what she knew was Nick's idea of a compliment.

"You haven't had any Botox injections or anything like that, have you?"

"Of course not, I'm not *that* vain. Why do you ask?"

"I was just thinking, you kind of have that glow you had when you were pregnant. Remember? Your hair and your skin were lustrous. Healthy looking."

She put her arm around him, saying, "Why, Doctor Andreas, you make a girl blush."

She looked down at a tour boat chugging through the harbor. "Remember?" she asked him.

"You mean, 9/11?"

"No! I was thinking of our first date."

"Oh. I was such a jerk. It's a wonder you went out with me again."

"You weren't a jerk. You got a call your mother was taken to the Emergency Room. You put me in a cab. I understood, it was our first date."

"And she died twenty-four hours later." Nick felt Beth's arm tighten around him as he recalled the hollow days of mourning and the mountains of personal belongings that he had to dispose of. They continued walking across the bridge, hand in hand, as cyclists blowing whistles and a couple of skaters doing spins and figure eights whizzed by.

He looked past her toward the Statue of Liberty. The evening sun was tipping toward the turreted horizon, reflecting gold and silver on the East River and the greater New York harbor. As a cruise ship made its way out of the harbor on her way out to sea, a pair of tugboats pulled away and saluted the great ship with their horns. The great vessel replied with a deep blast.

"Let's take a cruise," said Nick, pointing at the ship.

"What? You got sea sick walking on the Intrepid anchored in the harbor!"

"I'll take medication." He saw a skeptical look on her face. "Let's do it. This winter. We'll fly to Florida and cruise the Caribbean."

"Nick, I hope you don't feel you have to make up for anything that you've done. I never felt for a moment that you neglected me. As far as—"

He bent down and kissed her tenderly on the mouth. "I love you, Elizabeth Theresa Andreas."

She wrapped her arms around him and nuzzled her face into his chest. "I love you, too, Nickolas Andreas. More than ever."

As the couple strolled arm in arm along the bridge, a figure dressed in a jogging suit, watch cap and white running shoes walked several yards behind them. Watching the couple through dark glasses, Alex Germaine silently cursed their embrace.

He went over his phone conversation with Andreas's supervisor again. She'd acted as if she knew nothing about his study of surviving spouses. That didn't add up. Were the interviews part of a police operation, or was she just afraid to talk to the press? If the cops *were* on the case, why send a public health doctor? Why not send a detective?

Alex was at a loss, and not knowing what was going on made him seethe with anger. Controlling events was the cornerstone of his business. His operation was so beautifully thought out. So perfectly executed. And this flunky doctor might be gumming it all up by talking to the spouses.

He looked for solace in knowing his exit strategy was rock solid. Even if the cops sent a SWAT team to break down his apartment door, with his fake identity papers, his masterful disguises, and his stash of money, he could still hop a bus for Mexico and be out of the country before anybody was the wiser.

Alex decided it would be prudent to vary his method of disposing of the targets until he could nail down how much Andreas knew. If the cops were looking for him, a switch in modus operandi would throw them off the trail. In the meantime he'd stay close to Dr. Andreas and find out exactly what his game was.

Watching Nicholas and Beth walking along the bridge, Alex's fury grew. *The happy couple.* Did they think they had the marriage of the century?

Well, if his perfect business plan did come crashing down like the Twin Towers all because of that meddling, two-bit city bureaucrat, he, Alex Germaine, would exact his revenge before leaving the country.

And the revenge would be doubly sweet, because killing Andreas would not only satisfy his right to punish the man, it would also break the wife's heart. After murdering Andreas, he would attend the funeral just to watch the wife fall to her knees in hysterical sobbing when they lowered the casket into the hole and threw the damp dirt over him.

That image of the broken wife crying over the grave would take the sting out of leaving New York.

SIXTY-TWO

Beth let Fran and Stanley into the apartment, saying, "Nick will be down in a minute, he's in the shower. *We* walked across the Brooklyn Bridge."

"What a beautiful day for it!" said Fran. "The city must have looked wonderful."

"It was enchanting. The setting sun cast a pink glow over the city." She told them about the cruise ship heading out to sea and Nick's promise to book of passage for them over the winter.

"Let's make it a foursome," said Fran.

"I'll go if they let me fish," said Stanley stepping toward the stairs leading to the upper floor.

"Shouldn't you use the elevator?" Fran asked. "Nick can let you in upstairs."

"I'm not a cripple. I can make it one flight."

He grasped the hand rail and took a few steps, then stopped and waited for his heart to stop pounding. He slowly ascended a few more steps. By the time he reached the head of the stairs his face was flushed and sweaty. He pursed his lips, trapping air in his windpipe, and made his way into the spare bedroom.

"Check it out. I got Steven Reinhold's…Credit card receipts," said Stanley, unable to hold enough air to vocalize a complete sentence.

"Let me see—" Nick stopped in mid-sentence, seeing his friend's flushed face and pursed lips. "You okay? Why don't you sit down?"

"Good idea." Stanley sank heavily into a stuffed chair. He mopped his face with a handkerchief. "This guy Reinhold does some traveling," said Stanley, handing his friend the documents.

"How did you get the credit card receipts on the suspects?"

"Don't ask," Stanley replied, still short of breath.

"The receipts must be for his business, don't you think?" Nicholas laid out the papers on the desk.

"Maybe not. I can see one trip to Atlantic City for a vendor fair. Exercise equipment and all. But why so many trips? And always early in the month?" He pointed to the circled credit card reports.

"He was probably entertaining clients," said Nick.

"That doesn't explain all the cash advances. Three, four, five thousand dollars charged to cash at the Taj Mahal."

"He must have a gambling addiction," said Nick.

"That's what he *wants* us to think." Stanley placed a second batch of credit receipts in front of his friend. "Look at Jewel Solomira's records. And note *her dates.*"

Nicholas looked over the receipts. "She charged five thousand dollars on her credit cards at Trump's World on August eight."

"The same date that Reinhold was taking money out at the Taj." He made a gesture mimicking a coin toss and shook his head.

"You don't believe in coincidences," said Nicholas.

"No more than you." Stanley set the records in order on the desk. "Let's list the cash withdrawals for all the suspects."

Nicholas took notes while Stanley read off the banking transactions. All of the suspects visited an Atlantic City casino on the same day. Seven took out thousands of dollars; others charged a meal. Or gasoline.

Nick said, "If they were all in town the same day, that's evidence of a conspiracy, isn't it?"

"Definitely. What's the average amount?"

Nicks used his cell phone's calculator to do the math. "It's right around five thousand."

"They're making payments on their marker. They'll keep ponying up until the debt is cleared." He shuffled through the credit receipts. "Two of them visited the casinos in September. Five of them went down in August."

"They all had payments scheduled the same day," said Nicholas.

"It's gotta be the mob. They've got a great scam going. Look at how smart they were setting up the murders to look like accidents." Stanley told Nick about his theory on Zachariah Thorne's rollover based on his interview with the tire dealer. They reviewed Laura Metcalf's suspicious slip on the stairs, Vinnie Solomira's drowning, Meredith Hamilton's fatal kick to the head, and the rest of the deaths. It was clear all of the accidents could as well have been staged as happened by chance.

Stanley clipped the credit receipts to Nick's calculations and tucked them in a manila envelope. "I'm gonna call my contact in Organized Crime. He'll subpoena the financial records and find the same thing."

Stanley pushed himself up, took a few breaths, headed for the door.

"You want to take the elevator?" asked Nick, reaching for the outer door.

"Christ, I already did the hard one. Why would I ride *down?*"

They found Beth and Fran sitting on the terrace enjoying wine. Beth had lit candles as the night drew a purple cloak across the skyline.

"Isn't it a lovely night?" said Fran, looking up at the sky. "You're so lucky to have a unit with a terrace."

The street below was quiet as New Yorkers settled in for their dinner and TV news. Television sets flickered in windows across the street. Stanley told the wives about the suspects' common visits to the casinos, adding that he thought it was an organized crime operation.

"So much for my theory of depression and suicide," said Nicholas. He told them about Libby's concerns that he had interviewed a few clients without going through the proper channels, as well as her worries about the suspicious reporter asking about his interviewing Steven Reinhold and Forest Hamilton. Stanley added that the spouses must have complained to their contact in the organization, who would naturally want to check out anything that could compromise their operation. He was about to explain about the cash withdrawals when he saw that Beth had risen to her feet and was staring at him, her eyes wide.

"Don't give me any song and dance, Stanley. Is Nick in danger?" When Stanley kept silent, she said in a fierce voice, "*Is my husband in danger?*"

Stanley shaped his words with care. "I don't know. I don't *think* so." He saw Beth open her mouth to object. "As far as the conspirators know, he's just a city employee carrying out a routine Health Department survey. They don't know he has any suspicion that a murder even occurred."

"Then why did they call about him?"

"They probably wanted to know if it's anything they should worry about."

"Well it's sure scaring the hell out of me," said Beth. Holding back tears, she told Nick and Stanley she wanted them to turn everything they had over to the police and to stop the investigation. "The police are paid to stick their necks out, you're not."

Nicks got up and put his arm around her. "We already decided, Stanley is going to turn all our evidence over to the authorities today. And I won't take on any more interviews. Okay? You happy?"

Stanley added, "I'll call the paper in the morning and check out the reporter. He's probably just following a tip he got somewhere."

"You promise?" said Beth.

"Scout's honor," said Stanley with a snappy Boy Scout salute. As much as he hoped that whoever called Nicholas would believe it had been an innocent public health inquiry, he knew that the criminals in the organization were not that stupid. Which was why he was going to stay damn close to Nick until the case was over. It was time for him to give his doctor friend some TLC for a change.

SIXTY-THREE

In the street below Nick's apartment, Alex sat in his car looking up at the terrace where the two couples sat and talked. The telephoto lens of his camera gave him close-ups of the foursome.

He saw Nicholas step out onto the terrace and settle into a chair. The terrace was on the sixth floor, an excellent height for falling. But Alex could not think of a credible way to induce a fall. Andreas was a good-sized man. Six-two, at least, and at forty-three, probably in excellent physical shape.

Then he saw another man come out onto the terrace. "Stanley Bezlin," he mumbled, recognizing the detective from the Mystery Writers International dinner where he had struck Bezlin and nearly killed him. Seeing him, Alex was at first surprised, then anxious, and finally, furious. All he needed was an ex-cop hearing about Andreas's questions and there was no telling where it might lead.

The presence of the two men together was puzzling. If the business was already in the hands of the District Attorney, they would assign active members of the police to investigate, not a broken down ex-cop who was out on permanent disability.

It made more sense if Andreas's story was legitimate; that he was simply carrying out a study of grieving survivors, nothing more. But if that *was* the case, why hang out with Bezlin? Unless…

Alex tucked the camera out of sight, left his car and went to the lobby. Sure enough, not far from the name *Andreas* was *Bezlin*. The cop was just a few doors down the hall.

How about that for fucking bad luck. If the doctor happened to tell Bezlin about his interviews, and if Bezlin got suspicious and took it to his old boss…

Alex had serious doubts that all his clients would keep their mouths shut in the face of a serious police investigation. He knew how the cops worked. They promised that the first one to flip would receive a light sentence, and they threatened them with a hundred years in solitary if they kept quiet. Somebody was bound to spill the beans.

The only way to keep everybody's mouth shut was to put the fear of god in them. If the cops started asking question, he would tell all of them that going to jail was the least of their worries should they talk. His 'organization' had agents everywhere, and they would hunt down the rat and kill him, in jail or out. Even in witness protection, the organization would find them and deliver a slow and painful death.

If the time to fold in the business was coming soon, Alex was ready. He had his fake passport, a flop house to stay in, and his cash in a place he could access at a moment's notice, twenty-four seven. It would be a disappointment to pull the plug prematurely, but shit happens. The important thing was, he was leagues ahead of those two pains in the ass on the terrace, and he was going to keep ahead of them all the way across the border.

Besides, he had come up with another brilliant plan for raking in the money. And the beautiful thing about it was, nobody would ever connect the new business with the one he practiced in New York.

Nicholas was just going upstairs to bed when he heard a soft *tap, tap* on the front door. Opening it, he saw Stanley standing in the hallway with a package in his hand.

"Stanley. Are you sick?"

His friend stepped into the apartment. In a stage whisper he said, "I'm fine. Sorry to come by so late. I got something for you." He peeked into the apartment; saw that the first floor was empty but for the two of them. "Is Beth upstairs in bed?"

"Yes. What's this about?"

"I'll show you." Ushering Nick into the half-bath beneath the stairs, Stanley closed the door and began to unwrap the package.

"What's with all the secrecy?"

"Shh! Keep your voice down." Opening the package, Stanley revealed a revolver in a shoulder pouch.

"This gun is legal. It's registered to me. I can get you a permit in a couple of days."

Nick looked at the weapon. As a physician in training he had held scalpels, saws, lethal-looking needles that could pierce bone; even electric cautery probes that melted tissue. But he had never held a weapon.

"I don't know anything about guns. I'd probably shoot myself in the foot."

Stanley held the gun out to Nicholas. "Keep it loaded and nearby, but where Beth won't see it. I'll take you to a shooting range this weekend and give you some pointers."

Nick pushed the gun back to his friend. "I know you mean well, Stanley. I do. But this organization apparently kills people by staging accidents. I don't think a gun would help me."

"A gun *always* helps. For all you know they hold somebody at gunpoint and make them walk off a cliff."

Nick looked down at the weapon. It looked dangerous. Deadly. He weighed his choice for a moment. Up until this moment in the investigation he had not felt afraid. Somehow the gun brought a point of fear into him. He asked himself if he had been in denial about the risks.

"Thank you, but I'm not ready to carry a weapon."

"Okay." Stanley began wrapping the package. "But it's here if you want it."

Once Nick had closed and locked the front door behind his friend, he made his way upstairs to bed. Beth asked him who was at the door.

"It was Stanley. He thought of something and wanted my take on it. I told him it could wait 'til the morning."

"Good for you," she said. Beth felt an urge to tell him again how worried she was for his safety. But she knew better than to repeat herself, Nick would just get his hackles up. Better to let him think about her words, they would sink in eventually.

She kissed him on the cheek and curled up beside him. Nick picked up a book to read, but the words only jumbled up before his eyes.

Am I really in danger here? He didn't think that crazed killers were stalking his every move. He hoped that Stanley was too much the worrier. *A cop's occupational hazard.* He put the notion out of his head. He had enough to worry about just getting his life back together.

SIXTY-FOUR

Alex held his glass of scotch in his large hand and said to Harriet Durban, "I noticed in court the other day that your husband seems to have a short fuse. Is he always like that?"

"Short fuse?" said Harriet. "Archer has *no* self-control whatsoever. His mother tells me he was the same way when he was a kid. Why do you think I've had so many visits to the emergency room? "She had a self-pitying look in her watery eyes that made Alex want to slap her around. He wasn't surprised the husband had the same reaction.

"That's interesting," said Alex. He sipped his scotch and felt a plan emerging.

Harriet's face took on a hopeful look. "Are you thinking there's some way that his temper can land him in an accident? Is that it?"

"Perhaps. Whatever method we choose to solve your problem, I assure you there will be no police investigation *of you* other than the required queries: how long have you been married, where were you when he died. That sort of thing."

He looked hard at her, thinking of the interference Andreas might be drumming up. Would this be his last client? "We have to be certain you can stay calm under a brief police interview."

"Sure I can. I stood up to his abuse for fifteen years, didn't I? The cops don't scare me. I can play the tearful widow from now till New Year's."

"Good. Now I want you to tell me the make of your husband's car, the color, and the roads he takes to get to work."

Harriet had a playful look in her eye as she unfolded a napkin and drew the route.

After giving Harriet Durban final instructions, Alex got in his car and drove to Atlantic City for his monthly payments. He found Forest Hamilton at Trump's Casino feeding silver dollars into a slot machine at a furious rate. He stepped up to the adjoining machine, fed a dollar into it and coughed, drawing Hamilton's eyes.

A moment later Hamilton got up from his stool, leaving the plastic cup with chips in the well of the machine for Alex. As Alex slid into his place, he saw the client take a vacant seat beside him.

"The shit's coming down!" said Hamilton in a poor stage whisper.

"Keep your voice down," said Alex in a quiet voice. "You're referring to the Department of Health study?"

"Yeah! How did you know?"

"Our organization has contacts in every city agency. It's nothing to worry about. Some eager-beaver researcher published a paper about grief, and now the city is giving out a questionnaire. It means nothing."

"But why *me?* Why *now?*"

"Look," said Alex, picking up the plastic cup and stepping behind Forest. "The cops don't consider it a criminal matter; the Medical Examiner's ruling still holds; the insurance paid out in full. *There is nothing to worry about.*"

Alex stuck a finger hard into Hamilton's back. "Keep your mouth shut or you'll join your wife in eternity. We have agents everywhere, even in the justice department." Pulling his finger back, he added, "I'll see you next month. On schedule."

As he walked away, cup of chips in hand, Alex weighed the implications of Hamilton's near meltdown. The finger in the back, threatening a gun shot, was a bit theatrical, but a hard head like Hamilton needed a firm hand. Alex knew the key to his survival depended on projecting the image of a powerful, ruthless organization.

He walked to the Taj Mahal, where he found Steven Reinhold at a dollar poker machine. Once he caught Steven's eye, he walked toward the man and smoothly occupied his stool as Steven got up. The cup of chips awaited in the well of the machine.

Once again, Alex was annoyed to see his client occupy the next seat.

"What's going on with that city investigation?" asked Steven in a harsh whisper.

"Nothing's going on. We checked it out, it's a bullshit study. It's not a problem."

"I don't like it. They could get suspicious."

"Nobody suspects anything. Somebody's doing research. You're caught up this month, are you not?"

"Just about. I'm worried about the money. It could look like a pattern."

Alex picked up the cup of chips and leaned closer to Reinhold. In a harsh whisper he spit out, "*If you don't catch up in full next month, you'll end up buried beside your wife. Keep your mouth shut and pay up.*"

He locked his eyes on Reinhold for a few seconds, making sure the message was received, then got up and walked away.

At the bar, Alex felt heat rising to his face as fury erupted inside him. He had earned his fees by the sweat of his brow and the elegant turning of his mind. *Nobody's stiffing me out of my money. Not some frightened husband. And not some bureaucrat doctor with a clipboard!*

He ordered a double scotch on the rocks, and didn't even stop to admire the cleavage and long legs of the young bar maid. He had to collect the fees from the others and get back to New York. It was time to nip this public health bullshit in the bud. If the inquisitive doctor was going to disrupt his perfect business model, he was going to pay for it with his life. And the end would be filled with pain.

SIXTY-FIVE

Nicholas was planning the day's visits to the nursing homes when he answered his phone.

"This is Reed Kohlberg at the Medical Examiner's. Listen, I have another wrinkle on those accidental deaths you're working on. You want to hear it?"

"Of course."

"We queried all the funeral homes that received the bodies of the accident victims you're interested in. We believed the District Attorney may want to file subpoenas to exhume the bodies and we wanted to know where they were buried."

"Excellent. What did you find?"

"All of the bodies were cremated."

Nicholas realized immediately the implications of the information. "Do you know the incidence of cremation as opposed to burial for this population?"

"I asked at the funeral homes. They said cremation is ordered roughly thirty-five per cent of the time. That's a ballpark figure, but still…"

"It's a far cry from a hundred. Thanks, Reed, I'll pass on the information." As Nicholas hung up he smiled to think that this statistically improbable occurrence made their hypothesis even stronger. With the new information, the police would have to investigate the deaths.

He called up the database he'd constructed and made a note of the cremations. As he typed, he realized every key stroke was monitored by some shadowy government agency, and that his days at the Department of Health were certainly numbered.

I don't deserve to be fired, he told himself. The thought was accompanied by a new feeling. A *good* feeling. At least, it seemed to be good. Maybe he had done one thing right. One good deed that didn't cancel out his guilt, but it made him a little less of a failure. If his bringing the DOH data home gave Chrissie the chance to make it public, then *fine,* it didn't make him a *hero,* but he sure as hell was no criminal. *They* were the criminals, hiding the data and denying the cause of the diseases spreading among the first responders.

He was staring at the list when Libby came in. He watched her face sink as she recognized the list of accident victims on the computer screen.

"Nick, I told you to drop that study! You're in enough trouble as it is. Investigating suspicious deaths belongs to the Medical Examiner's office, not us."

"Actually, the ME just called me. He found a suspicious death of a man in divorce proceedings. Because of the information I brought them, they're reviewing all the autopsies on the accidental deaths. They asked *me* to send them everything I have on it."

"Well it's about time. At last the issue is in the appropriate hands." Stepping back out the door, she added, "Now go out and finish visiting the extended care facilities."

Once Libby had left his office, Nicholas turned off his computer, locked his desk and started for the elevator, determined to hold on to the new feeling that had buoyed his spirits. He would receive updates from Stanley as the police followed the investigation, and he would take enormous pleasure in being proven right when the police broke the criminal conspiracy.

SIXTY-SIX

Alex put on a black shirt, black jeans, and black boots, then tied a red bandanna around his neck. Having studied a World Wrestling Federation magazine, he had a pretty good idea of how a thug dressed. He'd considered shaving his head, but abandoned the idea, deciding he would be too conspicuous wearing a wig while his hair grew back.

Instead, he used a washable hair color to dye his hair an ash blonde. An earring in his right ear and a children's temporary tattoos on both hands was good for mis-identifying a suspect. The final and ultimate touch: a line of gold paint carefully applied to two front teeth, giving him a look of a poor white loser.

He drove to the Junker Rentals in Queens, leaving his car a few blocks away. After showing a fake driver's license, a handy item he'd picked up from a contact his bookie gave him, he picked out an old Ford Crown Vic. A real battle ax of a car. He had to pay a "surcharge" for not using a credit card. There were always expenses.

He got the Ford to start on the third try. A cloud of blue smoke belched from the tailpipe, the engine rumbled with a leaky muffler, and the rubber strip around the door let in sunlight, but it would perfectly serve his purpose.

Back in Brooklyn, Alex parked the car three blocks from his apartment building. He covered one of the rear taillights with red tape, making it look as if a broken lens cap had been cheaply repaired. Then he took a bumper sticker that read DON'T LAUGH, IT COULD BE YOUR DAUGHTER IN THIS CAR and fastened it to the bumper using double-stick tape. For the final touch, he replaced the old, rusty hubcaps with shiny new caps that continued to spin after the wheel stopped rotating. They were so flashy, any witness would be bound to describe them to the police.

Later that night when the street was quiet, he switched the license plates for a pair he'd taken off a car in the Bronx a week before, and *voila*, he was ready. Come seven in the morning, he would be following Archer Durban on the Henry Hutchinson from Queens. There was construction on the road, creating a bottleneck right where he wanted it.

As soon as he arrived home from work, Nicholas went to Stanley's apartment, finding him in the kitchen making a sandwich.

"Fran's got a class tonight," said Stanley. "You want something?" When Nicholas declined, Stanley led Nicholas to the study, where he had a large sheet of white paper taped to the wall. He'd made columns on the paper labeled SUSPECTS . . . METHOD . . . FLAWS . . . ALIBI . . . MONEY TRAIL.

"I thought we agreed to quit the investigation," said Nicholas.

"The Feds have taken up the case, but that doesn't mean we can't play with the information. Just for the hell of it." He tapped the column labeled FLAWS. "This is where your average criminal screws up. No matter how careful he is in the planning, there's usually a hole in the operation somewhere, if you know where to look for it."

Nicholas pointed to the row for Laura Metcalf. The entry read: *wet laundry soap on stairwell.* "You think my science experiment is valid."

"Hey, if I was the DA, I'd put you on the stand as an expert witness." Explaining that he'd gone back to Laura Metcalf's apartment building to speak to the residents, Stanley added that a resident who worked on Wall Street had seen a black UPS delivery guy going through the lobby around the time that Laura was killed. "UPS doesn't deliver to private residence at six am. I checked."

Stanley tapped the words *suspicious horse shoe* in Meredith Hamilton's entry. "I compared a photo of Meredith Hamilton's head injury with the shoe from the horse she was riding. Not a match." Stanley made the motions of a baseball player swinging a bat. "They probably nailed the shoe to a baseball bat or an ax handle."

Nick noted that the two suspects had been out of town at the time of their spouse's death. "I don't know how to derive a statistic for that parameter, but if that pattern holds up, it's got to be strong evidence of a conspiracy."

"It gives each spouse an alibi. The organizers didn't think about it establishing a pattern."

"I've got another pattern for you." Nicholas told Stan that every one of the victims had been cremated. "I understand the typical incidence is around thirty-five per cent."

Stanley chewed his sandwich as he added the word 'cremation' in the FLAW column for each suspect.

Nicholas asked about the entry, *suspicious tire* under Zachariah Thorne's name. Stanley explained that most blowouts on SUV's were from separated tread, not a weakening of the sidewall. They discussed how Vinnie Solomira's boat was probably doctored, causing it to sink when the engine was stopped.

"It's really quite an impressive set of crimes, don't you think?" said Nick. He thought about how much he'd enjoyed his investigative work, and how boring the liaison with the nursing homes was. "I wish I could interview the rest of the survivors, but I guess the police have already brought them in for questioning."

"They haven't talked to anybody yet. The Feds are slow as molasses getting into a new case."

"What are they waiting for, another ten victims in the morgue?"

"We have to wait for the U.S. District Attorney to issue subpoenas. They'll haul the suspects in and hold them. It only takes one to turn on the others and the whole organization comes down."

Nick was angry at the delay, but he understood there was nothing he could do to speed them up. It was the same with the city government, the bureaucracy moved at its own pace. Ranting and raving just seemed to slow it down further.

After they agreed that Stanley would summarize all the data for the DA, Nick returned to his own apartment, finding it empty. Beth was serving on a school committee, and Chrissie was probably off with Lucas doing he didn't want to know what. There was leftover Mexican food in the fridge. He warmed up the rice and beans and half a burrito, carried it to the living room and read the paper as he ate. The obituaries didn't mention any accidental deaths.

He wondered if the organization had canceled its murder business. Or had they taken up some new approach that no one had identified? He found a special satisfaction in knowing that the entire investigation had begun because of his long-standing habit of reading the obits. Now wasn't that ironic: an interest in natural deaths uncovering a murder racket.

In the street below a scruffy guy with greasy tangled hair and shabby clothes picked through a bag of recycling. As he collected bottles and cans worth five cents at the market, he kept glancing up at the Andreas apartment. He saw Nicholas settle into a chair and eat his dinner. The apartment seemed otherwise empty.

Alex decided to remain in the neighborhood as long as he could stay without attracting attention, in the hope that tonight Andreas fell into the trap he'd set. There was no way to predict *when* it would happen. Although this particular killing would be as brilliant as all the others, it's one drawback was that the timing was wholly unpredictable. Nevertheless, if the date and time of Andreas's fatal accident was uncertain, the outcome was a foregone conclusion.

SIXTY-SEVEN

Dressed in worn out clothes and an old baseball cap turned backward, Alex followed Archer Durban on the Henry Hutchinson Parkway, the trees on the side of the road showing their Fall colors. He rested his left arm on the windowsill of the old car, glanced at his hand and admired the fake tattoo of a snake. It was big enough to be seen by a driver in another car.

Traffic on the Hutch wasn't bad, he was driving against the bulk of the commuters coming into the city. The cocky son of a bitch stayed in the left hand lane, even when he wasn't passing someone.

Five miles before the Mamaroneck Road exit, Alex passed Durban on the right, then swerved into the left lane, just barely missing the other car's front bumper. Alex heard a long, loud horn blast as his quarry vented his anger.

Alex lowered the window and flipped Durban the finger. He let up on the gas and allowed the old car to slow down. In his rearview mirror he saw fury on Durban's face.

Finding himself forced to slow down, Durban brought his car within inches of the Crown Victoria's bumper and leaned on his horn again. He stuck his head out of his window and released a string of expletives, then pulled over to the right lane to pass.

When Alex saw Durban moving to the right lane, he hit the gas and swerved over as well, releasing a plume of blue smoke that entered Durban's open window. Durban released a fresh blast on the horn and another string of curses.

Switching in tandem back to the left lane, they passed a truck, with Durban inches from Alex's rear bumper and still leaning on the horn. Alex could see the truck driver watching Durban as they passed. Once they passed the truck, Alex slowed again, keeping in his lane. Durban jerked his steering wheel, passed Alex on the right, and swept back into Alex's lane.

Alex sped up, nearly hitting Durban's rear bumper. He passed Durban on the shoulder, eliciting more curses and honking. Durban tried to pass on the right and on the left, but Alex weaved across the lanes, blocking him every time, the truck driver watching the bizarre scene unfold. Alex was confident that the truck driver, now a considerable distance behind them, would be able to testify that a crazy blonde guy with tattoo in an old white car had driven like a maniac.

Approaching the exit that Durban always took, Alex raced down the ramp and came to a screeching stop at the stop sign. Durban pulled up beside him and leapt from his vehicle, his face red and contorted with rage. Durban charged at Alex's car, just as Alex knew he would. When Durban grabbed the handle to the door and jerked it open, Alex pulled the trigger on the pistol in his hand, sending two shots into the victim's chest. Durban fell onto the macadam, convulsed for several seconds as if jolted by an electric current, then lay still.

Putting his car in gear, Alex saw the same truck driver rubber-necking as he rolled past the exit with the body in the road. Alex pulled out onto the side street and gunned the motor just as a woman in a Toyota came toward him. Alex sped along the narrow street, putting distance between himself and the scene of the crime.

Having planned his escape route carefully, Alex drove south on secondary roads. He made his way back to the car rental, where he left the car, keys in the ignition, having removed the bumper sticker and replacing the hub caps and license plate. The gloves he'd worn left no fingerprints behind; if the cops *did* somehow identify the car, the fake ID and the disguise would send the cops searching for a non-existent driver.

He hurried along the street to a subway stop carrying a nylon gym bag. Passing through the turnstile, he found an empty spot behind a girder, where he removed the earring and took off his hat and ratty coat, revealing a neat suit jacket, crisp white shirt and tie, and dress pants. He dropped the clothes into the gym bag and took out a black raincoat. After using a disposable cleaning cloth to wipe away the tattoos on his hands, he emerged from the shadows, a nondescript business type waiting to make the commute into Manhattan. He crossed to the other side of the tracks and waited for the next train. Once safely aboard the subway, he would discard the bag of clothes in a dumpster far from the scene.

Seeing an ad in Spanish for a beauty school, with a foxy young woman showing her cleavage and smiling, he decided to hire a Hispanic prostitute. After all, if the heat was on and he had to leave for Mexico early, well, he could eke out a good life on what he'd already collected.

The one annoying issue was, he didn't know if Dr. Andreas had fallen into the trap. Was he lying on a stretcher waiting for the autopsy, or was he at work with the other drones? Alex decided to stop at the doctor's neighborhood and hang around, there was a tot lot and benches on the sidewalk where seniors sat and ruminated on their last days.

If Andreas was dead, it would be the talk of the neighborhood.

SIXTY-EIGHT

Nicholas sat in his office planning the route that would take him to another group of nursing homes. His distemper over the menial job was heightened by his anger over the FBI's lack of progress. Here it was the first week of December and the Organized Crime Task Force had still made no arrests. No charges filed. The suspects were still enjoying their inheritances.

What the hell were they waiting for?

He opened the file on the death rates of the divorcees and looked at the tables. The statistical analysis was strong; no one could believe that the mortality rates were a random occurrence. What's more, the hundred per cent rate of cremation was hugely improbable. The two surviving spouses he had interviewed being out of town at the time of the deaths was equally unlikely. It was a criminal conspiracy, no doubt about it.

He looked over the copy of the casino visits that Stanley had given him. Like the first Western epidemiologist, who noted that all of the victims of a cholera epidemic in London had drawn their water from the same well — a well that he closed, ending the epidemic — Nicholas had looked for patterns. Coincidences. Commonalities.

All the spouses had visited Atlantic City casinos on the same days. *Drinking from the same polluted well.* But they hadn't always visited on the same day of the month. That was puzzling. They'd gone to AC on the seventh of July; on the eight of August; the ninth of September…

He froze. The days of the month were a progression, each month one day later than the last. *And*, the *day* of the month was the same ordinal value as the month's number in the year. He kicked himself for being so stupid not to see it when Stanley showed him the credit card receipts.

He looked up at the calendar on the wall: It was December twelve. *The twelfth day of the twelfth month.* The FBI had to get this information immediately so they could capture the delivery on film and arrest the suspects in the act of paying.

He called Stanley, but the answering service was on. He tried his friend's cell phone and got voice mail again.

Cursing, he fished around his desk for Fran's number. He didn't have it, having never needed to phone her at work. What was the name of her company? Beltway, something or other. Or was it Thruway? Or Parkway?

Christ! Why didn't he keep numbers at hand the way Beth did. She was so organized. So—

He grabbed the phone and called his wife's cell. He had no idea when she would be out of class and in the teacher's lounge, but if he was lucky just this once...

At the third ring he heard Beth's voice say, "This is Beth Andreas."

"Beth? It's Nick."

"Hi." Her voice became tense. "What's wrong? You never call me at work."

"I'm fine. I need to get hold of Stanley, and he's not answering his phone. Have you got Fran's number at work?"

"Yes it's right here. I — " She broke off in mid-sentence. "Is this about that murder investigation? You promised to drop it, Nick."

"I did drop it. I just realized something important. I need Stanley to call it in to the Feds is all." She grumbled but gave him the number.

He called Fran, who told him that Stanley was probably at the sports gym. "His doctor okay'd him doing light weights." Like Beth, she made Nicholas promise that they weren't planning on doing anything themselves.

Nick called the gym and asked them to page Stanley Bezlin, saying it was a family emergency. The throbbing music that sounded when the secretary put him on hold gave him a headache. The music blared on and on. Why couldn't the secretary realize this was a matter of life and death. Especially death.

Nick was afraid that the secretary in the gym had given up trying to find Stanley, when he heard his friend's voice. He quickly explained what he had discovered about the dates of the payments, pointing out that the next set of payments was due today.

"That's not much lead time," said Stanley. "I'll call my friend on the Task Force. They might be able to put *some* kind of surveillance together."

"Call me as soon as you hear something," said Nick.

Stanley promised to let Nick know what the Feds would do and hung up, leaving Nick with nothing to do but go back to the mundane world of nursing homes and vaccinations, while the authorities were missing a chance to stop this gang from carrying out its methodical string of murders.

SIXTY-NINE

Alex sat across from Anna Darling in the midtown coffee shop. The blinking Christmas lights over the counter and in the front window gave the place a cheery look. Bing Crosby sang of a white Christmas, although the long term forecast was for cold rain, which suited Alex just fine. He wasn't expecting any gifts.

"What exactly did you mean outside the courthouse yesterday when you told me you were going to make my Christmas a merry one?" asked Anna. She was an aging forty-something who starved herself to retain the thin body of her youth, but years of hard drinking and smoking left her looking shriveled and cadaverous.

Alex had watched the lawyer appointed to represent the children's interests testify about Anna's drinking and her failure to attend a single parent teacher conference. Hearing about her leaving the pre-teens home alone with nothing but peanut butter and moldy white bread to eat while she sat in the local bar for hours had visibly annoyed the judge. Anna's protests of blackouts had only made her look worse. The writing was on the blackboard. Rupert Darling was going to get the kids.

Alex stirred sugar in his cup and took a sip. "It's very simple, really. Your husband, the Grinch, is trying to take everything you hold dear away from you. Your children, your home….Even your new car."

"Do you believe that bum stopped making the lease payments? *I love my Lexus.* How am I supposed to drive the kids to school?"

Alex offered a look of sympathy. "My organization has a simple, effective solution to your dilemma. We will remove him from your life, and from his own life. We will make it appear as an accident. And we will guarantee the results or you pay us nothing."

"You're kidding, right? You're working for the dick. Right?"

Alex's eyes twinkled with holiday merriment. "Oh no, my dear. This Christmas season I'm playing Santa, and I am giving you exactly what you wished for." He sipped his coffee and completed his pitch, seeing her eyes light up when he assured her she would be losing her husband with no police investigation.

"Tell me more about your husband. I need to know his habits. His hobbies. That sort of thing."

"He's a royal pain. He makes a big show about the Christmas spirit, but it's all about him. He has to have the biggest car. He's driving an Escalade, for god's sake. He was going to get a Hummer, but it wouldn't fit in our garage."

Alex pictured their Bay Ridge house, a modest colonial three blocks from the water.

"Tell me more."

"Every year he goes ape shit putting up Christmas lights around the house, over the garage, on the roof."

"Did you say 'on the roof'? Where, exactly?"

"Everywhere! He puts these stupid figures of Santa and his reindeer around the chimney like he was gonna climb down and burn his ass. Rupert always has to have the biggest and the flashiest display. He doesn't even go to church!"

Alex pictured the hapless fool tumbling off his roof. Falls were the number one cause of accidental death. "Tell me, Anna. Does he usually put up the lights during the day, or does he ever work on them at night?"

"During the day. Usually he puts them up on a Saturday morning. It's dark by the time he gets home from work. He'd be crazy to put the things up at night."

"Hmm. I want you to urge him to start his lighting during the week. Tell him you hear there's a storm coming on the weekend and it would be dangerous to go up when it was icy and wet. Get him to go up on the roof Wednesday after he gets home from work."

"Wednesday. It'll be getting pretty dark by then."

"Have him put on all the floodlights."

"How do you know about the flood–" Anna stopped when she realized that she was dealing with a professional organization that did their research before making a business proposal. That knowledge reassured her.

"Once your husband has started getting his tools together, go over to a neighbor's house and stay there until the police come looking for you."

"I could go across the street to Harriet's and bake Christmas cookies."

"That will do well. Next Wednesday, send your husband up to the roof as soon as he gets home and remain with your neighbor until the police find you." He dropped some money on the table and, turning to leave, added, "Oh, and, have a merry Christmas."

Anna Darling toasted him with her coffee cup. Pleased with the promise of a bright new year, she added a shot of Irish whiskey from a flask in her purse to her second cup of coffee.

SEVENTY

Nicholas sat at his desk, restless and irritated, waiting to hear back from Stanley about what the Feds were going to do in Atlantic City. He glanced at the clock on the wall. The second hand's advance mimicked the glacial passage of time. Any thought of going out to visit nursing homes was extinguished by the urgency of this call. It was maddening to think the Feds would let this golden opportunity slip by them.

The phone rang. He grabbed the receiver before the tone had completed.

"Talk to me!"

"I couldn't get through to my friend on the Task Force, he's in some kind of high-level meeting. I left a message for him to call my cell as soon as he got out."

"Jesus Christ! You told them this was no time to dick around, didn't you?"

"You don't tell the Feds to put it in second gear, it only makes them move slower."

Nick squeezed the receiver, his anger growing. He asked if Stanley could call the police in Atlantic City.

"No chance. It'd take somebody a lot higher up the NYD food chain than me to get them to set up a surveillance team, especially this fast. Besides, you don't know if the officer you're talking to has friends in the casinos."

Nick cursed. "What the hell do we do—*nothing?*"

Stanley was silent for a few second. "Wait a sec! I know an ex-cop who works in security at the Taj. I bet I could watch for Steven Reinhold from the surveillance booth. That's where he made his payoff. We couldn't make an arrest, but we'd have them on tape, it would make a slam dunk case for the Feds."

"All right, let's do it. I'm coming with you."

Stanley reminded Nicholas he'd promised Beth he was dropping the investigation.

"This is different," said Nick. "What do cops call it? 'Exigent circumstances'?"

"Christ. Another *Law & Order* expert."

"Besides, I need to keep an eye on you."

"Okay. I'll pick you up in thirty minutes."

Nicholas hung up. He wrote a note for his supervisor saying he had a family emergency and had to leave work. Then he hurried downstairs and out to the street. As he waited for Stanley to arrive, he called Beth and got her voice mail. Annoyed that he couldn't speak to her directly, he left a message that he was going to Atlantic City with Stanley and would call her when he arrived.

He could already hear his wife's furious voice. Well, if she didn't understand that the investigation was giving Stanley new life, too bad. Stanley needed to do it, and Nick needed to watch over his friend. End of story.

After leaving Anna Darling in the coffee shop, Alex went to a theatrical costume store, where he rented an old, worn out Santa Claus suit. He stowed the suit in the trunk of his car. As he opened the driver's door, he looked up and saw the gray sky. Even with the threat of freezing rain, Alex was filled with the Christmas spirit, knowing he was granting a miserable woman her fondest wish and that there were many friends in Atlantic City waiting to give him gifts.

Driving over the Verrazano Bridge, he asked himself for the hundredth time why that fucking Grinch, Andreas, had to stick his nose into his business and interview the clients? If the police *were* involved, it was time to cut his losses and split for Mexico. He wouldn't have the million bucks he'd been counting on, but there was enough to carry him for a long time. Life was cheap south of the border.

There was still a chance that Andreas's public health visits had been innocent after all. Stanley Bezlin lived down the hall from Andreas, so maybe their hanging out meant nothing. Maybe it was all just a coincidence.

Or maybe the police already *did* start questioning his clients, threatening to charge them with conspiracy to commit murder. He had little faith all of them would hold up under the pressure. Especially the women. They were emotional; they would crack under pressure.

If one of them had cut a deal and was wearing a wire, he'd show it in his face. And voice, liars always gave themselves away by talking too much. Alex planned to scrutinize each one of them for signs of nervousness, while he remained cool as ice.

It was risky, taking this last round of payments, but what other option did he have? He needed this round of payments before hitting the road. Then it was on to the next business startup. Life was full of opportunities, there was always a market for murder.

It would be a shame to miss watching Andreas go to his grave with the little woman sniffling behind the coffin, once the trap he had set was sprung. Well, it would all be in the news, he'd read the New York papers every day until it showed up. He might even send the wife a sympathy card.

He drove south through Staten Island and on to the New Jersey Turnpike. His senses were at their peak, his mind racing with possibilities. Opportunities. Strategies. He had never felt so alive. Putting the car on cruise control, he found a radio station playing Christmas music and settled in for the drive, secure in the knowledge that whatever the police did, he would come out on top.

SEVENTY-ONE

Driving south on the New Jersey Turnpike with Nicholas in the passenger seat, Stanley said, "These Federal agents are as useful as tits on a bull. They can't even answer a phone call that will blow their case wide open?"

"They're like the Department of Health, they're ruled by protocols," said Nicholas.

"And just to make things interesting, I heard about another death, and this one's a hoot."

"What was it, another motor vehicle accident?"

"Even better. It was a shooting on the highway. The witnesses say it looked like a case of road rage, but I checked on the victim and, guess what? He was facing a tough divorce."

"You think the gang has changed their method?"

"I would, if I thought somebody was investigating my crew, and we know at least one of the spouses told them about your interview or they wouldn't have known to call your boss and ask about it."

"I hope your ex-cop can get us in to watch for the payments from the security booth," said Nicholas.

"*I* can watch."

Nick gave his friend a questioning look.

"My buddy can get me inside on account of my being a cop. He's not gonna tell his boss I'm out on permanent disability. Getting you in won't be so easy."

"What if I show them my Department of Health ID?"

"They'll think you're looking for some kind of weird disease. Let's see how it plays out. Worst case scenario, you hang out at the bar and I'll keep you updated by cell phone."

"Fine. We'll start at the Taj Mahal, right? That's where Steven Reinhold made his payments."

Stanley said, "As long as you keep out of sight. You interviewed him. If he spots you, he won't make the payment and it'll show our hand."

Nicholas agreed to lay low at the bar, his cell phone on vibrate so as not to draw attention. And then he had another idea how he might walk through the casino unnoticed.

Beth listened to her cell phone voice messages after finishing her last class of the day. She was stunned by Nick's message about going to Atlantic City with Stanley. He had *promised.* Swore he was taking himself out of danger.

Nick had no idea how much it would devastate her and Chrissie if he were killed. She didn't think she'd be able to work. The thought of identifying his body made her feel cold and lifeless.

She was almost as angry with Stanley. *Some friend.* He probably proposed it, and Nicholas, mister I'm-not-afraid-of-anything, went right along with him.

Shaking with anger and fear, she left the school and walked to the subway. Finding a quiet spot outside the entrance, she called his cell phone.

"Hel-lo?" Nick's voice was a little broken up with static.

"Nicholas? *What the hell do you mean you're going to Atlantic City with Stanley?* You promised to leave everything to the police!"

"I know I did. We tried to contact the Feds, but Stanley couldn't get through."

"Then why didn't you wait until he talked to them? They're paid to put their lives on the line. You're not. And neither is Stanley, *he's* not on active duty."

"Because we realized that the conspirators will be making their monthly payments *today.* Stanley's going to sit up in the surveillance booth and watch them. I'm going to sit at the bar and wait for him to get it on tape. Then we'll turn the tapes over to the Feds. Nobody's going to be in any danger. I promise."

"Oh, great. You'll be sitting in a casino investigating a mob murder ring surrounded by who? *The mob!*"

"I'll be careful. I promise."

"Call me as soon as you're done. If I'm not home I'll be with Fran.

"I will. I—"

Click. She had hung up.

As the car approached the exit for Atlantic City, Nick looked at Stanley, who shrugged. "She's gonna worry. You can't stop 'em. I heard it the whole time I was on the force, even though I always said I was safer patrolling the neighborhood than somebody crossing Flatbush Avenue against the light."

They finished the last miles in silence.

SEVENTY-TWO

Alex drove into Atlantic City and parked his car in the street. He wanted to be able to get out of town in a hurry and not fool around with a parking garage. Besides, the garages had video cameras. Since 9/11 they'd been taping cars that came and went. That meant license plates. And faces.

As he walked across town to the strip, he felt a wave of sadness tingled with an electric current of anticipation. There might be a jackpot waiting for him or a pair of handcuffs. Even if there was no sign of police interest in his business, he knew this would probably be his last round of collections. The anticipation got his juices flowing. He felt light on his heels. Danger was his business, and murder was his game. He didn't rely on luck and he didn't need to play any odds; he was the master of his fate; the bringer of new life and old fashioned death.

In the Taj Mahal, Stanley introduced Nicholas to his friend, Ed Deas, and filled the security guard in on the case.

Deas said, "I'll tell you, Stan, if some crime group is using *our* casino to make payoffs, you better believe we want them outta here. Come on upstairs."

"What about me?" said Nicholas.

"Sorry, doc, my boss didn't go for it. If it were the kitchen you were lookin' at, okay, but our security offices are off limits."

Nick agreed to stay out of sight and wait for Stanley's call. Left on his own, he went to the gift shop, where he bought silver-reflective sunglasses, a Hawaiian shirt and a straw hat. He went to the bathroom and changed, stowing his own shirt in the plastic customer bag. He looked in the mirror, liked what he saw. *I'm going undercover.* Chuckling, he went out to the floor to wait for Stanley's call.

Upstairs in the surveillance room, Stanley sat with Ed watching the bank of cameras. He'd given his friend photos of the suspects. On the multiple screens patrons passed by in a constant stream. Several cameras viewed them from above, making it difficult to identify individuals, while others were level with them and gave a straight-on view.

"How do you like the security work?" Stanley asked.

"It beats riding a patrol car. Nobody's shooting at me."

"That's a plus."

"What about you? I heard you were real sick for a while."

"Ticker gave me trouble."

"Yeah? That's tough." Ed studied the cameras for a minute. He thought he saw one of the suspects, but after zooming in on the guy he decided it was somebody else.

"I'll tell you what. You ever need work, I can get you in down here. The hours are great and it's not as dirty as police work."

"Thanks. I don't wanna leave New York."

"I hear you. Well maybe they'll get the casinos."

"We already got 'em," said Stanley. "Wall Street."

"True."

Stanley sat forward and pointed at a shapely blonde moving through the casino.

"Victoria Hodges," he said.

"Damn, she's hard to miss," said Ed.

Stanley called Nick on his cell and told him where Victoria was heading. Nick spotted her just as she sat down at one of the poker machines. He took a spot across from her and fed a twenty into the slot machine. He made dollar bets as he watched her play.

Up in the booth, Stanley and Ed watched as Victoria sat at the poker machine playing a leisurely game. She fed a bill into the machine and played several hands, occasionally glancing around at the other players.

"She's looking for her contact," said Stanley.

Victoria played for another half hour. Finally she got up from her seat and moved away, leaving a joker in a cowboy hat to take her place.

"No contact," said Stanley. "She just walked out."

He followed Victoria's figure across several cameras as she walked across the casino. She passed through the exit, with Nicholas not far behind her. Stanley cursed when he saw the 'disguise' his friend had adopted. "Damn fool's gonna get himself killed," he muttered. He lost sight of them when they stepped out to the street.

Ed said he thought the pickup was going to be at his casino. Stanley shrugged, not sure what was going on. "Nick will stay with her. We'll know soon enough."

Stanley waited, tapping his foot on the carpet, anxious to hear from his friend. All he could do was sit in the booth and wait for a phone call, and hope that Nick was all right on his own. He wished his friend had taken the gun.

After an eternity of waiting, Stanley's cell phone rang.

"Talk to me," Stanley said.

"I followed her to the parking garage. She got her car from the valet and drove off. She didn't stop to talk to anybody."

"That's really weird," said Stanley. "Unless the valet was her contact."

"I don't think so. I got a good look, and she definitely only gave him a tip."

"Shit. You better come back inside. Steven Reinhold should show up any minute."

"I'm on my way." Nick cursed himself for missing the opportunity to catch Victoria passing her payment on. Where did she do it? At the cashier's? It was maddening to think she'd slipped through their fingers. He hoped the rest of the day would not be a waste of time.

And where the hell was the fucking FBI?

SEVENTY-THREE

After taking Victoria's place at the slot machine, Alex placed his hand on the plastic cup that was waiting for him in the well. He reached into his pocket for some quarters and fed the machine. As he pressed the button to select a card, he glanced around the room looking for anyone suspicious. Nobody seemed to be looking his way. There were tired seniors bent over their machines, and a young Asian couple sharing a seat chattering as they played.

Alex played the machine for exactly fifteen minutes; long enough to dispel any sense that he had only sat down to connect with his client. He rose, cup in hand with his cowboy hat low over his forehead, and walked to the cashier, where he cashed the thousand- and hundred-dollar chips. He folded the bills in a gold clip and tucked it in his pocket. The first of today's payments. So far there was no sign of the police. Maybe he was in the clear after all.

He walked through the casino looking for the other clients. After a few moments he spotted Steven Reinhold seated at a nickel poker machine. The cheapskate was playing the least expensive machine in the whole place. Unbelievable. Alex swore that if the bastard came up light in a payment one more time he would kill the man for the satisfaction, and damn the consequences.

When Reinhold saw him, he gave Alex a little nod of his head.

Subtle bastard, thought Alex. He took a seat at a nearby machine and began to play. Between hands he looked around the room, seeing nothing suspicious.

As Reinhold rose from his chair, Alex stepped around him to take the seat, muttering, "If you're light, I'm putting your name on the list. You'll join your wife at the cemetery."

Steven froze where he stood. "It's all there!" hissed Reinhold. The man squared his shoulders and walked away.

Alex looked into the plastic cup, saw a number of high value chips, but couldn't tell what their total came to. He rammed a quarter into the machine and punched the button. The machine dealt a hand of poker. Alex selected a card without caring if he won or lost and looked at his watch. *Fifteen minutes to play, and it was on to another payment.*

Stanley and Ed watched Steven Reinhold set a cup of coins in the well of the machine, then pull a bill from his pocket and feed it into the machine. Stan had alerted Nick, who again positioned himself close enough to see Reinhold, but not too close to be spotted.

"It's a replay of Victoria," Stanley said to Ed. "He's playing poker."

"Well, it *is* a casino."

They watched Steven play several more hands. He glanced around the room, his eyes seeming to look for somebody, then resumed his game.

"Watch his hands," said Ed. "You see how he reaches into his pocket and comes up with a bill, then he feeds the bill in and plays the credit on it?"

"Yeah…" Stanley peered at the figure on the video display. "He's not dipping into the cup of coins."

They watched the suspect play another hand. He did not once reach into the plastic cup in front of him. Finally he stood up and stepped back from the poker machine, leaving the cup behind as another patron wearing a cowboy hat took his place.

Stanley pointed at the screen. "Son of a bitch! He left his chips at the machine!"

Ed slapped his friend in the back. "Not only that, the guy with the cowboy hat taking his place is the same one who took the machine from the girl your buddy followed out the exit."

"The payment's in the cup," said Stanley. "It's pure genius."

They watched Reinhold walk away. The cowboy hat continued playing poker without looking up and never reaching into the cup for coins.

"I'll rewind the shot of Victoria Hodges," said Ed. He pulled up the video on another screen and moved back to the moment when Victoria got out of her chair. The guy in the cowboy hat was the same. Ed and Stanley watched as he assumed custody of her cup of chips.

"We need to follow the bag man," said Stanley. He called Nick on the cell phone and gave him a description of the guy.

"I see him," said Nick.

After several minutes the fellow left the machine and carried his cup of chips to the cashier. Stanley and Ed followed the man on the video screens as he received cash for his chips and then made his way to the exit. As he approached the doors, the camera caught him in profile.

"I don't fucking believe it," said Stanley.

"You know the guy?"

"Sure I know him. He's a drunk name of Alex Germaine. What the fuck is a two-bit, out of print writer doing collecting money for the mob?"

Stanley's heart sped up when he saw Nick in his Hawaiian shirt and mirror shades follow Alex out the door. He was afraid his friend had no idea what kind of people he was dealing with. Shadowing a mob bag man was a good way to get himself killed.

SEVENTY-FOUR

After following the man in the cowboy hat to Bally's, where the bag man settled into a seat at a slot machine, Nick called in his location to Stanley. Stanley warned him to keep his distance and to lay low, but to watch if he took charge of a cup of coins left by another patron at a machine. He reminded Nick that the people they were dealing with invented cement overshoes.

Nick smiled as he sat down at a poker machine with his back to the subject. Setting his mirrored sunglasses on the machine, he watched Alex Germaine in the reflection in the glasses. It wasn't long before Alex got up and took a freshly vacated seat. Sure enough, there was a cup of coins nested in the ledge of the machine. Germaine played the game for what seemed like an hour, but by his watch Nick saw that it was exactly fifteen minutes. The bag man got up, plastic cup in hand, and walked to the cashier's.

As Germaine repeated the scenario at another machine, Stanley joined Nick at a spot out of view from the suspect. They saw Forest Hamilton take a seat not far from Germaine. Since Hamilton was one of two spouses he had interviewed, Nick kept his mirrored sun glasses on and stayed hidden behind a slot machine.

When Forest Hamilton got up from his chair, Germaine took his seat. He played for several minutes, using coins from his pocket, then repeated the pattern, going to the cashier's to cash in the cup of money.

"Germaine knows you," said Nick. "I'll follow him if he leaves the casino and keep you posted on your cell."

"That's a *terrible* idea. I can't let anything happen to you, Beth would never forgive me. She would—"

"Gotta go," whispered Nick. He took off after Germaine, following him out of the casino, with Stanley keeping a safe distance behind his friend in the Hawaiian shirt and aviator glasses.

Stanley had a hunch that since the mob was using Germaine to collect their payments, they would watch their bag man closely. But as hard as he looked, Stanley could not find any tough guys appearing to take an interest in their quarry.

When Germaine left the boardwalk and walked westward, Nick followed, keeping his distance. A cold rain had begun to fall. After several blocks he saw Germaine get into an old blue Ford Escort. Blue smoke belched from the exhaust as the driver turned in the direction of the expressway.

Cursing, Nick took out his cell phone, only to find Stanley walking rapidly toward him.

"Christ, Nick, you're gonna give me two heart attacks and a stroke."

"Are you short of breath?"

"Short? I feel like there's a gorilla sitting on my chest." He took a moment to rest, adding, "You gotta remember, these bastards know a whole lot about you. That cheesy disguise wouldn't fool a ten year old."

"You're worried about those cement overshoes."

"Damn straight. Come on, let's get the car. Maybe we can catch up with mister moneybags. He's probably heading for the Atlantic City Expressway."

"You think he's going back to Brooklyn?"

"No way to know, but if he was gonna turn the money over in AC, I don't see why he'd drive to it."

Nicholas ran ahead and retrieved Stanley's car, saving his friend from any further exertion. Stanley took over the driver's seat and blasted out of the parking lot. He hit the highway and ran the car up to eighty, ignoring the danger of a wet road from the freezing rain. He passed a Honda on the right, crossed to the left lane and edged up to ninety. He ignored the entrance to the Garden State Parkway and continued west.

"You're betting he took the Turnpike," said Nick.

"I like the truck stops for a bag man. It's classic."

Stanley turned up the fan and blew air across the windshield, clearing a bit of fog. His eyes focused on the road ahead as if he were sighting along the barrel of a gun.

"You're lucky you don't have to sweat a ticket," said Nicholas.

Stanley chuckled. He weaved through traffic while his friend searched for the blue Escort. There was no sign of the car the entire stretch of the A.C. Expressway. They took the exit for the Turnpike and headed north to New York, passing trucks and cars of all types, but not Germaine's old Ford.

As he drove out of town on the Atlantic City Expressway, Alex congratulated himself on spotting Nicholas Andreas in the casino, despite the man's mirror shades and awful Hawaiian shirt. *Rank amateur.* He'd spied the physician just before collecting from Forest Hamilton. Alex suspected that the physician had been following Hamilton, having interviewed the man over that supposed grief thing. Since Andreas didn't know that Alex even existed, Germaine was confident he hadn't been spotted.

He had no doubt that ex cop Bezlin was around, too. How had they figured out where he was making his collections? The how didn't matter, it meant the game was up. It wouldn't be safe going home. He'd have to ditch his car as well.

It must have had something to do with work at the Department of Health. It didn't come from the Medical Examiner, the deaths were all ruled accidental. It had to have been something in the public health service. Maybe Andreas's questionnaire about mourning had uncovered some piece of information that raised a question. But what? How?

Or maybe it was the deaths themselves. Those pinhead bureaucrats kept all kinds of information on how many people died from different causes. How many gunshot victims. How many overdoses. How many children beaten to death in the home. They were filthy with statistics.

Did they count how many people died from accidents? Could they be *that anal?*

Whatever they did, something must have caught the pesky doctor's eye. The nosey bastard had told his cop neighbor, and now the two of them had ruined his beautiful business. After all the care and sweat it took to build it up, the retirement plan was beginning to unravel. Alex felt a rising tide of righteous indignation.

But if Andreas and Bezlin were shadowing him, why hadn't the police taken him while he was inside one of the casinos? And why hadn't they interrogated his clients? He was sure he would have seen the fear in their eyes if the cops had sweated them. Especially the women.

The only thing that made sense was that the cops were building a case against him and would be breaking down his door as soon as they had all their ducks in a row. The knock on the door could come at any time.

Which meant it was time to turn tail and split for Mexico. He had his money in a safe account under a different name. He'd don a fresh disguise and split under a new name, the fake ID was solid. Good enough to get him across the border where he could hang for awhile. When it was safe to come back north he had the new business plan ready to launch. It would all work out in the end. Right after pulling off one last job.

He had promised Anna Darling to take care of her husband, Rupert. The woman was counting on a merry Christmas. It wouldn't be fair to disappoint her.

As for Dr. Andreas, the meddling prick had stumbled upon the most elegant murder scheme ever devised and pulled the plug on it. He *had* to fall into the trap that was waiting for him, it was only a matter of time. The weekend promised fair weather. That should be enough to entice the bastard into his trap. It was a beautifully engineered death.

Patience: the mother's milk of success. Alex was certain his last murder in New York would be his most satisfying.

SEVENTY-FIVE

As Stanley hurled the car down the left lane of the Turnpike, he and Nick reviewed what they'd seen in the casino. They had no doubt that the cup of chips held the monthly payments.

"Fucking Alex Germaine," said Stanley. "How low can you go?"

"Isn't he the guy who sucker punched you at the mystery writers dinner?"

"That's him. He's a drunk. Been out of print for years."

"Could he be behind the operation?"

"That sleaze? I can't see it, his stories are derivative and his characters are one-dimensional. I don't figure him for the imagination. Or the balls."

"You don't see him carrying out the murders," said Nicholas.

"He's probably just a bag man for the mob. My guess is he came up short to his loan shark, he wasn't making any money on his writing, and they told him work for them or learn to get around the city in a wheelchair."

Nick told his friend that as much as he was enjoying the hunt, he'd promised Beth that they would turn the investigation over to the authorities. Stanley promised that he would call his contact in the Organized Crime Task Force as soon as they got home and tell him how to contact his friend Ed at the Taj. The security tapes would be enough to bring an arrest order on Germaine. The two-bit hack would no doubt sing like a canary as soon as he was arrested.

Spotting a rest stop, Stanley crossed three lanes and shot into the exit, raising furious complaints from several drivers. He drove through the lot, both men scanning the parked cars. When the blue Ford did not appear, he drove to the truck stop region and slowly cruised between the big rigs.

"Bastard's not here," said Stanley.

"Could he have gone south?"

"He would if he made us, but I don't see how, I kept out of sight and he doesn't know you from Adam." Stanley turned back toward the plaza. "They *could* make your face, they know where you work. Even with your expert disguise."

"Guess I should leave the tracking to the pros."

"You want I should take out your appendix?"

Nick removed his Hawaiian shirt and took out the staid dress shirt from the shopping bag, while Stanley eased the car back onto the highway.

Stanley said, "Ya know, if I haul ass, we can probably get back to Brooklyn before Germaine does. There's a pothole crew working the in-bound side of the Verrazano. I can park the car in front of their truck and we'll watch for him."

He accelerated onto the Turnpike and sailed around cars and trucks, smiling. "Nice to be doing eighty on the Pike again."

Whipping through Staten Island, they roared onto the high suspension bridge spanning the narrowest part of the outer harbor. Dark clouds hid an anemic setting sun, leaving the roadway dark. Half way across, they found the work crew blocking off the right lane. The men stood with bright orange vests filling holes and tamping down the asphalt, despite the lightly falling rain.

Stanley pulled to a stop past the crew, got out and went to talk to the crew chief. Returning to the car, he and Nick watched as drivers jockeyed for the open lanes. A truck blocked their view of the far lane, but as it passed they got a look at the cars on the other side. No blue Ford Escort. Stanley inched his car forward as the work crew crawled along the surface.

After a half hour of waiting, Nick suggested that Germaine had gone into Manhattan. "He might have crossed by the Holland or the Lincoln Tunnel."

"It was a shot in the dark. Let's give it another fifteen minutes."

When the time passed without spotting their suspect, Stanley turned the key. He put on his signal and was about to put the car in gear when Nick pointed his finger at the traffic. "That's him!"

"Christ!" Stanley opened the window and put out his hand to make room for him in the crowded lane. A woman in an Acura leaned on her horn, but Stanley forced his car into the lane, causing her to jam on her brakes. He accelerated hard and crossed to the far lane.

"If he keeps left he's on the Belt going home," said Stanley. "You watch the right lane."

Stanley pulled within inches of the car in front of him, swerved to the right just ahead of a family in a minivan, pushed ahead and passed back to the left lane. As the traffic divided, Nick saw no blue Ford in the right lanes, which meant Germaine was going to the Belt Parkway. "I think we're okay," he said.

"We'll know in a minute," said Stanley. He accelerated into the exit, pushing the car to the limits of the tires' adhesion thru the constant radius turn. Nick held onto the strap in the ceiling, admiring his friend's skill, and hoping that the elusive Alex Germaine would appear when they hit the Belt.

SEVENTY-SIX

Stanley shot out of the exit and accelerated onto the Belt, weaving thru traffic. The old highway, crowded beyond capacity, had no shoulder for long stretches, making it difficult to make up the distance. They passed a truck carrying newspapers and swerved around a Subaru when Nick pointed straight ahead. "I think I see him."

His arms fully extended racecar style, Stanley dove into gaps between cars, missing them by inches. As he roared past a dozen cars, passengers stared at him in disbelief through their windows. Nick smiled, knowing his friend was having the time of his life.

Stanley eased the car into the right lane, leaving one car between them and Germaine. At the Cropsey exit Germaine braked and got off the parkway without signaling. Stanley followed, keeping several car lengths away. He stayed with the suspect onto Surf Avenue. On their right the Atlantic appeared between apartment buildings, a black expanse separating the night sky from the darkening shore.

Suddenly the blue Ford emitted a puff of smoke and accelerated through a yellow light. Stanley braked for the red and inched into the cross lane, raising long blasts on the horns of vehicles crossing intersection. Stanley stuck the nose of his car into the lane, forcing traffic to screech to a halt. He inched through and floored the car on the other side.

Three blocks along the Ford suddenly swerved into the Aquarium parking lot, accelerated toward the building and slid to a stop at the end of the lot. A shadowy figure spilled out of the driver's side, his head low, and ran up the steps leading to the boardwalk. The figure disappeared in the shadows.

Cursing, Stanley's front wheel hit the curb as he muscled the car into the lot. Nick had his door open and his seat belt loose before coming to a stop beside Germaine's car.

"You better stay and watch the car!" Nicks called out as he broke for the boardwalk.

"Not on your life!" Stanley called after him. "I can't run, but I can still canvass the area."

Nick ran up the steps to the promenade, taking them three at a time.

He hit the boardwalk and started running. The freezing rain robbed the setting sun of its last light, providing deep shadows among the vendors. Most were closed, but a few hardy souvenir shops and an odd restaurant remained open, despite the biting cold.

Nick looked into each open establishment, but found no sign of the suspect. The cold rain was beginning to make his hands numb when his cell phone vibrated in his pocket.

"We . . . Lost . . .Him," said Stanley in a weak voice.

"Stanley! Are you okay?"

Nicks heard a loud crack, then silence. He called into the phone again, but there was no answer. His cell phone told him the connection hadn't been broken. Stan must have dropped the phone, which meant he was down as well.

Running through the cold rain, Nick cursed himself for not insisting that his friend stay in the car, where it was warm and dry. When he reached the stairs to the parking lot he saw that Germaine's car was gone and Stanley on the ground beside the car. He was on his back, the cold rain beating down on his face, the dim street lights reflecting on the puddles.

Nick ran to his friend, knelt and felt for a pulse, calling out, "Stanley! Can you hear me?"

Stanley turned his head toward his friend, opened his mouth, but made no sound. His dark purple lips betrayed the suffocation that was robbing his body of oxygen. He raised an arm slowly, then let it fall back to the wet pavement. His eyelids slowly closed. A curtain going down.

Nick felt for a pulse with one hand while calling for an ambulance with the other. The pulse was rapid and thready, the ambulance ten minutes away. Hanging up, he took a breath, pressed his lips to Stanley's mouth and blew. He could only force a small volume of air into his friend's lungs, the airway was so constricted by the cold, damp air. It was like trying to blow out a fire through a straw.

He took off his jacket and wrapped it around his friend. Then he resumed giving the mouth-to-mouth resuscitation, letting the small volume of air escape from Stanley's lungs, then blowing in again. Nick wished he could give his friend one of his lungs, with its rich blood stream carrying loads of oxygen. Stanley's skin was cold and clammy, perhaps the most apt medical phrase ever uttered. Apt, and chilling.

Kneeling on the cold pavement with the rain beating down on him, Nick thought the ambulance would never come. It was the loneliest, saddest spot in the world. The place where friendships expire.

SEVENTY-SEVEN

Nicholas stood at the bedside studying the numbers on the monitor. He tried not to look at Fran, the weight of guilt pressing down on him. He knew he was to blame. Knew he'd screwed up, and that Fran was angry to the point she couldn't speak to or look at him. She sat frozen in a chair watching her husband, too distraught to cry, too angry to speak.

Feeling that he had to say something, Nick said, "They're giving him maximum medications for his breathing. And broad spectrum antibiotics for pneumonia. I talked with the pulmonologist." This brought no response. "I mean, he's getting enough oxygen to support him."

Fran glanced at him. Numb, she turned back to look at Stanley.

"I'm so sorry, Fran. I told Stanley to stay in the car. I mean — "

"Don't." She held up a hand, a finger pointing straight up. "Just let me sit with him."

Nick stepped to the foot of the bed and watched the action of the ventilator. *Whoosh, whoosh.* The breathing machine's LED display revealed that it was delivering one hundred per cent pure oxygen. That was bad. Very bad. Nick knew it meant that Stanley's lungs were so diseased, they could not deliver adequate oxygen to the blood stream, even at five times the normal oxygen content of room air.

He scanned the numbers on the patient's bedside record. The record sent a chill through him. Stanley's blood oxygen level was only fifty-nine. *Fifty-nine!* On pure oxygen it should be three or four hundred. The cells of his body were screaming for oxygen that the lungs couldn't deliver. Screaming, and dying.

Nicholas couldn't bring himself to say anything to Fran.

If only there was some miracle drug that could restore the lungs. Bring back the thousands of tiny air sacs that had lost their elasticity. Open the airways and let the air flow free again.

But he knew there was no treatment on the planet for this terrible disease acquired at Ground Zero.

Later that day Nick was alone in the apartment, Beth having gone to sit with Fran in the hospital. He hated sitting alone. Couldn't focus on the newspaper. He decided to take the Avanti for a spin. Maybe push it to a hundred, hundred-ten, burn off the carbon in the cylinders; really let her stretch her legs. He walked down the stairs thinking about his experiment with the liquid laundry soap that had started the affair. He wished now he hadn't taken on the stupid investigation. Hadn't let Stanley get excited and start running around as if he were healthy and still on the force. As if he wasn't hanging onto his life by a worn out old shoelace.

Peeling back the dust cover and stowing it in the trunk, he opened the driver's door and stood admiring the car, with its black leather seats and the flourishing letters *Avanti* stitched in red across the seatback. The curious airplane style controls and stainless steel instruments.

A hundred-seventy miles per hour on the Bonneville salt flats in 1963. Stock! Now that's a muscle car. Nick recalled running his car the summer before with other Avanti's at the Indianapolis Speedway. He'd hit one-twenty before the engine ran out of RPMs. He had bought speed-rated tires, the street rubber on the car couldn't be trusted at that kind of speed.

What a thrill it had been thundering down the straightaway with the others, shaking the ground as they raced toward the first turn. Stanley had been his pit man and loved every minute of it.

He settled into the driver's seat, enjoying the way the thickly padded leather cushioned him. He put the key in the ignition and turned it. The starter turned, but the engine failed to start. He tried again. This time the engine came to life, but something was off. There was a skip to the rhythmic pulse of the cylinders, and the exhaust note stumbled in the pipes.

He pressed down on the pedal, bringing up the RPMs in an attempt to smooth out the engine. All of a sudden, he smelled gasoline. *Shit!* He wondered if the choke was frozen and he'd flooded the engine. But he hadn't pumped the gas pedal or run the starter for long, there shouldn't be *that much* fuel in the throat of the carburetor.

He eased off on the throttle, opened the car door and had placed on foot on the ground when he heard a load *whump.* Black smoke poured out from the engine compartment. Quickly he leaned into the back seat, lifted the hatch in the rear deck and pulled up the fire extinguisher, a safety item mandated by his classic car club. He aimed the extinguisher though the front grill, not wanting to feed the fire by opening the hood, and pulled the trigger. The chemical smothered the fire, leaving a smoking engine bay.

A fire alarm in the garage screamed its disapproval.

Stunned, Nick stepped back from the car. The fire department would be there soon. It would be embarrassing to have to tell them his handiwork on the carburetor had caused the fire. Well, he'd screwed up so much landing his friend in the ICU and letting a member of a criminal gang get away, what was one more humiliation?

When the firemen came to examine the car, they listened with great sympathy to his explanation about the carburetor rebuild. "Shit happens," a tall rangy fellow with a handlebar mustache said. He was beginning to tell Nick about his own mishaps rebuilding an old Ford pickup truck, when another fireman, his head and shoulders deep inside the engine bay, called out, "Hey! Come check this out!"

Joining the fireman under the hood, Nick saw the man shining a flashlight on a spark plug wire, which was hanging loose beside the carburetor. The fireman then turned the light on a loose connection where the fuel line entered the carburetor. "Looks like you didn't connect the line too good, and you left a plug wire disconnected. The fuel line came loose, and the unconnected plug wire sparked the fire." Shaking his head, the fireman added, "Man, you were lucky to come out alive."

Nick said, "There's no way I left the plug wire like that. I haven't worked on the electrical system since I put in new plugs last year." He explained that he'd secured the fuel lines with great care, making certain that the connections were tight.

"I ran the engine for thirty minutes after I put in the rebuilt carb. Everything was perfect. I haven't touched the engine since then. I—"

Nick suddenly saw the hand of the same criminal organization that was killing divorcing spouses at work. They had planned his death. Only his stepping out to examine why the engine was misfiring and quick access to the fire extinguisher had saved him from being burned. Or worse.

"You better call the precinct," Nick said. "Somebody wants me dead."

SEVENTY-EIGHT

Alex sat at the wheel of the car watching the firemen leave Andreas's apartment building. No ambulance had taken the doctor away, a bad sign. The plan had not worked. It was his first failure. Deciding to waste no mental energy or time dwelling on it, he would change his tactics and face the challenge head on. No more subtlety. Direct action was called for in the matter of Nicholas Andreas.

Driving to the Sheepshead Bay section of Brooklyn, he parked on a dark stretch of street several houses away from Ann Darling's house. He put on his Santa Claus suit and sat in his car watching the house. The wife came out of the front door and crossed the street with a bowl filled with baking paraphernalia. *Time to make the cookies.* A moment later Rupert Darling came out of the garage with an aluminum ladder.

Now there was only one possible glitch facing him. If Darling set the ladder at the front of the house, it would be exposed to view — not a good thing, even with his disguise. Alex had looked over the house carefully. It seemed as if the notch where the garage met the roof was the logical place to set the ladder, it was the lowest point of the room. Still facing the front, but recessed and out of the light.

Rupert extended the ladder, lifted it, and walked unsteadily toward the notch. He set the top of the latter in the notch and wiggled the feet of the ladder until they were firmly planted on the driveway. A cautious man. Always good to prevent accidents.

Rupert climbed the ladder, a thick string of lights on his shoulder and a line of reindeer tucked under one arm. He reached the roof, then carefully laid the gear down. He clambered bent over up the steep grade, unwinding the string of lights as he climbed.

When Rupert reached the chimney, he went back for the reindeer figures, which were lying near the top of the ladder. Cautiously he carried the figures up toward the chimney. He pulled out a ball of twine and wound it around the brick structure, securing the reindeer. Satisfied, he turned and bent down to pick up the string of lights, intending to plug in the reindeer. Suddenly he spotted a strange, magical figure walking toward him. The figure had a red suit, white beard and long red hat.

"Santa?" asked Rupert, confused by the ghostly figure.

Alex patted the reindeer. "This is a good likeness." He stepped toward Rupert. "Merry Christmas, my friend. I'm here with a wonderful gift."

"For, for me?"

"No, Rupert," said Santa, holding his white gloved hands in front of him. "For your wife."

Alex shot his hands forward, pushing Rupert back. The man rolled head-over-heels down the roof and off the edge. A brief shriek followed by a loud *thud* announced the body's impact on the driveway below.

Alex looked up and down the street. It was still empty, the windows of the nearest houses closed and curtained, music or television sets blaring within each house, obscuring any sounds from the street. He had counted on the isolation of the suburban lifestyle.

He climbed down the ladder and hurried to the crumpled figure on the pavement. He felt at the man's wrist for a pulse; found none. He placed his ear over the man's mouth to listen for a breath; heard nothing. Satisfied, he stood and walked briskly down the street.

At the corner he turned and passed two boys who were rolling a ball of snow in the thin cover of the front lawn, hoping to make a little snowman. The boys looked up and saw Santa.

"Hi, Santa!" the smaller of the boys cried.

"That's not Santa," said the other, poking his companion in the side. "That's some geek going to a little kid's party." He turned toward Santa, who was hurrying down the street. "Where's your stupid reindeer, Santa Claus?" he cried.

Alex gave the boys a wave of a gloved hand and continued on. He saw no one else as he approached his car, got in, pulled off his hat and beard, and started the engine. He made a U-turn to avoid the snowball-rolling children and drove out of the neighborhood singing White Christmas.

When Nick heard Beth come into the apartment, he dreaded having to face her, knowing how much he was to blame. She came into the bedroom, strode up to him and began striking his chest with her fists, crying, "You said you were through! You said you wouldn't be involved any more!"

He grabbed her wrists and looked into her eyes, seeing tears welling up. And fear.

"Try to understand. We had to go. There was a window of opportunity. If we let it slip by, who knows if the opportunity would ever come again."

"I don't care about the murders! I don't care about the crimes! Stanley is dying and you could have been killed. I met the super in the lobby and he told me about the fire. *Nicholas,* they tried to *kill* you. You promised me you would be safe!"

He put his arms around her and held his wife. No words could express the regret that he felt. No confession could expiate the guilt.

His one consolation was that he had given the police a description of Alex Germaine and the name of the security guard who had helped Stanley monitor the exchange of money at the Taj. He told the police that Stanley had been certain the surviving spouses would cave under pressure when they were told that the bag man had been captured. From there the criminal organization would come down like a house of cards.

SEVENTY-NINE

Anna Darling carefully pulled a cookie sheet from her friend's oven. Beverly pressed a mold into cookie dough for more cookies, while the children laid around in the living room watching cartoons.

"Kids!" called Anna. "Don't you want to help bake the cookies?"

"We'll put the sprinkles and gum drops on when the show is over!" called the oldest girl.

"Okay!" called Anna. "But anybody who doesn't help with the baking won't get to lick the icing off the spoon."

The children ignored her threats.

As Anna began transferring the cookies from sheet to cooling rack, she heard a loud knock on the front door. The dog leapt up onto the windowsill and yipped and growled. Beverly called, "Somebody get the door!"

A moment later the eldest daughter came into the kitchen and said, "There's a policeman at the door, mommy."

Beverly looked at Anna, who shrugged her shoulders. The two women walked into the living room. At the door they found a young patrolman, his shoulder-mounted walkie-talkie squeaking.

"Sorry to disturb you, ladies. Would a Mrs. Anna Darling happen to be here?"

"I'm Mrs. Darling."

She looked past the officer through the open front door, saw the flashing red lights of an ambulance across the street in front of her house. She clutched at her chest with a fist and said in a stricken voice, *"What is it? What's happened?"*

"I'm awful sorry to have to tell you this ma'am. It's, uh, your husband. Rupert Darling?"

"That's his name! That's my husband's name!"

"I'm afraid that he took a tumble off the roof and hit his head, and, well, the paramedics tried to revive him, but he was too far gone. They think he was on the ground too long, not breathing and all." The officer reached a hand out to the wife. "I'm afraid your husband is dead."

Anna let out a sob that only she knew was a cry of relief. The tension she felt in the kitchen had been unbearable. She didn't dare look out the window and down the street; could not risk watching for the agent who would stuff her stocking with the best Christmas gift of all.

Through her tears she sobbed, "Those stupid Christmas lights! I *told* him to be careful! I told him!" She threw herself into Beverly's arms and cried, raising real tears, much to her surprise. Then she slowly pulled away and stepped to the door, saying, "I want to see him. I want to say good-bye."

The officer held the storm door open for her and walked with the grieving widow across the street.

After dispatching Rupert Darling to the great toy land in hell, Alex buried the Santa suit in a dumpster, changed to a black sweater, black jeans and sailor's cap and pea coat. In a day or two he would make tracks for Mexico using his fake ID. For now he found a cheap hotel in the Bronx. The creep at the desk had asked if he wanted to pay by the hour or the night. Alex paid a week in advance; that would give him time enough to carry out his last hit.

There was just one piece of unfinished business he needed to complete. He wasn't going anywhere until he'd exacted his revenge on that trouble maker, Andreas. And this time he was going to make damn sure he looked into the bastard's face before taking his life.

EIGHTY

On the subway ride in to work, Nicholas saw in the morning paper an article about a Queens man who fell off his roof while stringing Christmas lights. Beneath a picture of the distraught wife, the caption read, *"The wife was across the street baking cookies!"*

Even though the article didn't say that the couple had been in divorce proceedings, Nick had a good idea that they were, the fall from a roof fit the gang's pattern too well to be an actual accident. As soon as he reached his office he called the Medical Examiner to alert them to the suspicious nature of the death. The ME had already added a protocol to question the marital status of any adult suffering an accidental death.

A moment later Libby poked her head into his office. "How are you coming with the Nursing Home survey?"

"Thirty-four down," he said, looking over a list of facilities in Brooklyn. "I'm just going back out on the road." While he was unhappy to have been shunted to such a low level assignment, he was surprised to still have a job with the DOH. The Feds really did move at a snail's pace.

"Any problems with the visits?"

"Seeger's Home in Canarsie had suspicious records. Their health service records say they vaccinated ninety-six clients and thirty-five staff members, but their pharmacy only has a record of one-hundred doses purchased, and they have doses left over."

"The Seeger family's been cited by the City a dozen times. They're probably dividing the doses in two, or maybe three. You better follow up with them."

"I'll go back tomorrow." He stuffed his files into his attaché and left.

The first Home was a small affair with thirty residents. He found it clean and tidy and free from foul odors, evidence of a diligent nursing and custodial staff. Their vaccination program was comprehensive and complete.

The second Nursing Home was larger and also well kept, with an energetic head nurse who ran a tight ship. Noting her military manner, Nick assumed she'd been trained in somebody's army, though he couldn't be sure by her accent which one.

The third facility was a big one in Fort Greene. The security guard's desk stood inside the entrance to the Sacred Sisters Convalescent Home. After showing his DOH identification and signing in, he waited until Joy Falang, the Infection Control nurse, came down and met him. The nurse offered to give Nick a tour of the facility.

"That won't be necessary. I just need to see your vaccination program."

She led him to her office on the second floor, passing the physical therapy room, where elderly men and women were bending and stretching on mats. "That is our yoga class. You would be amazed how flexible some of our clients have become."

An elderly woman with a Foley bag was watching the class, a vacant smile on her face. The smell of urine hung in the air.

"We are very proud of our program, Doctor Andreas. This year we have a ninety-eight percent compliance with our clients and a seventy-five percent compliance with our staff."

"Call me Nick." He was impressed with her program; health care workers in hospitals and nursing homes were notorious for refusing the flu vaccine, which made employees the number one source of influenza among patients and long term residents.

He asked if she had enough stock to immunize any new clients who were admitted to the facility. She showed him a copy of the pharmacy purchase order documenting a robust number of remaining doses.

"You have a very good program," he told her.

"Yes. We try very hard to convince our people to take the vaccine."

When Joy offered to accompany him out, he told her he could find the entrance by himself and set off down the corridor. He passed the gym, where the seniors in the yoga class struggled to bend over.

As he turned a corner, Nick bumped into an elderly man with a shock of snow-white hair shuffling along with a walker. He was wearing a blue cardigan sweater and gray sweat pants. Nick thought the man must be anemic, he was bundled up in so many layers of clothing.

The old man grasped the walker to steady himself. The frail fellow tilted forward onto the walker and was about to fall when Nick grabbed his arm and steadied him.

"What're you trying to do, kill me?" the old man barked. He smelled of sweat and urine. Nicks could see the blue plastic of an adult diaper poking out from his baggy sweat pants.

"I'm terribly sorry. Are you all right?"

"No, I'm not all right!"

Nick released the old man, who grasped his walker and slowly inched forward. The man's trembling hands had age spots and brown smudges on the fingers that Nick assumed was fecal matter.

"You might as well help me back to my room," said the old man.

"Is it far?" said Nick, looking at his wristwatch. "I have a lot of appointments to make."

"*Appointments*? First you try and kill me, and then you tell me you don't have time to help me! What kind of a person are you?"

"I'm a doctor, actually."

"Hmmph. Should have known."

The old man took hold of Nick's arm and pointed down the corridor. "My room's around the next bend."

Nick picked up the walker with his free hand and walked slowly down the corridor, the old man shuffling along beside him. They walked in silence until they reached an empty room.

"In here," the old man said.

Nick pushed the door wide open and went in first.

"Put the walker by the bed and hand me the pillow," said the old man, taking his arm out from Nick and grabbing the open door.

Nick set the walker down beside the bed and picked up the pillow. As he turned around and held out the pillow, he heard the click of the door closing. The old fellow stepped forward and grabbed the pillow out of Nick hand.

"Doctor Andreas, I presume," said the old man. An evil grin animated his face. As Nick looked into the laughing eyes, he saw beneath the layers of make-up, penciled wrinkles and white wig the face of Alex Germaine, and in Germaine's hand, which was no longer trembling, a gun pointed at his heart.

EIGHTY-ONE

As Nick looked at the gun in Alex Germaine's hand, he pictured the path the bullet would take through his chest and the damage that would ensue. Puncture the skin and soft tissue, shatter a rib and perforate the lung. The rapidly collapsing lung would trigger a sudden drop in his oxygen level and blood pressure. The bullet would almost certainly strike a major artery, producing rapid intra-thoracic hemorrhage and shock.

He estimated that without an immediate surgical intervention and blood transfusion he would suffer irreversible brain death in three to five minutes. Unless the bullet perforated his heart, in which case death would be immediate.

"If you pull that trigger, a lot of people are going to come running."

"That's why I asked for the pillow, it'll muffle the sound," said Germaine, pressing the muzzle into the soft fabric. "Besides, they're all at lunch gumming their tuna melts."

"The nurse will hear."

"She's on the phone yakking to her boyfriend." He waved the gun in a half-circle. "Clasp your hands behind your head."

"Look, you don't need—"

"Just do it! I was going to wait to kill you until we had a little chat, but you can die now if you prefer."

Nicholas raised his arms and placed his hands behind his head. He kept the hands overlapping, not interlocked.

"It makes no sense killing me. I'm not in a divorce. Nobody's paying you."

"This one's personal."

"But *why?*"

"*Why?* You ruined a perfect business model! You killed the goose just when she was laying beautiful golden eggs!"

"I'm just a public servant. I was only conducting a survey for the city. I–"

"Don't bullshit me, Andreas! *You* were the fucker who figured out my game. It all had to do with the numbers, didn't it?"

"I don't do the statistical analysis. That's somebody else."

"Don't insult me with lame shit. Somehow you picked up on the accidents and you realized there were too many of them. I should have known some stupid city flunky would keep track of this kind of thing."

"It wasn't personal," said Nicholas.

"Oh *no?* What's more personal than destroying a man's greatest life's work? What's more personal than killing the golden goose just when I was getting some real money socked away?"

Nicholas glanced at the gun in Germaine's hand. It seemed to be pointing lower, at his abdomen, or perhaps his hip. A hip wound wouldn't be fatal, unless the bullet struck a major artery. If he leapt forward and grabbed the gun…

"Listen, Germaine, all the deaths so far have been ruled accidental. With a good lawyer you can beat the rap on those. Killing me will clearly be a homicide. You'll never get off if you shoot me."

"One more body won't make me any less guilty. Lethal injection or life sentence, either way, I'm not interested."

Nick took in a breath and tensed the muscles in his legs preparing to leap forward and fight for the gun. His eyes locked onto the black hole of the barrel. He was about to dive forward and try to grab the gun when he heard a sound.

Crack!

The door to the room suddenly flew open, knocking Germaine forward. The gun exploded, flashing fire from the barrel. Nick felt a sting in his hip as he thrust out his hands for the gun. He grabbed the barrel and pushed Germaine back, catching a glimpse of an old woman's shocked face in the hall before Germaine's body slammed into the door, shutting it on the stunned senior.

Nick cocked his free arm back and threw the hardest punch he could muster, connecting with Germaine's jaw. The blow drove Germaine's head back; the gun fell to the floor. As Nick kicked it away under the bed, Germaine turned, ripped open the door, and pushed past the old woman standing in the hallway as he raced away.

Stepping into the hallway, Nick saw Germaine turn a corner and disappear. The old woman in the hall had a confused look on her face.

"I left my teeth in the room," she said in a tremulous voice. "Can I come in now and get them?"

Nick ignored her as he hobbled after Germaine, pain lacing through his hip. When he reached the corner, he saw his adversary disappearing into a stairwell. A few doors past the stairs, an Asian nurse sat at the nursing station talking on the phone.

Nicholas hurried to the station, the pain in his hip growing in intensity. He looked down, saw a dark stain on his pants. Felt a trickle of warm blood running down his leg. He realized he was like the boxer in the ring who doesn't feel the pain until the fight is over. Now he felt it all right.

"Jesus Christ," he said, reaching the station. "Nurse! Call nine-one-one. And get me some gauze and two inch tape."

The startled nurse looked up at him, not understanding who he was.

"I'm Doctor Andreas. I need gauze and the police!"

When the nurse still looked perplexed, he added, "Don't just stand there, I've been shot. There's a madman running through your facility!"

As the nurse hung up on her friend and dialed the emergency number, Nicholas spied a supply cart behind the station. He stepped around the counter, ripped open a drawer, and fished for gauze pads and tape. He dropped his pants, tore open several gauze packages, and pressed a wad of them over the bullet wound, which was oozing crimson blood. He estimated the crest of the hip was probably shattered. Well, it wasn't a weight bearing part; he could still walk on it.

"Give me the phone and tear off some tape," he told the nurse. Holding the phone to his ear, he gave the nine-one-one operator a description of Alex Germaine, explaining that the man was a suspect in a murder case.

While the nurse stretched the tape over the improvised bandage, Nick finished explaining to the operator who he was, the name of the facility, and the clothing that Germaine was wearing when he fled.

When Nick hung up the phone and began pulling up his pants, the nurse said, "Doctor! I must call an ambulance for you."

"I'll be all right. Tell the police I've gone down the stairs. I'll check the lobby."

"But, doctor, you are *bleeding!"* She watched helplessly as he lurched toward the stairs. Nick hobbled through the door, the pain shooting through his hip, and hurried down the stairs. Each step sent greater waves of pain through his body and threatened to bring on more bleeding. He knew he was crazy to go running with a bullet wound leaking blood, but he was angry. Really angry. Nicholas had taken insults and threats from fellow New Yorkers, but a bullet was going too far.

He wanted to get his hands on Germaine before the police did and do a makeover with his fists. He would give some radiologist an opportunity to identify a *depressed skull fracture.* Reaching the first floor, he opened the door and saw the security guard at his post.

"Did you see an old guy come out of this stairwell and run out the door a moment ago? Blue sweater, gray sweat pants, white hair?"

"Nope. Nobody's come out of those stairs since I been on duty."

"Shit! Thanks."

Nick turned and hurried down the steps to the basement. As he reached the door on the lower landing, he felt a new rivulet of blood run down his leg. The dressing had pulled loose.

He was bleeding to death.

EIGHTY-TWO

Nick pressed the flat of his hand firmly over the bullet wound and hobbled out of the exit. He found himself on a loading dock that was smeared with grease and dirt. There was a wheeled trash barrel along the wall. Inside was a white wig.

"Christ, he's slick," Nick swore. At the end of the loading dock was a short metal stair to the street. He made his way down slowly, the pain shooting up from his hip. His shoe had filled with blood.

He reached the street, looked up and down. Five blocks away a figure in a blue sweater was getting into a blue car.

Nick stepped into the street and was nearly struck by a van. The driver leaned on his horn, cursing as he veered around Nick and sped past. A woman in an SUV talking on her cell phone swerved from her lane and nearly clipped him without interrupting her conversation.

Hustling through a break in the traffic, he hobbled toward the blue car, only to see a cloud of smoke belch from the tailpipe as Germaine pulled out into traffic and sped away.

Nick looked around for a cab, saw nothing yellow. He had given up hope of ever catching his foe when a siren filled the air and flashing lights approached the nursing home. He stepped into the middle of the street and waved the police car down. The car roared toward him. For a moment Nick thought the cop would run him down, but the vehicle came to a screeching stop just in front of him.

The passenger side window came down. A burly cop with deadpan eyes poked his head out.

"You Doctor Nicholas, something or other?"

"Yes! I'm Doctor Nicholas Andreas. The man you want just took off in a blue Ford Escort." He told him what Germaine looked like, having discarded the white wig.

"Did you get the plate number?"

"No, it was too far away."

"That's okay, get in, maybe you'll spot him." The officer opened the back door for Nick, who fell into the seat as the car accelerated hard, slamming the door shut. The siren screamed as the driver picked up speed, slowing at red lights and pushing through the crunch of vehicles in the cross street.

The burly officer called in a description of the car and the suspect and their current location and direction, while the driver, a tall fellow who gripped the steering wheel straight-armed, shot the car through gaps in the traffic.

The burly cop turned toward the back seat. "You look like shit, doc. I better call for a bus."

"It can wait. I want to get the bastard first."

The cop looked Nick up and down. "You must do a lot of ER work."

"In my day." Nick pressed hard on the wound, staunching the flow of blood.

The driver weaved around cars, buses, vans and a cyclist making deliveries. At Atlantic Avenue he avoided a collision with a Volvo by inches, braking hard and veering around the offending vehicle, then accelerating hard past the train station.

Nick scanned the cross streets looking for the car. At Washington he spotted a blue car that looked familiar. The driver was elderly, had gray hair and a blue sweater.

"That's him!" Nicholas cried, pointing at the cross street.

The officer at the wheel slammed on the brakes, the tires screamed and the patrol car fishtailed, striking the sign for a bus stop. In reverse, the tires screeched and sent up blue smoke, propelling the vehicle backwards against the flow of traffic. Startled drivers veered into the middle of the road, raising a half-dozen horns and curses in several languages.

The cop pointed the patrol car into the side street and accelerated hard. Siren blazing, the car ran up on the sidewalk going around a slow-moving sedan, bounced onto the street and picked up speed.

"It's a fricking Escort," the cop said with derision. He began closing the gap, swerving around cars and nearly scraping a big SUV. The blue Ford ran a red light. As it reached the middle of the intersection a UPS truck caught the Escort's rear bumper and spun it around. The Escort came to a stop facing the way it came, with the police car barreling down upon it.

The driver stumbled out of the car, slipped and caught himself on a lamp post. He righted himself and started to hustle down the street. The two officers gave chase, reaching him half way down the block. They threw his against a parked car, jerked his hands behind his back and cuffed them, and dragged him back to their patrol car.

The cop holding Germaine's arm said, "Good news, doc, we got your perp."

Nick leaned out of the car, looked at Alex Germaine. Even with his failing eye sight, he could see there was something seriously wrong. The killer was grinning at him as if he'd won the lottery. As if he was the luckiest man on earth.

"What the hell do you have to be smiling about?" Nicholas said.

Staring at Nick half dead in the back seat of the police car, Germaine began to laugh. It was an insane, unceasing laugh. The sound grew louder and louder until it drowned out the noise of the city.

Nick pushed open the car door and put one foot down on the ground. Fighting the pain and the dizziness, he said, "You slimy bastard! It's 'cause of you my friend is dying, you scum bag."

Germaine's laughter slowly died away, though his smile never wavered. He looked at the crowd gathering on the sidewalk and the growing number of police officers surrounding the area, seemingly satisfied with all the activity swirling around him.

An ambulance pulled in behind the police car, the rear doors burst open, and an EMT began unloading a stretcher. The burly cop took Nick by the arm. "Time to get you to the hospital, doc."

Feeling faint, Nick let the officer assist the paramedics settle him onto the stretcher and load him into the ambulance. In seconds the ambulance sped away, the driver hitting the siren and racing to the hospital. The bumps in the road reverberated through the ambulance, sending new waves of pain through Nick's hip and back as the paramedic pressed a fresh dressing over the wound.

"Why was he laughing?" Nick asked the paramedic, who shrugged, knowing nothing about the case Nick had been so wrapped up in. "And smiling. What did he have to smile about, he's going to prison."

"Probably just a crazy fuck, don't worry yourself about it, doc."

Arriving at the hospital, the paramedics hurried Nick into the ER. The physician began barking orders for an x-ray, blood typing and antibiotics. Nick was whisked away to an x-ray room within the ER. He asked to see the image on the digital screen as they shot his hip, but the technician told him he would have to speak to the radiologist, and Nick was too weak and too tired to argue.

He hadn't been back in the ER long when the cop who had driven the car and his partner came in. "Hey, doc, how ya doin'?" the burly one asked. "We got to get your statement. Whenever you're up for it, 'o course."

"I am a bit dizzy, still," said Nick. "Perhaps after the pain killer kicks in."

"Sure, no sweat." The cop who drove the car told them he was going for coffee, he'd be back in a few. The second cop found a chair next to the stretcher and settled into it.

"Ya wanna hear somethin' really crazy?" the cop asked. Nick nodded his head. "You'll never believe what that freak Germaine was laughing about back at the scene."

"Oh? What was it?"

"The guy must be a first class nut job. On the ride to the station he asked if he could make a phone call, only it wasn't to his *lawyer*, it was to his *agent.*"

"You're kidding me."

"F'real. He wanted to talk about a book deal. Seems he wants to sell his memoir about being a 'successful professional killer.' The scum bag thinks he can get published. Is that nuts or what?"

"I thought you couldn't profit from a criminal act with your writing," said Nick.

"That's just it, he says he's not in it for the money, he wants to be on the New York Times bestseller list. That's all that fucking matters to him. Do you believe this shit?"

Nick asked the nurse caring for him if she would call his wife and tell her he was okay. He was surprised to realize that for the first time in a very long while he was genuinely glad to be alive. In fact, he was thrilled so much, he started to laugh.

The cop gave him a questioning look. "Not you, too, doc."

Nick grinned. "No, I'm not going crazy. It's just so good to be alive."

"Amen to that, brother," said the cop. "There ain't nothin' beats taking a gun shot and living to tell the tale."

EIGHTY-THREE

The physician in the Emergency Room who reviewed the x-rays of Nick's hip wanted to send him up to a room, but the patient refused. He wanted to stop and see Stanley first, who was in the same facility. The physician appealed to his wife, who begged and threatened and cried, but Nick wouldn't have it. He would see Stanley first, then go to bed.

Riding to the Intensive Care Unit in a wheelchair, he found Chrissie and Lucas in the family waiting room. Nicholas started to rise to his feet, but the pain stopped him. Chrissie ran to him. When she wrapped her arms around him, he was so relieved at the expression of affection, he felt tears well up in his eyes as they hugged her.

Releasing his daughter, Nick said, "You were right about the Trade Center stuff. I was wrong. I was a coward. I should have spoken out a long time ago."

"Dad! How can you say that? You said yourself, nobody knew what to expect. The Feds promised the air was safe to breathe. It wasn't *you.* It *wasn't.*"

"But I still knew better. I *knew*. When everybody was drawing a circle with the wagons, trying to get things back to normal, I should have spoken up." He glanced at Lucas, then back to his daughter.

"I'm going to work with the Trade Center support group. I'll help them analyze the data that they have. I'll testify for them if need be, even if it's from prison." Chrissie took Luca's hand, nodding her head, unable to speak.

Beth asked Nick if he was ready to go in to Stanley's room. Nick nodded. She wheeled him through the electric doors into the ICU, with Chrissie and Lucas behind them. Fran was standing at the foot of the bed talking to a physician. By his gray hair and weathered appearance, Nick assumed he was the senior physician in charge of Stanley's care.

Stanley was lying flat in bed, his mouth connected to a breathing machine. His face was swollen and pale, his lips and tongue blue. His head bobbed slightly with each breath of oxygen, a sign of severe oxygen starvation.

Rising from the wheelchair, Nick hobbled to the bedside and gave

Fran a hug. She clung to him for a long minute, trembling.

Nick almost wished it was him in the ICU bed instead of his friend. Guilt and fear and sadness washed over him. He felt Beth's hand on his shoulder.

The doctor reached out his hand to Nick. "Doctor Andreas, Fran has told me what a good friend you were to her husband. How much you cared for him over the years."

Nick said nothing. He couldn't see how he could take pride in helping Stanley when his failures had led to his friend's long illness.

"Mister Bezlin was admitted with multi-lobar pneumonia and septic shock. I'm afraid we were never able to adequately oxygenate him."

Nick nodded his head, understanding that the underlying lung disease made Stanley exquisitely vulnerable to infections.

"I asked for a neurology consult, but it's really not necessary," said the physician. "His pupils are fixed and dilated. He doesn't respond to painful stimuli. There's a vestigial degree of brain stem activity, but in my opinion any further treatment would be futile."

Fran bent down and kissed Stanley on the top of his head. She brushed back a stray lock of hair, tears running down her face.

Nick reached for Stanley's hand, felt the cold fingers, saw the darkened nail beds. The digital display on the intravenous pumps showed they were administering the maximum doses of stimulants. The heart was barely holding a pressure, despite being bathed in adrenalin.

Nick released Stanley's hand and stepped away from the bed. He knew that of all the body's organs, the brain was the most sensitive to prolonged oxygen deficits. Once damaged, it never recovered.

When Beth opened her mouth to speak, Nick held his finger to his lips, urging her to be silent. He knew she, too, wanted to comfort him. As he looked at his friend lying in the bed so close to death, he was overcome by two conflicting emotions. Pain at the loss of a good and noble friend; and relief. Relief, because for the first time in a long time he knew deep down in his soul that this death was *not* his fault. He would bear some responsibility for Stanley's exposure to the toxins at Ground Zero, but he was not responsible for Stanley's decision to pursue one last case. He would not take the blame for Stanley's refusal to stay in the warm, safe car when a killer was escaping into the cold, rainy night.

Stanley made his choices. He followed his heart, and his heart was set on bringing a killer to justice. They had done that. They had won. Stanley chose how he would leave this world. Nobody else could make that choice for him.

Fran looked from her husband to Nick. Choking on the words, she said in a husky whisper, "Pull the plug, Nick. Don't leave him to suffer, he wouldn't want it."

Nick looked at the physician in charge of Stanley's care, who nodded his head in agreement. Feeling proud at being able to do this one last act of kindness for his friend, Nick stepped toward the ventilator.

THE END

Made in the USA
Charleston, SC
24 April 2011